Bello:

hidden talent rediscovered

Bello is a digital-only imprint of Pan Macmillan,
established to breathe new life into previously published,
classic books.

At Bello we believe in the timeless power of the imagination,
of a good story, narrative and entertainment, and we want to
use digital technology to ensure that many more readers
can enjoy these books into the future.

We publish in ebook and print-on-demand formats
to bring these wonderful books to new audiences.

www.panmacmillan.co.uk/bello

Richmal Crompton

Richmal Crompton (1890–1969) is best known for her thirty-eight books featuring William Brown, which were published between 1922 and 1970. Born in Lancashire, Crompton won a scholarship to Royal Holloway in London, where she trained as a schoolteacher, graduating in 1914, before turning to writing full-time. Alongside the *William* novels, Crompton wrote forty-one novels for adults, as well as nine collections of short stories.

Richmal Crompton

CHEDSY PLACE

B E L L

First published 1934 by Macmillan

This edition published 2015 by Bello
an imprint of Pan Macmillan
Pan Macmillan, 20 New Wharf Road, London N1 9RR
Basingstoke and Oxford
Associated companies throughout the world

www.panmacmillan.co.uk/bello

ISBN 978-1-5098-1009-3 EPUB
ISBN 978-1-5098-1007-9 HB
ISBN 978-1-5098-1008-6 PB

A CIP catalogue record for this book is available from the British Library.

Typeset by Ellipsis Digital Limited, Glasgow

Chapter One

THE girl stood on the lawn, looking up at the house, from which ordered rows of sash windows seemed to gaze down on her dispassionately in a facade of warm red brick.

The house had been built at the end of the eighteenth century, and there was about it that subtle charm of dignity and proportion that characterised the period—a period when the slavish worship of Palladianism was waning, and its incongruous grandeur being replaced by a suggestion of modesty and repose.

The front of it faced a wide gravelled carriage sweep, from which the drive wound away out of sight among the trees. The carriage sweep continued along the side of the house in the form of a terrace, flanked by a stone balustrade, in the middle of which a broad flight of steps led down to the lawn where the girl stood.

The girl was of medium height and firm build, with dark hair, blue eyes, and a pleasant mouth. She looked neat and compact, capable and good-humoured.

"Robert!" she called softly, without taking her eyes from the house.

A man came strolling, hands in pockets, pipe in mouth, from behind a small shrubbery that adjoined the lawn.

He was tall and loose-limbed, with ginger hair, freckled sunburnt skin, and tawny eyes. His brown suit was shapeless, his brown shoes worn and shabby, but there was an unmistakable air of breeding about him. He appeared at home and in his natural element in this rather stately setting of country mansion, broad terrace, and smooth sweeping lawns. The girl, who was his wife, looked less at home in it, despite her well-fitting tweed costume and slender upright figure. Something of hard bright efficiency that lurked in her eyes and in the curves of her lips seemed to strike an alien note in the slumbering peace of her surroundings.

"Yes?"

"It's—ever so much bigger than I thought it was."

He stood by her and surveyed the house in a leisurely fashion. Everything he did, his slightest movement, even his deep pleasant voice, held that suggestion of leisureliness, almost of indolence. His mouth—a long mobile mouth with a lazy, good-humoured twist at the corners—curved into a faint smile.

"I didn't realise you'd not seen it before," he said.

"I've seen pictures of it, of course, but somehow they don't give one any idea how beautiful it is."

"Nothing could do that."

"Tell me about it." She slipped her arm through his. "It was an Elizabethan building originally, wasn't it?"

"Yes. Burnt down in 1770. They saved the family portraits and some of the furniture and valuables, but nothing was left of the building. Then they built this. . . ."

Looking at him quickly, she caught something in his eyes before he had time to veil it.

"You love it, don't you?" she said.

"The place where one's lived as a child naturally means a lot to one," he replied, "especially if it's a place like this."

"And now it's yours."

He glanced down at her with his faint smile as if amused by her earnestness, her vividness, her dramatising of the situation and his feelings.

"Hardly," he said. "A place you can't afford to live in isn't really yours."

"How I wish you could live in it!"

Her eyes lost their keenness and became dreamy as though she saw him actually in possession.

"You belong . . ." she said.

He knocked out his pipe against his boot, still with that faint indolent smile.

"I don't," he said. "I'm nearer belonging to the workhouse at this moment."

"Nonsense! The farm's doing splendidly."

"I know, but—compared with this!"

She made a quick impatient movement.

"Let's go inside and look round."

He didn't stir, didn't even seem to hear her.

"When I was a kid," he said slowly, "I used to envy Cyril because it was going to be his. I once read a story in which it turned out that the heir and his cousin had been changed at birth, and so the cousin ended by having the whole show, and I used to dream of that happening with Cyril and me. It somehow made it worse that Cyril never cared two hoots for the place. Mean little beast I must have been. Of course, the idea of owning it, but not having a bean to keep it up, never occurred to me in those days."

She stood, tapping her foot on the grass, obviously eager to start on the tour of inspection, but restraining her impatience, reluctant to break in upon his reverie.

"Darling," she said at last, "let's go and look over it now. One feels it ought to be a much more impressive ceremony somehow—miles of servants forming a sort of avenue and the flag out and someone presenting an illuminated address of welcome."

"Old Mother Hubbard's still there," he said. "She was housekeeper when I was a child. She had an army of servants then. I expect she's hardly any now. I wonder what'll happen to her when it's sold."

"She probably has a nest-egg that could buy us all up. You know what tips those old servants used to get from visitors." She began to draw him with gentle urgency across the grass towards the terrace steps. "Come along, darling. We can't stand here staring at it all day."

They walked slowly up the stone steps, along the terrace, and round to the front of the house.

There again he stood for a moment, looking up at the Venetian window just above the door. He had always loved that window.

"What an imposing entrance!" said Celia.

3

He felt a momentary irritation. Imposing was the last word that she should have used about it. Though in proportion with the rest of the house, it had a charm, an elegance, a certain winning sweetness, which had appealed to him, even as a boy.

The stone steps that led down from the front door were flanked by balustrades of delicately wrought iron, curving outward in a graceful sweep. Under the moulded pediment was a fanlight of exquisite tracery. The door itself, solid and massive enough, had yet always seemed to him to have an indefinable welcoming quality about it, as if it had been made to let people into the house rather than to keep them out. No, Celia should not have said "imposing."

He followed her up the short flight of steps, laying his hand on the wrought-iron balustrade in a gesture that was almost a caress.

In the middle of the door was an old brass knocker, made in the shape of a lion's head.

He was in general singularly devoid of imagination, but such imagination as he possessed had always been called into play by this house, and in his childhood he had thought of the knocker as hurt and saddened by the presence of the modern interloper, the electric bell. He used to linger about the front of the house when visitors were expected and whisper to them mysteriously, "Knock, don't ring," which many of them did, thinking that the bell must be out of order.

It seemed to smile down at him now in rather weary welcome. Before he knew what he was doing he had whispered, "Knock, Celia, don't ring."

She looked at him in faint surprise and put her finger on the bell.

"I'll knock if no one comes," she said, "but surely they haven't let the bells get out of order."

A very old woman in a black silk dress opened the door. After staring at them a moment in astonishment she started forward with outstretched arms.

"Master Bob!" she said.

He clasped her to him and kissed her.

"Mother Hubbard! Old Mother Hubbard!" Then he remembered

Celia and, releasing the small black figure, said, "Mother Hubbard was like a mother to me when I was a boy, Celia."

He spoke awkwardly. Celia had never belonged to this part of his life. He felt shy of admitting her to it—shy and in some strange way afraid, as if uncertain what her hard bright efficiency might do to it.

The old woman drew out a handkerchief and wiped her eyes.

"Excuse me, ma'am," she said in an unsteady voice. "It took me by surprise. I haven't seen Master Bob for so long. I didn't know you were coming. . . ."

"I'm sorry," said Robert. "We ought to have sent you word, of course, but we only got the news this morning, and we drove over at once. We left the car in the road and came in through the kitchen garden. Well, how are things?"

"You'll find a sad change, sir," said Mrs. Hubbard, standing aside to let them enter. "It's been empty so long since the last tenant. Times are very difficult, I hear, and few people have the money to take a big house like Chedsy Place."

She spoke as the inhabitant of a desert island might speak of the fabled doings of a far-off continent. She had lived so long in this little world that life outside it seemed unreal and legendary to her.

"They say times are very bad indeed, sir," she said again, shaking her head.

Then she turned to Celia with an air of quiet dignity.

"I wish I could welcome you in a different fashion, ma'am, but with the place unlet so long we manage with as few servants as possible. Only just enough to keep things clean. Would you like to rest, ma'am? I'll have a fire lighted at once in the small drawing-room. I'd have seen about lunch, of course, if I'd known you were coming, but there's soup, and I can send out for chops and——"

"No lunch, Mother Hubbard," put in Robert. "We've only dashed over to see the place, and then we're going straight home. I shall have to make arrangements with the lawyer, of course, but I just wanted to see it first once more and show it to my wife. I've got a farm in Somerset now, you know, and I'm a real regular right-down working farmer. I was a lazy little blighter when I lived here, wasn't I, but I have to be up with the dawn now. We make it pay, too—just pay." He smiled at Celia. "It's my wife, of course, who's the brains of the thing."

Mrs. Hubbard sighed, a gentle melancholy sigh. "Real regular right-down working farmer." Times had changed indeed. She did not understand it. She did not even try to understand it. She accepted it with resignation and a faint distasteful wonder. What had people been about to let things come to this pass? She'd done her duty within her own little world, upholding the old traditions, maintaining the old discipline. Why hadn't other people done their duty in the big world outside? The system in which people knew their places had been in her eyes perfect and unassailable, but, however perfect, it hadn't proved unassailable. People didn't know their places any longer. The whole world was upside down.

They followed her through the hall. A log fire burned in the great open fireplace, and in its light the polished surfaces of chairs and chests and tables shone like crystal.

"How beautifully everything's kept!" said Celia, and added, "I suppose you've been here a long time, Mrs. Hubbard?"

"I came as kitchen-maid when I was fifteen," replied the old woman.

She must be nearly eighty, thought Robert, glancing down at her. He had thought at first that she had hardly changed since the days when she had presided over his boyhood, always respectful, always in the background, yet somehow always more important than the nurses and governesses who had been his official guardians. Looking at her closely now, he saw that she had altered more than he had noticed in the first excitement of meeting. Her eyes were red-rimmed, her skin was covered with tiny wrinkles, her mouth was sunken, but her eyes, beneath the gold-rimmed glasses, were as keen as ever, and she held herself as erect as a young girl. More erect, indeed, than any young girl holds herself nowadays, he thought. Despite the slightness of her figure and the deference of her speech and manner, she had always had about her a secret dignity of

6

which even as boys he and Cyril had stood in awe. She opened the door of the big drawing-room and stepped aside for them to enter. It was a lofty spacious room, with a fireplace at each end and an elaborate candelabra hanging from the centre of the ceiling. Robert closed the door and examined it.

"Look at this door, Celia. It's solid mahogany, inlaid with ebony. And the handle. . . ."

"It's lovely," she said, but there was a far-away look in her eyes, and he knew that she was thinking of something else.

In the dining-room the huge mahogany table that ran down the length of it was covered with holland, and somehow its shrouded shape made Robert think of a coffin, in which the glory of the Beatons lay buried. Faded oil paintings of Beatons looked down from the walls—men with ginger hair, sunburnt freckled skins, tawny eyes, and the long indolent humorous mouth. It was not a weak mouth, but it explained perhaps the gradual decline of the family fortunes.

"The mantelpiece is an Adam," Robert was saying, "and the panelling was all made from wood on the estate. In the days when there was an estate, of course."

Again Celia threw a glance round the room, dreamy, speculative, with an odd underlying shrewdness.

"The man over the fireplace," went on her husband, "was killed in a duel in Elizabeth's time. . . . The old lady herself was supposed to be involved in it somehow—no one quite knows how. Anyway she gave the place to his son—and anything else he wanted, apparently."

She looked at the portrait with her faint abstracted smile.

He thought: It doesn't mean anything to her. And felt disproportionately hurt.

They went round the other rooms—the library, its walls lined from top to bottom with books, its long windows overlooking the rose garden; the small drawing-room, the morning-room, the gunroom, the billiard-room.

They followed their guide up the broad shallow staircase and saw the best bedroom, with its great four-poster bed and rich silk hangings dim with time; the blue bedroom, with the brocade panels that had faded to a colour that was neither blue nor grey but as lovely as the first evening mist; the Chinese bedroom, with its lacquered furniture, Oriental jars, and framed panels of embroidery. Everywhere the air was sweet with the aromatic perfume of the pot-pourri that stood in open bowls on window-sills and chests.

Robert put his hand into one of them and let the ghost-like petals fall slowly through his fingers.

"You still make it?" he said.

"Yes, sir. Every summer just as usual," said the old woman.

Whatever happened in the strange alien incomprehensible world outside, the rites of her own little world must be performed punctiliously and regularly as they had been performed for centuries.

But the subtle glamour that the place had always had for him was laying its hold on him again. He had forgotten how strong it was, how it seemed to enter his very veins, to steal over his senses like an enchantment. His body ached as if with desire for a woman. It frightened him, and he gathered together his defences.

"There's no point in going through the other bedrooms . . ." he said to his wife.

But Celia, who had seemed aloof, almost bored, in all the rooms they had entered, now insisted on seeing everything.

"I'll go on. Wait for me here if you don't want to come."

So she went on with Mrs. Hubbard, and Robert stood, leaning out of the window, gazing over the garden and park towards the far-off hills. He looked placid enough, his eyes fixed dreamily on the distance, his pipe between his lips, but his heart was a riot of emotions. He had forgotten that it was like this, that a mere heap of stone and brick and mortar could tear so at one's heart. . . .

Celia came back, looking purposeful and alert.

"It's very good of you to have taken me round, Mrs. Hubbard," she said. "We'll explore the garden alone. We ought to be going, oughtn't we, Robert? No," as Mrs. Hubbard anxiously murmured something about "soup" and "chops," "we honestly can't stay for lunch."

They went down to the front door, and Robert again impulsively kissed the little old woman.

"Good-bye, Mother Hubbard," he said. "I'll write or come round and see you as soon as I've settled with the lawyers."

Mrs. Hubbard stood watching them till they had disappeared round the house, then she went slowly back to the hall, through a green baize door, and down a flight of stairs to the kitchen regions. The housekeeper's room was the largest room in the basement except the kitchen itself. In it was a square table covered with a red serge cloth, a comfortable basket chair, and a big old-fashioned fireplace. An enormous dresser took up one side of the room, and there was a sink, with taps and drying-board, beneath the window. On the window-sill, catching what light there was, stood several bowls of lilies of the valley just coming into flower. Except near the window the room was so dark that, it had to be lighted artificially all day, but there was about it, when lighted, a cheerful cosy air. It had been Mrs. Hubbard's home for fifty years.

A young girl, dressed in a print dress and white apron, was kneeling on the hearth-rug, putting coals on the fire. She raised her face, the round rosy face of a country girl, and said:

"Was that Mr. Robert?"

Mrs. Hubbard took the basket of household mending that stood on the dresser and, sitting down by the hearth, went on with the task of darning a fine linen pillow-slip at which the visitors had interrupted her.

"Yes," she said slowly.

The girl's eyes were bright with excitement.

"What's going to happen to the place, ma'am?" she said.

Mrs. Hubbard drew out her thread from the almost invisible darn before replying. Then she said, "That's neither your business nor mine for the present, Kathleen."

Kathleen put another piece of coal onto the fire. Though temporarily checked, her curiosity was too insistent to be extinguished.

"He lived here when he was a child, didn't he, ma'am?" she said.

Mrs. Hubbard let her mending fall onto her knee.

"Yes," she said, speaking so dreamily that she seemed to be talking more to herself than to the girl. "He was old Mr. Beaton's nephew, and when he was left an orphan old Mr. Beaton brought him up with his own son."

"With Mr. Cyril?"

"Yes. He was always more of a Beaton than Mr. Cyril, and Mr. Beaton always liked him the better of the two, though he did his best to hide it."

"Did you like Mr. Cyril, ma'am?"

Mrs. Hubbard shook her head.

"No ... there was something not quite straightforward about him. He wasn't a real Beaton. He and Mr. Robert never got on even as boys, and when Mr. Beaton died and the place came to Mr. Cyril they had nothing more to do with each other."

"Mr. Cyril never lived here, did he, ma'am?"

"No. He was abroad when his father died, and he only came home to see about letting the place, then went back again. I'm afraid he was rather wild. He gambled a good deal. Now that he's dead and the place has come to Mr. Robert, there's very little money with it, I believe. And, even if he tries to let it again, few people are wealthy enough just now to take a house as big as this."

"It's, been empty three months, hasn't it, ma'am?" said Kathleen.

"Yes. They can't afford to let it stand empty any longer. Mr. Robert never had much money. His father invested foolishly."

"Then the place will be sold?" said the girl.

"I expect so."

"What will you do, ma'am?"

Mrs. Hubbard drew herself up, as if realising for the first time to whom she was talking.

"That's not your business, Kathleen."

"I'm sorry, ma'am," said the girl, then, seeing that the old woman was not really offended, went on:

"I only just caught a peep at them. I'd like to have a proper look."

"Well, you can't," said Mrs. Hubbard shortly. "They've gone. So you may as well get on with your work."

But they hadn't gone. They were standing by the wrought-iron gate that led into the walled kitchen garden, looking back at the house.

"I'd meant to tell Mother Hubbard that there'd be a pension for her when the place was sold up," Robert was saying, "but somehow when it came to the point I couldn't. It seems indecent to talk of money to her. She must have a pension, of course, when things are settled."

"Of course," said Celia absently, and added, "Christmas is only a month off now, isn't it? I don't suppose that anything will be settled before Christmas."

"Christmas . . ." he echoed slowly. "It seems odd to think of the place standing empty at Christmas. It used to be chock-full of people then in the old days."

She said nothing, only continued to look up at the house with that dreamy speculative gaze. He stirred uneasily. Again there had come to him an insistent desire to get back to his farm as quickly as he could. This place, with its subtle, all-pervading charm, was like a mistress, the farm was his wife. He wanted to forget the mistress and return to his fidelity. He loved the farm and felt often an odd secret kinship with the earth he tilled. Its slow leisurely processes satisfied something deep and fundamental in his nature. They couldn't be hurried, couldn't be turned from their course. . . .

"Let's go, Celia," he said. "There's nothing to see in the gardens. They never were much, and now they've run to seed altogether."

But Celia seemed to think that there was something to see in the gardens. In the kitchen garden, at any rate. She went round it slowly, examining every plot of ground, ignoring his impatience.

"Darling," said Robert, "if you want to watch cabbages growing you can do it just as well at home."

She smiled at him, still continuing her slow, deliberate scrutiny.

"The kitchen garden's been kept up quite well," she said at last. "I suppose the man sells the stuff." She turned to him abruptly.

"Robert, there's no reason why we shouldn't spend Christmas here."

"My dear, we couldn't possibly," replied Robert patiently. "Surely you understand that. It's simply running away with money standing empty like this. We've got to sell it, lock, stock, and barrel, at once and get what we can for it—precious little, I expect—and be satisfied. What would be the point of pigging it in two rooms with Mother Hubbard and a woman from the village?"

"I didn't mean pigging it in two rooms," she said. "I meant opening it out, and engaging a proper staff."

He threw her a puzzled glance.

"You know we couldn't afford it."

"We could, if we took paying guests."

He was silent for a moment. The smile had faded from his face.

"Paying guests?" he repeated slowly.

"I mean nice people," she said hastily, "really nice people. I don't see that it would be any different from the old days. Lots of your uncle's friends who came down for Christmas must have been strangers to you personally. Nearly everyone with a house this size has to take paying guests nowadays."

He looked away, so that she should not see the sudden horror in his eyes. It was less horror at her suggestion than at the gulf that it had opened up between them. Or rather that it had revealed—for the gulf must always have been there.

"It's impossible," he said shortly. "You don't understand."

"I do," she pleaded. "It's your place. I want you to have it just for a few weeks, and that's the only way."

He understood, with something of amazement, that it was her love for him that had given birth to the project. He tried to find words to tell her how abhorrent the idea was to him, but could find none. About anything beyond the superficialities of life he was strangely inarticulate. He abandoned the attempt and instead sought some practical objection that would appeal to her.

"We haven't got the money even for that," he said. "It would want a lot of doing up."

"No, it wouldn't," she countered. "There's nothing that I couldn't do myself or get done quite cheaply. The rooms and furniture are just right."

He realised that her dreamy air when going over the rooms had not meant boredom, as he had imagined. She had been thinking even then of filling the place with paying guests. The grace and beauty of the rooms had meant little or nothing to her, but she could probably have given their exact proportions, she probably knew just what pieces of furniture the strange holland shapes concealed, she had probably already in her imagination arranged each room to its last detail for the reception of her "guests." He felt a fear that he had often felt before—a fear of her quiet purposefulnness and determination. It was incalculable, irresistible, beyond the reach of his love or even of his understanding.

"We couldn't leave the farm," he said, but, as he said it, he knew that she must have already considered and settled that point.

"Yes, we could," she said, "for a week or two, at any rate. We could easily leave Halliday in charge. He's the best foreman we've ever had." She turned to him suddenly. "Darling, didn't the Harveys ask you to go and stay with them? Why not go and spend the next month there? It will do you good. You need a change. I'll make all the arrangements for the Christmas party here while you're away, and you shan't have any of the bother of it. You do agree to it, don't you, darling?"

He yielded, because he had always yielded to her, because he loved her so much that he could never deny her anything, and also because it was his nature to take most readily the way of least resistance.

At his consent she glowed into a flame-like eagerness, and her whole body seemed to quiver with impatience.

"Come along, then," she said. "We're going to be awfully late home."

He went with her through the green wooden door that led from the walled kitchen garden to the lane outside, where the battered old Standard awaited them. He took his place at the wheel, and they drove off. She had lost her air of dreamy abstraction. She was bright and entertaining, commenting on things they passed, making plans for the farm. She did not once mention Chedsy Place or her idea of taking paying guests. Had he not known her so well he would have thought that she had completely forgotten it.

Chapter Two

CELIA stood in the hall, looking about her with critical appraising eyes.

Through the open door could be seen the large drawing-room, where a log fire burnt at each end and where bowls of flowers and flowering bulbs stood on tables, mantelpieces, and window-sills. Over everything was the pleasant acrid scent of burning logs, mingled with the sweetness of early hyacinths.

For the last four weeks she had worked almost without rest. Even when she slept her mind was at work, for she generally awoke with some of the many problems that confronted her solved, some plan ready to carry into action. During the day, dressed in overalls and dustcap, she had polished, scoured, moved furniture with the servants, and even repainted the shabbier woodwork.

The whole undertaking had been more difficult than at first she had realised. She had decided that the place should combine the amenities of hotel and country house. The country-house element was to be in the foreground. There were to be a butler and footmen instead of the usual uniformed porters, and Celia herself intended to play the part of hostess of a private house party, but the guests were to sit at separate tables in the dining-room, except for the Christmas dinner, and tea was to be served to them separately in the drawing-room or library. She had engaged a large staff, all of whom had worked indefatigably to get things ready in time. Celia never had any trouble with servants. As Kathleen said to Mrs. Hubbard: "You don't mind working yourself to death for someone what's not afraid of working themselves to death alongside of you."

Mrs. Hubbard, too, had worked hard in her basement stronghold, looking through piles of linen that had not been used for years, darning, sorting, airing, renovating.

"And this, ma'am," she had said, drawing her wrinkled fingers over the priceless lace of an afternoon tea-cloth that had once formed part of a bride's dowry, "is this to be used?"

"Oh yes," Celia had replied. "I want to use all the nice things. I want it to be just like the Christmas parties in the old days."

"Very good, ma'am," said Mrs. Hubbard, with an only just perceptible tightening of her wrinkled lips.

In spite of her willingness to help, Celia had a dim, unformulated feeling of disappointment with regard to Mrs. Hubbard. She had wanted someone with whom she could relax, someone who, in this affair at any rate, would be more or less her equal, someone with whom she could discuss her arrangements unofficially, at her ease. And Mrs. Hubbard had refused to be that someone. She was respectful, uncommunicative, infinitely detached. While willing to work to her uttermost in order to help Celia's venture, she seemed in some subtle way to dissociate herself from it. She had withdrawn into an impregnable fortress, and all Celia's attacks upon it were in vain. Celia would come down to Mrs. Hubbard's room and talk to her in a kindly confidential manner, but she could not get beyond the barrier of the old woman's aloofness, beyond the armed defences of her "Yes, ma'am," "No, ma'am," "Very good, ma'am."

In the end she shrugged her shoulders and left the old woman to herself. She's been buried here so long, I suppose, she thought, that she's almost mummified. She hasn't an idea in life outside the kitchen and the household linen.

The butler—Cummings by name—was an intelligent man, who had at once grasped the whole situation. As he had been butler in titled families as well as porter in an exclusive West End hotel, he could be trusted to combine the two roles with tact and discretion, and already he had made of the heterogeneous collection of servants under him a well-drilled, well-disciplined little army.

In appearance he was a tall man with shoulders that were just too broad even for his height, a square sallow face, a straight narrow mouth, and a knowing humorous eye. He had an air of understanding at once any situation in which he found himself, of being slightly amused by it, and wholly equal to it.

Turning to cross the hall, Celia glanced at her reflection in a Queen Anne mirror that hung by the fireplace. She looked pale and tired, but she didn't feel tired. She felt excited and stimulated. She had enjoyed this work more than she had ever enjoyed the management of the farm. There had always been something about the farm that she had secretly resented. The very slowness of the processes of Nature, their refusal to be hurried or bent to her will, had irked and irritated her. This was different. . . . In four weeks she had transformed this barracks of a place into something that was, she firmly believed, perfect and unique. She had always been aware that she possessed unusual organising powers, and she had found an intense satisfaction in this outlet for them. So absorbed had she become in carrying her plan into effect that already she had forgotten the impulse of love for Robert that had inspired it.

She entered the little room at the end of the hall that had been the gun-room and that she had now made her office. A list of the "guests" lay on her writing-table. Her carefully worded advertisement had had a large response, and the house would be full for Christmas.

On the wall over her desk hung a list of "festivities." Christmas Day was on the Monday, and the short programme began on the Friday evening.

Friday evening	Whist Drive
Saturday evening	Dance
Sunday evening	Carol Singers
Monday evening	(Christmas Day) Dance

She had made no arrangements for the Tuesday, as all the guests intended to leave for home on that day. The whole thing was to be as informal—as much like a private Christmas party—as possible, the arrangements subject to any sort of change at the last minute.

She took up the list of guests and the dates of their arrival. Five of them were coming to-day.

Wednesday 20th   Miss Nettleton

	Mrs. Lewel and Mrs. Nightingale
	Mrs. Stephenson-Pollitt
	Mr. Mallard
Thursday 21st	Miss Kimball and Miss Lattimer
	Miss Wingate
	Mr. and Mrs. Fielden
	Rev. H. and Mrs. Standfield
Friday 22nd	Miss Bella Torrance
	Mr. Ellison
	Mr. and Mrs. Paynter and family
	Mrs. Kellogg
	Mr., Mrs., and Miss Downing
	Mr. and Mrs. Osmond

Robert was coming to-morrow. He had gone to stay with the Harveys a few days after their first visit to Chedsy Place, and she had not seen him since. She had told him nothing of her arrangements in her letters, because she wanted them to be a surprise to him.

She put down the list and turned to the window.

Already a taxi was drawing up at the door, and Miss Nettleton was descending from it.

Chapter Three

MISS NETTLETON was tall and thin, with a surprisingly youthful figure, a surprisingly old face, and a brown wig that must have shrunk in the cleaning, for it showed a distinct line of white hair all round the edge. She was dressed in a shapeless brown tweed costume and a battered brown felt hat. After greeting Celia rather vaguely, she went up to her room to unpack and came down again in a few minutes, carrying a map and guide-book.

Celia, who was waiting for her in the hall, showed her into the drawing-room.

There the new-comer sat down in the armchair nearest the fire and crossed her legs, revealing voluminous grey knickers that came down well below her knee.

"So I'm the first, am I?" She had a resonant drawling voice that somehow consorted oddly with her wrinkled face. "Perhaps you can help me arrange my expeditions," she went on. "I always like to get those fixed up as soon as possible. I've never done this part of the country before, though I've done most others."

"You've travelled about a good deal?" ventured Celia curiously. There was certainly an elusive suggestion of flotsam and jetsam about the visitor.

"I'm always travelling," replied Miss Nettleton. "I live in hotels. *Hotels!*" She sat up as if galvanised into sudden life. The drawl left her voice, the vagueness her eyes. "I simply can't *tell* you what I've suffered in hotels. The one I was in last month. . . . Cabbage day after day, day after day. Simply day after day. Cabbage. Never any other vegetable. Only cabbage. I said to the waitress: 'Take this away and bring me some other vegetable.' She said: 'There isn't any other vegetable, madam.' I said: 'Then you must get some other vegetable, and I'm staying here till it comes.' So they sent me a tablespoonful of tinned peas. And when I spoke to the manager about it he was most insolent. I went on to Marlton the next day and stayed at the Bridge Hotel. The cooking was all right, but the *beds*! So many lumps you simply couldn't get comfortable between any two of them. It was an expensive hotel, too. I went on after two days. I never stay long anywhere. I find that people get on one's nerves so. . . ."

"This, of course, isn't exactly a hotel," said Celia gently.

Miss Nettleton, having left the only subject that could rouse her passions, resumed her slow drawl.

"No. I thought it would be a change. I liked the sound of your advertisement. I didn't want an ordinary hotel for Christmas. I generally stay with relations, but—well, my arrangements fell through this year. My uncle—he's a judge—isn't well and has to be kept very quiet, and my brother's had to let his place this year. It's too big for them to keep up. I don't mind about that, really, because I don't like his wife. . . ."

Despite the oddity of her appearance, something in her speech and manner proclaimed that she came of good family. She was evidently one of those eccentric elderly spinsters who drift from hotel to hotel, and whose families are glad to pay a small allowance in order to rid themselves of further responsibility.

Her eyes were roaming round the room again with vague approval.

"We had two fireplaces in our drawing-room at home. So sensible, isn't it? . . . Now, Mrs. Beaton"—she jerked her long thin figure to an upright position—"I must plan my little expeditions. I don't like to lose a minute when I'm in a new part of the country. I've been studying the guide-book, and I've made a list of the things one ought to see, and I'd be so glad if you could tell me about 'buses and things."

Celia fetched the time-table of 'buses and trains and was just putting them on the table by Miss Nettleton's chair when Cummings announced the arrival of the next two guests.

Mrs. Stephenson-Pollitt—taller and thinner even than Miss Nettleton—was dressed in an old-fashioned travelling-cloak that she threw carelessly aside as she entered the hall, revealing a loosely fitting green garment, heavily smocked at waist and yoke—a garment of the sort once affected by the Pre-Raphaelites. Indeed, thirty years ago she must have been a beauty of the Pre-Raphaelite type, but, though she still cultivated the type, the beauty had run to seed. Beneath the broad-brimmed hat could be seen frizzy black hair bound round her brow so low as almost to obscure her sight. It had a frowsty unbrushed look, as if it had been done up in that fashion several years ago and never taken down since.

Her eyes, or rather what one could see of them through the obscuring mist of hair, were beautiful—black, velvety, heavily fringed with thick, curling lashes.

The rest of her face was uninteresting. The mouth and neck lacked the exotic beauty of the Rossetti type, and the teeth were irregular and discoloured.

At first Celia felt slightly alarmed when, replying to her greeting, Mrs. Stephenson-Pollitt placed her hand on her arm and approached her face so close to hers that there was only an inch or so between them, but she soon found that this was the only attitude in which Mrs. Stephenson-Pollitt could carry on a conversation. Moreover, she generally sank her voice to a sibilant confidential whisper, even when merely commenting on the weather.

"It's all beautiful," she whispered.

"I'm glad you like it," said Celia, conquering a strong desire to withdraw from the close proximity of the frowsty hair and blazing black eyes.

"I love it. I knew I should. I'm psychic, you know. As soon as I saw your advertisement, I heard a voice telling me to write about it. I always obey my psychic voices, so I wrote at once. I knew it would be congenial. ... I suffer so terribly in uncongenial surroundings. One has to pay for being psychic, you know. Oh, this is my nephew, Brian Mallard."

The handsome, sulky-looking boy who had been glowering in the background bowed stiffly. Mrs. Stephenson-Pollitt approached her face still nearer to Celia's and lowered her voice till it was a thin, penetrating whistle.

"He's at a theological college. Going in for the Church, you know. I always say that institutional religion is a step. It helped me before I came to a fuller knowledge, came, one might almost say, into direct contact with the Infinite. . . . I retire into the silence every afternoon after lunch."

The nephew made an impatient movement, and Celia said: "Won't you come up and see your rooms?"

Mrs. Stephenson-Pollitt gathered together her trailing skirts and accompanied Celia upstairs. At intervals she stopped, closed her eyes, sniffed, and said, "Yes ... sympathetic ... distinctly sympathetic. . . . Of course, I simply couldn't breathe if it weren't. I've often had to go straight home the minute I've arrived at a place, haven't I, Brian?"

Brian muttered something inaudible.

"Brian isn't psychic," explained Mrs. Stephenson-Pollitt in her piercing whisper. "He lacks spiritual sensitiveness. His aura's almost colourless. . . ."

Celia was glad to show the unhappy boy into his room and go on alone with Mrs. Stephenson-Pollitt.

"Brian and I," continued the new-comer, "aren't quite *en rapport*. He's my brother's son, and my brother and I were never quite *en rapport*. Brian's like him in many ways. He's not even set foot in the psychic world, as yet. He hasn't got *vision*. ... I've brought him up since his parents died, you know. When he chose the Church as his career, I said: 'Brian, I shall never try to influence your choice, but think, think deeply, before you dally with institutions. Institutions are soul destroying.' I still hope that he may change his mind. I thought early this year that his aura was getting a little more colour, but——"

"This is your room," said Celia.

Mrs. Stephenson-Pollitt entered, closed her eyes, and sniffed once more.

"Yes, the whole house is sympathetic," she pronounced with an air of finality.

Then she took off the floppy hat and pushed back the furze-bush of hair from her eyes. "I write, you know, and that's the difficulty

I find in writing in strange houses. An atmosphere that isn't sympathetic paralyses me. Literally paralyses me."

Celia glanced at the little writing-table.

"Will that do to write at?" she said. "I think that some of the others are larger. I could easily have it changed."

"No, it will do very well, thank you," said Mrs. Stephenson-Pollitt. "I don't intend to write much while I'm here. Don't go, my dear," as Celia began to edge to the door. "Just stay with me while I put away my things. I find you very sympathetic. Your aura's got just the right shade of blue. . . . Do you know my books?"

"No, I don't think I do," said Celia.

"Oh, my dear, you must read them," hissed Mrs. Stephenson-Pollitt earnestly. "I know you'd like them. Everyone does."

She had unstrapped a battered leather bag and, drawing out a photograph in a silver frame, handed it to Celia. It was the photograph of herself taken about thirty years ago in the heyday of her beauty.

"That's me, my dear, when I was young. People tell me that I've hardly changed at all. It was my husband's favourite photograph. That's why I carry it about with me. I've always had the gift of beauty."

She spoke in a tone of superb detachment—too calm and remote even to approach vanity.

"It's very nice," said Celia, "but I think I really must go now."

"Well, my dear, if you must . . ." hissed Mrs. Stephenson-Pollitt confidentially. "But we'll have a long talk together soon. And you must read my books."

"You'll ring for anything you want, won't you?" said Celia from the door.

"Yes . . . there's only one thing, my dear. I told you that I went into the silence every day from two to half past. It will be quiet up here then, I hope? I can't stand noise when I'm in the silence."

"Oh yes, I'm sure it will be quiet. I'll see that it is."

"Thank you, my dear. I once had a housemaid who hummed. You could hear her all through the house. It was a hum without any tune in it. Just on and on. You know the sort. And if there's one thing more disturbing than another when one's in communion with the Infinite, it's humming. I told her that she'd have to go if she couldn't conquer it. She tried hard to conquer it, but she couldn't. She could stop while she thought of it, but as soon as she began to think of anything else the hum came on again, so she had to go. I was sorry, because in lots of ways she was more satisfactory than the cook. The cook drank and had men in the kitchen, but, as I explained to her at the time, that didn't interrupt me when I was communing with the Infinite and humming did."

"I'll see that it's quite quiet," Celia assured her again and, ignoring an "Oh, and another thing . . ." from the new-comer, made her escape.

On the landing she drew a deep breath. It was dreadful. Suppose the whole lot of them were cranks. Perhaps a thing like this—neither hotel nor country house—was bound to attract only cranks. She'd expected Mrs. Nightingale to be rather odd (the daughter, Mrs. Lewel, had said that her memory was failing), but both Miss Nettleton and Mrs. Stephenson-Pollitt had written perfectly normal letters.

A heavy depression stole over her spirit. It was the reaction, she told herself. . . . Till now she had been so busy that she had had no time or energy to waste on anxiety for the future. But now the moment to which she had been directing all her efforts had arrived, and she felt, instead of exultation, a desperate fear of failure.

She wandered aimlessly in and out of the rooms, shaking the cushions, altering the position of chairs and ornaments, a prey to "nerves" for the first time in her life.

She was relieved when the sound of wheels on the gravelled drive warned her of the arrival of Mrs. Lewel and Mrs. Nightingale.

Forestalling Cummings, she was standing at the open front door when the taxi drew up.

Mrs. Lewel descended first. She was a thick-set, middle-aged woman, with brown, short-sighted eyes, thin brown hair streaked with grey, a sallow face, and an air of resigned weariness. Her navy-blue costume was well cut, but showed signs of long wear.

Her mother, on the other hand, was a gay, brightly coloured, little old lady, with silver hair, blue eyes, and rosy cheeks. She wore a long black cape and a bonnet trimmed with bunches of violets and bows of lace. A slight affection in the nature of paralysis agitans kept these trimmings dancing continually, and so gave their wearer an odd air of gaiety. She smiled at Celia and kissed her affectionately.

"How *nice* to see you again, Bertha darling," she said.

"It's not Bertha, mother," said Mrs. Lewel patiently. "It's Mrs. Beaton."

"Of course, my dear," said Mrs. Nightingale vaguely.

She threw a rather bewildered glance round the bedroom into which Celia showed her.

"This isn't the bedroom we had last time, is it?"

"We've not been here before," said her daughter.

"But, darling, we *always* come to the Grange for Christmas."

"This isn't the Grange. It's Chedsy Place."

Little Mrs. Nightingale wrestled with the problem for a moment, her brows drawn together over puzzled blue eyes, then seemed to dismiss it. She smiled brightly at Celia, and the violets and lace bows in her bonnet danced merrily together.

"Anyway, it's so good of you to have asked us, Janie dear," she said, "and I'm so looking forward to seeing your dear boys again. . . ."

Mrs. Lewel drew Celia out onto the landing and closed the door.

"She won't be any trouble," she said, rather anxiously. "It's just that she forgets."

"Of course," said Celia. "I shall love having her."

"Christmas is such an awkward time for us," went on Mrs. Lewel. "You see, her companion goes away, and maids want a holiday at Christmas nowadays. . . . We went to a hotel last Christmas, but it wasn't a success. When I saw your advertisement I thought that it would be just what we wanted. I'll try not to let her annoy people. It isn't that she means any harm, of course. It's just that she—forgets."

There was something vaguely depressing about the dining-room that night, with only three of its fourteen tables occupied. Miss Nettleton had not changed her shapeless skirt and jumper, but she had put on another wig—a tidier and larger one that completely hid her white hair.

Mrs. Stephenson-Pollitt wore a dress of ruby velvet, made in a mediaeval style, whose long sleeves almost touched the floor. A tiara gleamed fitfully through the tangled meshes of her hair, and she had on an enormous necklace of barbaric design that reached her knees.

Her nephew walked behind her, with an air that seemed to protest dumbly but passionately against her whole existence. He scowled ferociously round the room when they entered, as if daring anyone to laugh at her.

No one, however, took any notice of them. Miss Nettleton had brought her guide-book and was absorbed in reading it and making pencil notes. Mrs. Lewel was intent upon her mother's dinner. Mrs. Nightingale had had a refreshing sleep since her arrival and had awakened full of energy and a certain childish, mischievous obstinacy. She wore a dress of black moiré silk, with a graceful medici collar of white lace and heavy lace cuffs. A lace cap, trimmed with imitation red berries, covered her white hair. Her blue eyes were bright, her cheeks rosy. She looked, in fact, exceedingly pretty.

"But I want it," she said. "I like lobster mayonnaise."

"No, dear," said her daughter patiently. "You know it doesn't suit you."

"It does suit me," persisted the old lady. "Anything suits me. I've got a wonderful digestion."

"You were ill the last time you had it, and the doctor said——"

"Nonsense. I don't believe in doctors. I never have believed in doctors. They've only got one idea in their heads and that is spoiling people's pleasure. I'm going to have——"

Her voice trailed away uncertainly. She had quite forgotten what it was that she had decided to have. Whatever it was had disappeared, but the footman was offering her a plate of chicken. She began to eat it with an air of triumph.

"Of course it won't do me any harm," she said. "I can eat *anything*."

Celia did not join her guests for coffee, but had it alone in her little office. She was still feeling physically exhausted and nervously apprehensive. In an attempt to conquer her depression, she took up the next day's list of arrivals and studied it.

Miss Judith Kimball and Miss Sidney Lattimer . . . Miss Kimball had written to make the arrangements, and her letters had been charming.

The Rev. Humphrey Standfield, a country clergyman in Wiltshire, had engaged rooms for himself and his wife in a small scholarly hand.

Miss Wingate, M.A., was a college lecturer, and, surely, Celia told herself, only a young and quite human lecturer would wish to join a Christmas party of this sort. Mr. and Mrs. Fielden. . . . Mr. Fielden had been blinded in the war. . . .

She went into the drawing-room and stood in the doorway for a moment, unseen.

Mrs. Stephenson-Pollitt was sitting next to Miss Nettleton, one hand on her arm, speaking earnestly in a low, tense voice.

"I have psychic dreams, you see. That's how I get my plots. . . ."

Miss Nettleton listened in an abstracted manner, her pencil poised over the paper on which she was drawing up her week's programme of sight-seeing.

Ostentatiously aloof from them, in a chair by the window, sat young Brian Mallard. He looked bored and sulky. His legs were crossed, and he seemed to be completely absorbed in watching the toe of his crossed leg move alternately up and down, and round and round.

Mrs. Lewel and Mrs. Nightingale sat side by side on the sofa. Mrs. Lewel was knitting a nondescript sort of garment that seemed by its colour, shape, and texture, to be destined for Charity. Mrs. Nightingale sat next to her, her eyes shut, evidently asleep. But, though asleep, she still quivered slightly, so that the berries and white lace bows danced and her whole figure still had that curious air of gaiety.

As Celia watched she opened her eyes and looked about her.

"We're at Bournemouth, aren't we?" she said.

"No, dear," said her daughter, "we're at Chedsy Place."

Again a slight bewilderment clouded the smiling blue eyes.

"I thought we were at Bournemouth, staying with Cissie."

"No, dear."

The old lady suddenly caught Brian Mallard's eye and beamed and nodded at him delightedly.

"*Dear* Peter!" she said, then to her daughter: "He's exactly like his mother, isn't he?"

Celia withdrew again to her office. She must remember to order cars to-morrow for Miss Wingate and the Standfields. Miss Kimball and the Fieldens were coming in their own cars. Mr. Fielden had sent innumerable instructions about diet. His vegetables must be steamed. His bread must be wholemeal. He breakfasted on an assortment of nuts, raisins, raw carrots, and apples. There must be a weighing apparatus and two hip-baths in his bedroom. He was bringing his own violet-ray apparatus, which his wife would manipulate.

She went through the list of his somewhat complicated requirements, ticking them off in her mind. Yes, she'd seen to everything. Suddenly she remembered that Robert, too, was coming to-morrow, and, at the thought of Robert, all her depression vanished.

Chapter Four

CELIA heaved a sigh of relief as Miss Kimball's car drew up at the front door. No cranks here. A correct, luxurious car. A correct, well-uniformed chauffeur. Inside, glimpses of a woman and girl, both fashionably dressed and wearing expensive furs.

As soon as the car had come to a standstill, the chauffeur sprang alertly from his seat and threw open the door.

Celia's eyes roved over him in half-unconscious approval. He was young and good-looking, with humorous eyes, a blunt nose, curly hair, and a wide mouth dented at the corners. He held out a gloved hand to help the woman descend, but she stepped out alone without looking at him.

Celia's approving eye moved on to her. A beautiful woman, beautifully turned out. The chic of the grey costume with its enormous fur collar suggested Paris. The small grey hat showed sleek waved hair of that shade of auburn that seems specially designed to set off a dazzlingly white skin. There was a hint of disdain in the modelling of the exquisite lips and the heavy lids that drooped over the hazel eyes.

Her obvious poise and sophistication made the girl who followed her seem almost pathetically immature.

She was a pretty girl, with dark hair, grey eyes widely spaced, and a sensitive, delicately formed mouth. Despite her look of youthful eagerness, there was something of diffidence and uncertainty, something almost of apprehension, in her manner as she followed the woman into the hall.

"I'm Miss Kimball," the woman was saying to Celia, "and this is Miss Lattimer."

The girl shook hands with Celia, then threw a shy smile round the flower-filled hall.

"How nice it all looks, doesn't it, Judith?" she said.

There was an odd propitiatory note in her voice that agreed with the faint diffidence of her manner, and she spoke tentatively as if she were ready—not only now but always—to withdraw at once any opinion of which her friend did not approve.

"Darling, I've left my muff in the car. Go and get it for me, will you?"

The girl went out to the car, where the young chauffeur was taking the luggage from the carrier.

"Miss Kimball left her muff in the car, Bennet. . . ."

He came round to the door of the car, moved the rugs from the seats, and handed her the small grey muff, smiling at her as he did so. There was something comforting and reassuring in his smile. He looked kind and human, as Dime, their real chauffeur, had never looked. Judith had been furious about Dime's illness, had said that temporary servants were always insolent and inefficient, had been as disagreeable (Sidney took back the word in loyal haste and substituted "cold" in her thoughts) as she could be—and that was saying a good deal—to Bennet ever since he had arrived yesterday to take Dime's place. But from the minute Sidney saw him he had given her a strange feeling of protection. Even on the rather dreadful drive down to this place the sight of his back—the square shoulders, the well-shaped head, the hair that curled irrepressibly beneath the neat cap—had made her feel, she didn't know how or why, sheltered and cared for.

This holiday seemed to have been doomed to failure from the beginning. Three weeks ago Judith had handed her a newspaper and, pointing to an advertisement, had said, "How would you like to spend Christmas there?"

Sidney had read it, laughed, and replied:

"I think it would be dreadful. Neither fish, flesh, nor good red herring."

And then it turned out that Judith had actually booked rooms at the place, and had been keeping it a secret from Sidney till everything was settled, so as to be a pleasant surprise for her. . . . In vain Sidney protested that she had been joking, that she hadn't read the advertisement properly, that she had spoken without thinking, that she would love more than anything else in the world to join the Christmas party at Chedsy Place. Judith had been cold and withdrawn for several days, not speaking unless it were absolutely necessary, and speaking then in that cold contemptuous voice that always set Sidney's heart racing and gave her an odd sick feeling in the pit of her stomach.

Quite suddenly, however, she had seemed to forgive her, had become again the Judith—all charm and kindness—whom Sidney had worshipped since their first meeting. But to-day, during the journey, she had changed again. Several times when Sidney had spoken to her she had not answered, and whenever she had spoken it had been to say something so carefully calculated to hurt that one would think she must have taken days to prepare it. But hurting came naturally to Judith in some moods, just as sympathy and tenderness seemed to come naturally to her in others. And, even when she was most unkind, that odd elusive charm that was like a chain binding you to her never weakened for an instant.

She must still be brooding over those unfortunate words of Sidney's. . . . Judith was like that. She would seem to forgive you for something, even to forget all about it, and then quite suddenly you would discover that she was still secretly holding it against you, that she hadn't quite stopped punishing you. Of course, Judith always hated journeys. They bored and irritated her. She was at her worst on a journey, and Sidney was the obvious person to vent her irritability on. Sidney tried not to mind. She would say to herself: "It's not Judith. It's just her nerves. She doesn't mean anything at all." And in the earlier days of her infatuation she had even felt a sort of fanatical pride in being thus used as an outlet for Judith's weariness or irritability.

She lingered by the door of the car, the muff in her hand, unwilling to leave the friendliness that lurked behind this young man's smile.

"It was a lovely journey down, wasn't it?" she said.

"Yes. . . . There's nothing to beat Devonshire."

"And I think most places look their best on a fine day in winter, don't you? The bare branches are so lovely."

"And the bare earth."

"Yes. I can't understand how people can put away their cars for the winter and then go tearing about the country in the summer when everything's covered with dust and every road thick with people. . . ."

"I can't, either. . . ."

They smiled at each other—a smile that seemed to cement their alliance. He had said nothing that a complete stranger might not have said, and yet it was as if he had said something intimate, momentous: "Don't be frightened. It's all right. You're young, and it's a beautiful world. Don't be frightened." Her fear and depression vanished. Everything was all right. . . . They were going to have a wonderful holiday.

But the look that Judith turned on her as she entered the hall sent her soaring spirits to earth again. It was a long cold stare, the sort of stare that one might give to a stranger who has insulted one.

"Darling," she said—and no one could make the word "darling" a more venomously hostile word than Judith, just as no one could make it when she chose a more caressingly tender one—"*need* you be all afternoon just fetching my muff from the car?"

The blood flamed into Sidney's face. Judith must be furious with her to speak like that in front of Mrs. Beaton. Generally she was rather careful not to snub her when other people were there, however nervy she felt.

"Will you come and see the drawing-room?" said Mrs. Beaton, obviously trying to cover the awkward moment.

They went to an open doorway and looked into a large, finely proportioned room. A log fire burned at each end, and the air was sweet with the scent of hyacinths. A woman with the most beautiful eyes Sidney had ever seen, wearing an appalling sack-like dress of green velvet, with a bird's-nest of hair that came right down over her forehead, sat on a sofa next to another woman, who wore a brown wig slightly askew, revealing a large expanse of white hair. Two more women sat on a larger sofa by the window, one of them knitting, the other sleeping. The one who was sleeping looked very old and wore a white lace cap with red berries that quivered slightly as if it were dancing a little jig all by itself.

The woman in the brown wig was talking in a loud deep drawl.

"I had to wait three-quarters of an hour for the 'bus coming back. Three *quarters* of an *hour*! And nothing to do there once one had seen the church. I was simply chilled to the bone. Quite an ordinary church, too. I mean, one's seen hundreds like it. . . ."

The old lady in the white lace cap woke up suddenly, looked round the room, saw Sidney standing in the doorway, beamed, nodded, and blew her a kiss. They withdrew to the hall.

"Tea's at half-past four," said Mrs. Beaton. "Perhaps you'd like to unpack first. I think that your luggage will be upstairs now."

"Yes, we'll unpack, I think," said Judith, and they all went upstairs together.

"Here's your room, Miss Kimball." Celia opened a door on the first floor. "Miss Lattimer's is next to it."

It was a large sunny room, with chintz-covered chairs, chintz curtains at the tall narrow windows, and a dressing-table with a chintz "skirt." A fire burned on the hearth, and a bowl of lilies of the valley stood on a gleaming Sheraton commode.

"You'll ring for anything you want, won't you?" said Celia and went downstairs to her little office.

The Rev. Humphrey and Mrs. Standfield would be the next arrivals. She must be ready to greet them. How beautiful the woman was, but how she'd snapped at that nice little girl! She shrugged her shoulders. Well, it wasn't her business. . . . They were a good-looking, well-turned-out pair, and they would do her party credit. They were very welcome after yesterday's arrivals.

Upstairs Sidney stood rather uncertainly in the middle of the room, looking around her. Then she took off her hat and coat, threw them onto the bed, and drew a bunch of keys from her bag.

"Sit down and rest, Judith," she said, "and I'll unpack. I know you're tired."

Judith turned from the window. Her hazel eyes were still cold, her beautiful lips tight.

"In what particular way," she said, "do I give the impression of being tired?"

Sidney flushed again. It had been the wrong thing to say, of course. She was always saying the wrong thing to Judith. She unlocked the suitcases and began to take out Judith's things in silence. Judith stood by the window, drawing off her gloves with quick jerky movements.

"I asked you in what particular way I gave the impression of being tired," she said again clearly.

The flush faded from Sidney's face, leaving it pale. She must have annoyed Judith terribly—she couldn't think how. She was much more annoyed than she'd been on the way down. On the way down she'd just been nervy. Now she was definitely angry about something.

"You don't," she said. "I'm sorry. I meant—I only thought . . ."

Her voice trailed away. Judith said nothing. She had taken off her gloves and stood gazing out of the window, frowning, tight-lipped. Sidney struggled against the sense of desolation and misery that was overwhelming her. She must say something. Not to say anything seemed as if she were sulking, and Judith hated one to sulk. Sometimes one could charm her back into good humour by talking ordinarily as if she hadn't just hurt one almost more than one could bear.

"We came down in good time, didn't we?" she went on in a little breathless voice.

"Quite," said Judith curtly.

"He drives just as well as Dime."

"Does he?"

"Oh yes." And, because in her bleak misery the memory of those kind, reassuring eyes was like a lifebuoy thrown to a shipwrecked sailor, she added: "I think he's awfully nice, Judith."

Judith turned to her.

"I noticed you did," she said. "I wonder if it would be too much to ask you not to stand gossiping with servants at the front door. It's one of the things that are not done."

Her voice was smooth, but her pallor had lost its usual clear

34

transparency and had taken on a dull heavy opaqueness. Judith never went red, but in moments of anger or emotion the texture of her pale skin seemed to grow thick and lifeless, and her hazel eyes turned green. This, then, was what she was angry about. She had seen her standing talking to Bennet after she had got the muff. It was not the first time that Sidney's friendliness with servants had caused trouble between them. Judith herself never spoke a word more than was necessary to her servants and seldom even looked at them when giving orders. . . . But there was something more than that. It wasn't just that Bennet was a servant. It was that he was a personable young man. Sidney had already learnt that she if could commit no greater crime in Judith's eyes than to appear to enjoy the society of a personable young man. She realised this only vaguely and at the back of her mind. All she was conscious of was a feeling of shock and dizziness, as if the stinging anger and contempt of Judith's voice had been a physical blow. Her heart stood still at the words, then began to race tumultuously.

Judith came across the room and took up Sidney's hat and coat from the bed.

"I wish you wouldn't throw your things about my room," she went on. "You know how I hate untidiness. And please leave my unpacking. I'd rather do it myself and know that my things are put away properly."

Judith didn't mind how unfair she was when she was angry. Only yesterday she had told Sidney that no one had ever packed and unpacked for her as well as she did.

"But, Judith——" she began, then the tears started to her eyes and she went abruptly from the room. In her own room she unpacked her bag, fighting back her tears, digging her teeth into her lip to keep it steady. She was trembling, and her breath came in little gasps, as if she were being choked by her misery and desolation. . . . I can't bear it, she thought. I wish I were dead. . . .

Suddenly the door opened, and Judith stood there.

"How long are you going to be, you little slowcoach?" she said. She spoke in a voice of gay tenderness that crept over Sidney's nerves like a drug, drowning all the memory of Judith's unkindness and her own unhappiness.

"Oh, Judith!"

Judith smiled at her. It was very seldom that Judith smiled, and when she did it made of her beauty something indescribably rare and exquisite.

"Come along, little silly," she said. "Let's have tea before we unpack. I've ordered it in my bedroom. We won't have it with those old frumps downstairs."

She slipped an arm through Sidney's and drew her along the corridor to her bedroom. An ecstasy of happiness swept over the girl.

"I had a foul headache on the way down," went on Judith, "but I'm all right now."

Sidney knew that Judith had not had a headache on the way down, but this was always her nearest approach to an apology, and Sidney felt grateful for it.

"I'm so sorry," she said.

Judith had taken nothing out of her box, but already the whole room seemed to be full of the subtle enchantment of her.

"We'll finish the unpacking after tea," she said. "Another frump's just arrived, by the way, in the most appalling of appalling red toques. I think it's going to be quite fun, however, despite the frumps."

"It's going to be lovely," said Sidney.

"'Neither fish, flesh, nor good red herring,'" quoted Judith, slipping an arm round Sidney as she said it, to show that it was only friendly teasing.

"Oh, you *know* I didn't mean it," pleaded Sidney.

The door opened, and a trim housemaid entered, carrying a tray of tea which she put on a low table by the fire.

Judith inspected it. "Toast . . . sandwiches . . . home-made cakes. . . . It looks quite nice. Come along, darling."

This time it was a "darling" that thrilled one like an actual caress.

Sidney was still upheld by that feeling of radiant happiness. How wonderful Judith was! As to the afternoon—well, naturally someone as fine as Judith couldn't help being irritated by someone as stupid and clumsy as she, Sidney, was. The marvel was that Judith was generally so patient.

She had taken her seat on the armchair, the little table between her and the fire, and she moved her exquisitely shod feet towards the hearth, so that Sidney could sit on the floor as she loved to, leaning against her knee. Sidney nestled down happily on the hearthrug beside her.

"It's going to be *lovely*," she said again.

Chapter Five

THE woman in the badly made red toque paid her taxi, entered the hall, and stood peering shortsightedly around.

There was an air of deliberate preciseness about her that included her features, her movements, and her dress. One felt that a good deal of trouble had been taken to get her nose exactly in the centre of her face, and her eyes and mouth at exactly the right distances from it. Her eyes were screwed up, her mouth pursed. Her brown hair was arranged in a neat bun at the back of her head and the red toque secured to it by means of a long hat-pin.

As Celia approached she pulled out a pair of pince-nez at the end of a thin gold chain and set them on the bridge of the small tight nose. The pursed mouth relaxed slightly—a relaxation that evidently did duty as a smile.

"Good afternoon," she said. "I'm Miss Wingate."

Celia smiled a welcome in return.

"I'm Mrs. Beaton. . . . I'm so glad to see you. Will you come up to your room? I'll have your luggage sent up at once."

"Thank you."

The preciseness of Miss Wingate's manner and appearance was as nothing to the preciseness of her speech. It was clipped and emphatic. She exploded her consonants, not vulgarly but with a refined incisiveness, and she enunciated her vowels with a peculiar distinctness of which "in these days of slovenly speech" (one of her favourite expressions) she was very proud. The whole of her small pursed face moved convulsively when she spoke without ever, under no matter what stress of eloquence, unpursing itself.

She accompanied Celia up the staircase, casting keen, peering, short-sighted glances around her as she went.

"This is your bedroom. . . ."

The little screwed-up eyes darted round the room. Flowers and a fire. Quite luxurious. Though, of course, flowers weren't healthy in a bedroom. Still, one could always put them out at nights.

"I've brought my hot-water bottle," she said anxiously. "I suppose that the maid will fill it?"

"Certainly," said Celia, "and you'll ring for anything you want, won't you? Tea is at four-thirty in the drawing-room. Unless, of course, you'd like it brought up here. . . ."

"Oh *no*, thank you," said Miss Wingate, as if horrified by the idea.

It was one of her boasts that she had not had breakfast in bed or a meal of any sort in her bedroom for over fifteen years.

Celia smiled again pleasantly and withdrew. Miss Wingate took off the badly fitting red toque and the equally badly fitting grey tweed coat and began to unpack her things. She was not interested in clothes, and she employed dressmakers and tailors, not on their merits as such, but according to their necessities. Her dressmaker, who had also made the red toque, was employed by her solely because she had rheumatism in her hands, and so, having lost most of her clients, was badly in need of money. The tailor who had made the grey tweed coat was employed by her solely because his wife suffered from diabetes, and the necessary treatment was a drain on his small income. Miss Wingate often said that as long as it was plainly made and of good material one dress was the same as another to her. Certainly the fact that a dressmaker was a success in her profession, and therefore prosperous, would have been to Miss Wingate the very reason for not employing her.

When she had unpacked her things, she washed her hands and face and went to the dressing-table to tidy her hair. She combed back the front of it, tucking in the ends neatly where it met the bun and carefully pinning together the loose wisps about her neck. Then she took the hairs from the comb and again peered round her short-sightedly. There wasn't a hair-tidy. How annoying! She felt quite disproportionately perturbed by the absence of a hair-tidy. She ought to have brought her own, of course. For some extraordinary reason people didn't provide hair-tidies nowadays.

She couldn't understand it, because surely even if you had shingled hair it came off on the comb sometimes. Still—she took the copy of *The Times* that she had bought for the journey, tore off a neat square, and wrapped up the two or three dark hairs that she had removed from her comb. She would put her other combings with them, make up a parcel, and bury it somewhere when she went for her walk to-morrow. And then she would call at the village shop to see if she could buy a hair-tidy there.

She must now discover where the bathroom and lavatory were. She wished that she had asked Mrs. Beaton. ... It was rather awkward having to look for them. Putting on her pince-nez, she opened the door a few inches and peeped out cautiously. One naturally didn't want to be seen looking for the lavatory. No one was in the corridor, so she ventured forth, still very cautiously, and made her way down to the end of the passage. Yes, there they were—a bathroom and a lavatory side by side. With her peering, short-sighted eyes, she measured the distance between her bedroom door and the bathroom. It wasn't very far. When she took her morning bath, she would have to peep out first to ascertain that no one was about, then make a dash for it. She hoped that there weren't any men on the corridor. As she was passing the door next to hers it opened suddenly, and a maid came out, carrying a tea-tray. The opening of the door disclosed a woman sitting by the fire, and a girl on the hearthrug at her feet. The girl laughed at something the woman said as the door closed.

They looked smart worldly people—the sort of people with whom Miss Wingate wanted to mix. For Miss Wingate had come to Chedsy Place simply in order to mix with people. She had told no one that she was coming. It was a secret spiritual adventure.

Miss Wingate had been appointed to the staff of her old college only four years after leaving it as a student, and she had been there ever since. The time had passed so quickly and indeed so pleasantly that Miss Wingate had hardly noticed its passing. She was very friendly with two other members of the staff, Miss Raikes, who lectured on history, and Dr. Masters, who lectured on physics, and they owned jointly a small but delightfully picturesque cottage in

Sussex, where they spent their vacations, accompanied sometimes by a few favoured students who were reading for their final examination. At Christmas, however, they generally each went home—Miss Wingate, who had no parents, to an uncle of eighty-eight, who till this year had officially carried on his duties as spiritual guide to a scattered parish of two or three hundred souls in a remote part of Cornwall.

But last term, suddenly and for no particular reason, it had occurred to Miss Wingate that she was getting into a rut. She had had in fact a horrible feeling that, however pleasant the process—and no one ever took more kindly to the academic life than Miss Wingate—she was being slowly buried alive. She remembered the amused if tolerant contempt with which in her own student days she and her fellows had regarded those prematurely aged lecturers whose outlook was bounded on every side by the affairs of the college. And a terrible suspicion had begun to grow in her mind that if she were a student now she would regard her present self with just that same amused and tolerant contempt. And Miss Wingate had always been a determined character. To realise a thing had always been with her to act on it. She was only forty-five. She wasn't surely so deep in a rut that she couldn't get out. She would go into the world and mix with people. It was to be partly the answer to a challenge and partly a task. She'd *prove* that she wasn't in a rut. She'd *learn* to mix with people. . . . The difficulty was, of course, to find some way of going into the world to mix with people. She shrank from the idea of an ordinary hotel, and she had no friends outside the college. Then she saw the advertisement of Chedsy Place in *The Times,* and it seemed exactly what she wanted for her purpose. The old uncle had conveniently died, so that she was quite free for Christmas. A bedridden great-aunt had asked her to stay with her, and she had allowed Miss Raikes and Dr. Masters to think that she had accepted the invitation.

She took off her outdoor shoes and put on a pair of sensible, roomy, ward shoes, straightened her skirt and jumper, and went downstairs to the drawing-room.

Mrs. Beaton was just showing a clergyman and his wife into it.

"Perhaps you'd like to have tea now, would you?" she was saying, then, seeing Miss Wingate just behind her, introduced them as Mr. and Mrs. Standfield. In a few moments, somewhat to her surprise, Miss Wingate found herself sitting with the new arrivals at a small table, having tea.

Well, it was all right so far, she told herself encouragingly. This was certainly "mixing."

The clergyman was a thin, delicate-looking man of about fifty, with a pleasant, somewhat wistful expression. His wife was short and thick-set, with a long nose and a slightly receding chin. Despite the receding chin her small mouth spoke of determination—a wholly good-tempered determination, for it curved always into a faint but cheerful smile. She talked vivaciously and incessantly, telling Miss Wingate about their parish and parish work, describing several incidents connected with them at what seemed rather unnecessary length, laughing herself heartily at such of them as were intended to be humorous. She explained that her husband had had influenza and that the doctor had ordered him away for a change of air.

"Of course, one doesn't like to be away at Christmas," she said. "For one thing I really can't trust anyone but myself to do the pulpit properly. They just smother it in holly, you know. I was short of helpers last Christmas and had to leave the pulpit to the churchwarden's wife, and she put holly simply everywhere. Poor Humphrey got quite badly pricked several times during the service. But the doctor was very firm about our coming away now, and I just happened to see the advertisement of this place and thought it would be much better for a convalescent than an ordinary hotel. Fortunately we were able to arrange with a retired clergyman in the neighbourhood to take the services."

She proceeded to tell Miss Wingate all about the retired clergyman and his family, describing in detail the careers and characters of his seven children. Occasionally she broke off her monologue to bully her husband good-humouredly.

"Are you sitting in a draught there, Humphrey?"

"No, my dear."

"Yes, you are. Change places with me."

"Honestly, Lucy. I'm quite all right here."

"Change places with me, Humphrey. You know you mustn't sit in a draught. . . . And do have another piece of toast. You've eaten nothing, and the doctor said you must eat."

Miss Wingate began to watch the people around her. Two women—one old, the other middle-aged—sat side by side on a sofa near. The old woman had been asleep, but she woke up suddenly and said, "What day is it, dear?"

"Thursday," said her companion, looking up from her knitting.

"What month?"

"December 21st."

"I must write to Aunt Cissie, then. It's her birthday to-morrow."

"No, dear. Aunt Cissie's dead."

"*Dead!*" said the old woman indignantly. "Nonsense! When did she die?"

"Ten years ago."

"Why wasn't I told?"

"You were told. You've forgotten."

"What nonsense! Of course she isn't dead. You're thinking of Aunt Emmie. . . . Aunt Cissie would be most hurt if she didn't hear from me. I'm going to write to her at once."

With that the old woman leant back on the sofa and went to sleep again.

At a table near the window sat two more women and a young man. The young man's legs were crossed, and he was moving the foot of his crossed leg up and down, round and round, scowling at it fiercely as he did so. One of the women was rather striking-looking, with untidy black hair, and the other wore a very obvious brown wig that showed her own white hair at the back. The striking-looking woman with untidy hair was saying: "As an author I believe in keeping *en rapport* with the reading public. I mean the ordinary man in the street. I always talk to them and listen to them. You know, a man who came to mend my bookcases the other day said to me: 'There's a new intelligentsia springing up that you authors have got to cater for—the intelligentsia of Peckham and Penge. People who've gone on educating themselves after they've left the board schools. They're as literary and as cultured and as able to appreciate good style as the intelligentsia of Bloomsbury and St. John's Wood. And you've got to cater for them,' he said."

She ended impressively, and there was a short silence. Then the young man said, in a jerky irritated way, "Well, then, why do they want catering for specially? Why can't they read the books that the intelligentsia of Bloomsbury and St. John's Wood read?"

"I don't know," said the woman. "He didn't say," and the intensity of her expression, together with the deep earnest tones of her voice, made her reply seem wholly satisfactory.

Mrs. Standfield had gone across to the small writing-table by the window and was engaged in writing a letter to the churchwarden's wife:

"The Vicar looks better already, and I'm sure the change will do him good. This place is not a hotel but a beautiful old country house. There are some very nice people staying here. If you happen to be passing the Vicarage, I'd be so grateful if you'd go in and just remind Cook to have the sweep before we come home. The study chimney's been so awkward lately. And would you also remind Mr. Mellow to keep an eye on Bobbie Brewston during the service on Sunday? He was sucking bull's-eyes all last Sunday, and it looks so bad in the choir. The Vicar spoke to him about it, but he may try to take advantage of our being away. . . ."

Brian Mallard had gone over to the window and stood looking out at the darkening garden. Though it was certainly better than the places his aunt generally fixed on for her holidays—they were usually ghastly holes of the Vegetarian Guest House type—it was going to be pretty awful, as indeed all the holidays with his aunt were. He needn't have come, of course. She had said, "If you've made other plans don't break them. I should like to have you with me, however." He generally managed to wangle invitations or arrange walking tours or reading parties for the other two vacations, but he felt that in common decency he ought to spend Christmas with her when she asked him to. After all, she had paid for his education since he was seven, and she gave him a pretty liberal allowance. He frequently told himself how grateful he ought to be to her, but the fact was that ever since he had first gone to live with her as a child he had disliked her intensely, and he had by now almost given up trying to conquer his dislike. He felt that she made him, as well as herself, ridiculous, and, lacking a saving sense of humour, he could not forgive her for it. Certainly she had cast a shadow over his whole childhood. His sufferings, when she visited him at school, had been beyond description. The days before her visit he had crept about literally sick with apprehension. Her actual visits had been nightmares, of which even now he could not think without a hot flush of shame. She had cherished a delusion that his schoolmates adored her. She invaded all their groups to talk to them. She trailed about the school—a strange figure in exotic garments with her hair coming down—and talked volubly and confidentially to everyone she met. She gave a set of her novels, suitably inscribed, to the headmaster. . . . And, of course, the days following her visits had been literally torture to her nephew. If he could himself have taken it as a joke it would not have been so bad. But he couldn't. He was desperately, agonisedly, ashamed, and the other boys, seeing it, pushed home their advantage with the cruelty of their kind. He had been as a child so acutely sensitive that even an exceptionally understanding person would have had need of subtlety to gain his love and confidence.

Things were better now, of course. One's relations did not matter so much at college. At college one could not be disgraced and humiliated for ever by the visit of an eccentric aunt. . . . He was going on to a theological college next year, and after he had taken Orders he meant to apply for a curacy in the North and see as little of her as possible.

He was by nature deeply religious, but his lonely childhood had made his religion unbalanced and fanatical. He practised many secret austerities, submitting himself frequently to fasting and even physical pain. He would have worn a hair shirt had he known where one could be procured. Occasionally he almost welcomed the shame and irritation his aunt caused him, looking upon them

45

as a sort of martyrdom; sometimes he even went beyond this and tried, ineffectually enough, to love her, but generally he remained the sulky small boy at the prep, school who had looked on her with horror and shrinking. He was very young and blundering and earnest and well-meaning, and had been so spoilt by lack of understanding treatment that he took a slightly distorted view of almost everything. He had long ago vowed himself to celibacy and shrank from women with a sort of panic, being deliberately rude from sheer nervousness whenever he met one.

He heard his aunt's voice upraised.

"Yes ... he's going into the Church. ... I always say that institutional religion is a *step*. ..."

He rose abruptly and went out of the room, snatched his hat and coat from the hall, where he had left them, and strode fiercely down the drive.

Miss Wingate, feeling much refreshed by her tea and having learnt all she wished to know for the present about the Standfields' parish, house, garden, and domestic arrangements (Mrs. Standfield had returned to her after writing her letter), decided to go in search of the other reception rooms of which Mrs. Beaton had told her. In the hall, which looked very cheerful with its bright log fire, stood a young chauffeur, talking to Mrs. Beaton.

"I just wanted to know if Miss Kimball had left any orders about her car for to-morrow, madam," he said.

"I don't think so," said Mrs. Beaton, "but I'm going up, so I'll look in and ask."

"Thank you, madam."

There was something merry and impudent about his smile, thought Miss Wingate, and his saying "Madam" to anyone seemed a joke. He was just the sort of boy one would like to have had for one's nephew, if one had had a nephew (Miss Wingate was too modest to consider any relation nearer than a nephew in such a connection). He stayed on the hearth-rug, cap in hand, looking up the stairs where Mrs. Beaton had disappeared. Miss Wingate went across to an ordnance map that hung on the wall next the mantelpiece. The woman in the brown wig was already standing in front of it, taking notes in a small battered notebook. She greeted Miss Wingate with a vague smile and spoke in a startlingly loud drawl.

"I'm going to try to do Felpham Rocks to-morrow," she said. "As far as I can make out it will take all day and I shall spend most of it waiting for 'buses."

"Why do you go, then?" said Miss Wingate.

"I must," said Miss Nettleton, with an air of weary resignation. "It's one of the places that people ask you if you saw when you say you've been staying down here."

With this explanation she shut up her note-book and went back into the lounge. Miss Wingate remained, gazing at the map. Maps had always had a fascination for her.

Suddenly the girl she had seen in the bedroom next hers came running downstairs. She was like a flame, eager, vivid, happy. The chauffeur stepped forward.

"Oh, Bennet," she said, laughing breathlessly, "Miss Kimball says you can bring the car round about ten o'clock to-morrow."

"Yes, miss," said the chauffeur.

He, too, looked somehow like the girl—eager, vivid, happy, as if the flame of her had set him alight.

"Do you know where she wants to go?"

"No. She didn't say. . . . You've got a map, haven't you?"

"Yes, miss."

"Look out a nice drive for us. Of course, she may not want to go, after all, but find us somewhere really nice to go to in case she does."

"Yes, miss."

He was smiling at her, and she was smiling back at him. Neither made any movement to depart.

"Do you like the car?" said the girl.

"Yes. Nice smooth engine. Good-tempered car altogether."

She laughed.

"Oh, do you feel like that about cars?"

"Yes, rather! Some cars are vicious, and it doesn't matter how much you've paid for them or how up to date they are or how much trouble you take over them, you're never really safe with them for a second anywhere."

She laughed again delightedly. How nice he was and how nice everything and everyone was and what a lovely holiday it was going to be and how adorably, adorably sweet Judith had been to her ever since they made up their quarrel!

"I must go now . . ." she said, her grey eyes still smiling happily at him. "Ten o'clock tomorrow, then."

"Yes . . . ten o'clock to-morrow."

Even then it was quite an appreciable time before she turned and ran up the stairs, and he did not go away till she had vanished from sight.

Miss Wingate, now left alone in the empty hall, continued her explorations. The library must be behind that door. She was just crossing the hall to it when the front door opened suddenly, and a man and woman appeared. The man wore blue glasses and had a massive, square, rough-hewn face, across which his mouth—set and aggressive like a prize-fighter's—ran like an ugly slit.

Miss Wingate turned and scuttled back to the drawing-room.

Chapter Six

CELIA stood motionless for a moment, dismayed by the appearance of this new guest. The letters she had received from him—letters containing minute instructions about diet—had led her to expect to meet one of those thin, dyspeptic-looking individuals who are seen anxiously consuming vitamin-and-proteid-infested food in health restaurants.

This man was thick-set, tall, and muscular. The blue glasses emphasised rather than concealed the aggressive scowl of his hidden eyes, but it was his mouth that seemed to dominate and express his whole personality. It was grim, bitter, ruthless, determined, set permanently in lines of strained and unremitting effort.

His wife had probably been pretty once, but she was of the type that fades early, and her rouged face, peroxided hair, and over-youthful style of dress, only succeeded in stressing the fact that she was many years older than her husband.

She shook hands with Celia.

"This is Mrs. Beaton, dear," she said to her husband.

He moved his grim mask of a face vaguely in Celia's direction with no relaxing of its grimness.

"How do you do?" he said.

"Would you like to come straight to your room?" said Celia. "It's this way. . . . The stairs are just here. . . ."

His wife took his arm and guided him to the foot of the staircase. She kept her hand on his arm a second too long, however, for he turned on her sharply.

"That's all right," he rasped. "I can manage now."

In the bedroom Celia stood irresolute. The woman was watching her husband, warily, anxiously, as though he were some dangerous animal of which she found herself the keeper.

"Would you like tea?" said Celia.

"Wait a minute," snapped the man, and began to feel his way from piece of furniture to piece of furniture, obviously engaged in memorising the room, his face still grim and set, his whole attention concentrated on it.

At one moment, when he stood groping rather uncertainly for the bed, his wife started forward to help him, but, even before she had touched him, he turned on her with a scowl, and she fell back. When he had completed his examination, he stood for a moment silent, as if finally committing his discoveries to memory, then said:

"I'll have a glass of orange juice, please. Would you like some tea, Maud?"

As he spoke, he went without a second's hesitation or faltering to the chest of drawers, laid his gloves on it, then returned to the fireplace and stood with his elbow resting on the mantelpiece. No sighted person could have moved more surely about the room.

"Yes, I'd like some tea," said Mrs. Fielden plaintively. "I'm tired."

"I'll see to it at once," said Celia.

Somehow she was glad to escape from the room.

Half-way downstairs she stopped with a cry of glad surprise. Robert was standing by the fire in the hall. She'd forgotten about Robert's coming, but the sight of him standing there set her pulses racing. She flew down the remaining stairs into his arms.

"Oh, *Robert*!"

He held her closely to him, kissing her eyes and lips and hair. She freed herself, laughing.

"Oh, Robert, you mustn't. . . . Not here. . . ."

"Why on earth not?" he said.

She put her arm through his and drew him across the hall to the gun-room. There she closed the door, and he held her at arms' length, his hands on her shoulders.

"What have you been doing to yourself?"

"Nothing. Why?"

"You're as thin as a rake."

She laughed.

"Rubbish! I've been busy, of course. But I've enjoyed every minute of it. Robert——"

She hesitated, aware for the first time of a dim feeling of apprehension. Something deep down in her had known from the beginning that Robert would dislike this scheme of hers. She had ignored the knowledge, refused to admit it to her consciousness, but—it had been there all the time.

"Yes?" he said, and there was a sudden constraint in his voice. He, too, was shirking the subject.

"Haven't we simply resurrected the place from the dead?" she said lightly. "Don't you think I deserve a pat on the back?"

She must go very carefully. Nothing could now make her surrender her plan—already it stretched in her mind far beyond the bounds of this experimental Christmas party—but she mustn't lose Robert either. She must strain every nerve, exert every atom of acumen and cunning, to keep them both.

"Oh, rather!" he said. The lightness of his tone was as carefully assumed as hers, but he was less clever at acting a part, and so it rang less true. "You've made the place look wonderful. . . ."

He gave her, indeed, all credit for that. When first he entered the hall, it had looked so exactly as it had looked in the old days—the log fire on the hearth, flowers everywhere, the surface of the lovely old furniture shining in the firelight—that he had stood for a moment dumbfounded, carried back into his boyhood, or forward into some dream in which his beloved Chedsy Place was his at last. Then a woman whom he had never seen before had come out of the drawing-room, stared at him as if he had no right to be there, and passed on with an air of owning the whole house. His dream had been abruptly shattered, and the blood had flamed into his cheeks. That odd sense of outrage still lingered with him. He dared not let himself think of the situation, still less discuss it with Celia. His love for Celia stood apart, inviolable. It was as inalienable from him, he felt, as his own body. And yet he had glimpsed more than once the gulf that, despite their love, divided them, and he shrank from anything that might reveal that gulf again. He fidgeted about the room, taking up papers, glancing at them without reading them, putting them down again, avoiding her eyes. They must come to grips about the thing sooner or later, but not just now, not to-night, not till he had got his bearings.

"Did you have good sport?" she said. "You told me hardly anything. You're quite the world's worst letter-writer, aren't you, darling?"

He smiled. They were on safer ground now.

"You didn't write much yourself if it comes to that," he said. "Yes . . . it wasn't bad. Not quite as good as usual. They've been building a lot on the edge of the estate, and it's made the birds shy. They've begun to run 'buses, too, and Harvey says he simply can't keep trippers out of the woods." He rose. "Well, I'm rather grubby. I think I'll go and have a wash."

"Yes, do. . . . We're in the best bedroom. You remember it, don't you?"

She was glad now that she had stuck to that. She had been tempted to give the best bedroom to the guests and put herself and Robert into one of the small bedrooms overlooking the stables. For herself she would not have hesitated, but some instinct had warned her to try to disguise from him as far as possible the "paying guest" aspect of her party. Already it was proving more difficult of disguise than she had anticipated. Her first idea of "paying guests" had been much less hotel-like than the reality. It was impossible, however, to fill the house with really congenial people, and, of course, English people hated being made to "mix." She had had to alter her plans to meet circumstances. Moreover, there was no doubt at all that her advertisement had attracted a certain number of cranks and oddities. . . . It was best to keep them apart.

"Dinner at eight," she went on. "You and I are having it alone in here. I thought it would be cosier the first evening."

"That'll be splendid."

He went to the door, then turned.

"I called at the farm, you know," he said. "Spent last night there, in fact."

The farm. . . . She could hardly believe that once it had formed her whole world, that only two months ago all her energies had been given to thinking and planning for it. Already it belonged to the past, and, though in a way she had loved it, she felt no regret at leaving it. For left it she had, she knew, and for ever.

"How were things?" she asked.

"Fine," he said. "Halliday's managed wonderfully."

He looked at her, beyond her, and saw the old farmhouse, the rolling expanse of ploughed field, the bare trim hedges ... saw cowman and shepherd going about their tasks with lanterns in the winter dusk, heard the cattle moving in their stalls, caught the faint cry of the first lamb. ... A wave of homesickness swept over him. Though he had never expected to set foot in Chedsy Place again, he had always in his heart looked upon it as his home, and the farm as a sort of exile. Now he was back in Chedsy Place as its master, and, strangely, it was Chedsy Place that was the exile, and he longed with all his heart to be back on his farm.

"Good!" she said, but, despite the enthusiasm of her tone, he knew that she was not really interested.

"Mrs. Hubbard's in her old room," she went on. "She's been an absolute brick about things."

"I'll go and see her."

But he felt oddly reluctant to go and see her, had to make an effort to conquer the temptation to put off the interview till later.

He found her sitting by the fire in her little room, wearing her black silk dress. Something about her seemed to restore the world to its equilibrium. She made him think vaguely of a rock left standing in its original position after an earthquake. It wasn't just that nothing about her or her room had altered. It was something much deeper than that.

He bent over to kiss her. "Hello, Mother Hubbard——"

Though her old face did not change, he had the impression that she was deeply moved by his coming.

He sat down in the chair on the other side of the fireplace.

"I hope Celia's not worked you to death yet?" he went on lightly. "She tells me you've been splendid."

"There is so little I can do . . ." she said. She laid down her sewing, gazing into space.

"You oughtn't to be doing anything," he said vehemently. "Look here, I'm going to find a nice little cottage for you, and you're going to live there. Somewhere where I can come and see you at least once a week. I know my uncle meant you to have a pension, and I——"

She interrupted him, drawing herself up with gentle dignity.

"No, Mr. Robert. You mustn't speak of anything like that, please. As long as there's work I can do here . . ."

She stopped, and he knew that she was waiting for him to speak of his plans for the house. He took up the poker and began idly to poke the fire in order to hide his embarrassment.

"I've just come on from the farm, you know. I've only seen Celia for a minute. . . . She's done wonders with the place, hasn't she?"

"She has indeed, Mr. Robert. She's worked night and day, one might say. I wouldn't have believed it possible to get done what she's done in the time."

Robert glanced at her. She spoke with an odd detachment, a guarded impersonal appreciation of another's efforts, while reserving all comment on the aim of those efforts. There was about her no ghost even of the enthusiasm that had quivered in every line of Celia's small eager frame, overworked and tired as it obviously was. Celia looked like someone engaged in the making of a new world, Mrs. Hubbard like someone who gazes back sadly at the ruins of an old one.

He glanced at her window-sill. "Still busy with your bulbs?" he smiled.

She glowed at last into a faint enthusiasm.

"Yes, Mr. Robert. They're more successful this year than they've been for a long time."

He went over to the window to examine her bulbs, feeling glad that the poor old woman should have this comfort at least in her tottering world.

"They're splendid," he said, as he returned to his seat.

He had been reluctant to pay this visit, but now that he was

54

here he was still more reluctant to go. He had a curious feeling that this small basement room was the only part of the house that really belonged to him. In the silence he became conscious, too, of something else—the bond that united him to the withered old woman opposite. Incredible as it seemed, she was in some ways nearer to him than Celia.

She on her side was watching him covertly. The ginger hair, the sunburnt freckled skin, the puzzled hazel eyes, the pleasant, sensitive, indolent mouth. . . .

He'll let her do what she wants, she thought. They've always let their women do what they wanted.

He roused himself with an effort.

"Well, I must go and change, I suppose." She sat motionless, gazing into the fire, long after he had left her.

Chapter Seven

BRIAN MALLARD walked out of the French windows of the drawing-room onto the terrace. He had spent an exhausting morning with his aunt, "but she had now withdrawn into the silence (a process he always suspected to be the same as that referred to by other people as "taking a nap"), and he was free for the afternoon.

His freedom gave him a sense of exhilaration, but something of the morning's irritation still remained with him like a faintly acrid taste. His aunt had asked him to go for a walk with her, and he had not liked to refuse. She had then changed her mind and decided to take a drive. She had then invited Mrs. Lewel and Mrs. Nightingale to join them, and he had found himself sitting on an uncomfortable tip-up seat in a taxi, riding backwards, while Mrs. Nightingale addressed him as Percy and asked him how his girls were getting on, and his aunt expounded her "religion" to Mrs. Lewel. Her "religion"—a blend of Theosophy, Christian Science, Buddhism, and Spiritualism, with a dash of an American cult called Unity, all strictly subservient to her own psychic powers—could and frequently did exercise her eloquence for hours together.

It was partly the irritation caused by her constant exposition of these vague tenets that had made her nephew embrace a religion of firm doctrine and clear-cut outline. It was, moreover, her belief in the equal efficacy of every faith, or rather the equal inefficacy of every faith—for, as she often said, there wasn't any evil in the world, only the appearance of it—that had made the rigidity of the Thirty-nine Articles so infinitely satisfying to him. He could even feel a kind of affection for Satan himself after listening to his aunt discoursing on the non-existence of evil. Secretly he was considering joining some strict silent Order when he had had a few years' experience as a parish priest.

Mrs. Nightingale had finally fallen asleep, and he had nothing to do but listen with growing exasperation to his aunt's monologue.

"There's no evil, no sin, no suffering," she was saying in her penetrating confidential whisper. "If only people would realise that, the world would be a so much happier place. What seems to us evil is only the appearance of evil. There's no reality in it. Everything is beautiful if only one can learn the right way of looking at it."

Mrs. Lewel made no comment. Mrs. Nightingale awoke from her doze, smiled at Brian, leant forward in her seat, and said, "You know, dear, I never thought that Uncle James was quite fair to you about Amelia's money. I *know* she'd meant you to have something."

He glared at her, then remembered that she was afflicted and that he ought to feel love and pity for her. But it was hard to feel love and pity for people who made one ridiculous, however much afflicted they were.

The terrible morning was now over; his aunt, after an excellent lunch, had withdrawn into the silence, and he was free.

He walked round the house, hoping that he would not meet anyone. Several new people had arrived since breakfast. He had noticed a stout, over-dressed, middle-aged woman, an elderly man of the type generally referred to as a man-about-town (he had heard someone address him as Mr. Ellison), and a girl who seemed to be alone. Yes, there she was standing on the terrace with Mrs. Beaton.

She had narrow slanting sloe-black eyes, black hair, plucked eyebrows, and vividly reddened lips. Something about her—it might have been the slanting eyes or it might have been the bold carmine of her lips—gave an elusive impression of bravado and experience. She glanced restlessly to and fro, and fidgeted with the handle of her handbag as she talked.

The boy flushed with embarrassment as he approached her. He hated himself for flushing, hated her for making him flush, was possessed by sheer panic as Mrs. Beaton glanced at him, obviously wondering whether to introduce them, scowled heavily at both of them, and strode on. The encounter over, he turned to deal with the emotional disturbance that it had left in its trail, deciding finally that all he had felt had been impersonal disapproval of women, natural and proper in one vowed to celibacy.

But the elderly man was now coming round the side of the house. He had a pleasant, sensitive face and an upright figure that he evidently put into the hands of a good tailor. He gave the boy a tentative smile as he approached, but the boy, overcome again by panic, plunged past without looking at him. He always disliked men like that—well dressed, with easy assured manners. They made him hotly conscious of his own uncouth manners and inexperience. Again he examined the emotion that had seized him and decided that it was righteous indignation at the thought of the self-indulgent life that such a man must lead, and the waste of money that such an air of elegance and good tailoring must represent. The boy gave a large amount of his allowance to charity and bought cheap clothes on principle, but he always felt fiercely resentful of men who were better dressed than himself.

He had hoped that the drive would be empty, but a car stood at the front door, and a woman and girl whom he had noticed at dinner last night were just getting into it. The chauffeur spread a rug over their knees. The two were talking and laughing together and didn't even glance in the boy's direction. Their absorption in each other sent a wave of desolate envy through his heart, which he translated as disapproval. All that money spent on cars and chauffeurs and fur rugs and fur coats and expensive clothes when there was so much poverty in the world! He had long ago decided that he was a Socialist, and now he almost decided to be a Communist. After all, there was a lot in the Bible in support of Communism. He hated the rich. The only difficulty was that, though he loved the poor in theory, he found it difficult to love them individually and in practice. He had spent a week working in a mission last year, and he had in the course of it come across some extremely disagreeable and ungrateful specimens of the poor.

The car drove off, and immediately the blind man appeared at the front door, followed by his wife. The boy stood watching them. How savage the chap looked with that grimly set mouth and square jaw and that odd suggestion of an aggressive stare, though his eyes were hidden by blue glasses! He, too, of course, was one of the afflicted, and as such the boy felt that he ought to offer him sympathy and help, but the very idea of offering sympathy and help to that jaw sent cold tremors up and down his spine. The blind man hesitated on the top step as if not quite sure of the distance between that and the second step. His wife started forward instinctively to help him, then as instinctively recoiled, almost before he had refused her help by an abrupt gesture.

The boy set off quickly down the drive, then made his way up onto the common. The pale winter sunshine poured down upon it, turning the tangled bracken to gold, and the slim trunks of the birches to gleaming silver. As he walked, all his irritation vanished, and by the time he turned homeward he felt at peace with the whole world.

He came back by the lane that ran behind the house and took the short cut to the house through the kitchen garden. As he passed through it he lingered, noticing with half-unconscious delight how the sun lit up the mellow red of the brick wall and the little tufts of grey-green and orange lichen that grew on it. In the summer, he was sure, there were ferns in the crevices along the top. . . .

Just as he was coming through the wrought-iron gate into the garden he ran into a girl whom he had not seen before—a girl with ash-blonde hair, blue eyes, and a sweet immature mouth. She was small and slender and wore a green woolly suit with a little green cap set at a jaunty angle on her silvery curls.

"I'm sorry," he gasped, putting out a hand to steady her.

She laughed, a laugh that was slight and silvery like the rest of her and that had in it no trace of embarrassment or self-consciousness.

"I'm sorry . . . it was my fault. I was running. I felt excited, and I always run when I feel excited. It's such a lovely place and such a lovely day. My name's Angela Paynter. We've just arrived. Are you staying here?"

"Yes."

"I'm exploring. I like to explore the minute I get to a place, don't you? Where does this path lead to?"

"The gate goes into the kitchen garden, but the path leads onto the park. There's a sort of ditch—I think it's called a ha-ha—between the garden and the park, but there's a little bridge across it, and there's a path through the park to the road."

He felt vaguely surprised by his communicativeness. Generally he was curt to the point of rudeness to strangers from sheer nervousness. Oddly enough, he didn't feel nervous with this girl, he didn't even feel as if she were a stranger. It must be because she was hardly more than a child.

"Do come with me and show me the little bridge," she pleaded. "It sounds so fascinating. I am glad we came. It was Mummy who saw the advertisement and thought it would be nice for us. We've never been away for Christmas before, but Mummy had had bronchitis, and the doctor said she ought to go away, and she thought that this would be nicer for us than an ordinary hotel. As a matter of fact Daddy and Mummy never care where they are as long as they're with each other. But Cicely and Ian and I have been frightfully excited about it."

"Are they your sister and brother?"

"Yes. Cicely's my twin. She was coming out with me to explore, but she got caught by someone in the hall—a dreadful woman, very fat, with very golden hair, and a lot of jewellery—and I suppose she can't get away. Cicely's fatally kind-hearted, you know. It's always getting her into trouble. She can't bear the thought of hurting anyone's feelings, so she's always pretending to be interested in things that no one could possibly be interested in. She's always having recipes for quince jelly and that sort of thing sent to her by post by people she's been talking to the day before, and she doesn't remember even having pretended to be interested in quince jelly, but, of course, she must have or they wouldn't have sent the recipes. She tries awfully hard not to be like that, but she can't help it. I mean, though she really loves being with exciting people, she always makes a bee-line for the very very dimmest ones, so that they won't feel out of it, and has a terribly dull time herself, poor darling."

"And Ian?" smiled Brian.

"Oh, Ian's *quite* young. He's in his last year at Winchester. He's going to Cambridge next year. He wants to be a barrister like Daddy, but he's not as clever as Daddy. Daddy's *terribly* brilliant, of course. Cicely and I are twenty-one, and Ian's seventeen, and then there's Jill, the infant. She's three. We haven't brought her because hotels aren't good for children. She and Nanny went to Granny's yesterday. They're staying there while we're here. It's such fun coming away for Christmas, isn't it?"

The little ripple of laughter seemed to ring out for pure joy of life.

To his surprise he joined in it. The light-hearted youthfulness of her was so infectious that for the first time in his life he, too, felt young. The weight of dreary responsibility that he generally hugged to him so jealously, the sombre feeling that the world was all wrong and that he must waste no further time before putting it to rights, fell from him. It was a pleasant world, after all, full of pleasant things and pleasant people. An odd exhilaration that he had never known before seized his spirit.

She had caught sight of the bridge, and again that gay little trill of laughter rang out.

"Oh, what a darling!" she said.

Before, the bridge had seemed to him a very ordinary part of a very ordinary landscape. Now it was suddenly transformed, invested with unearthly glamour.

"Yes, isn't it!" he agreed.

"I ought to be going back," she went on. "They'll wonder where I am, but I *must* run over it. Isn't it a duck?"

She ran over the bridge and back like a child, then looked up at him. There was a delicate wild-rose colour in her cheeks, and her lips were curved into a faint smile. He felt a sudden almost uncontrollable impulse to take her in his arms and kiss her. The thought of the yielding softness of her lips against his sent an odd pang through his body. He had never had an impulse like that in his life before. He had always prided himself on the fact that he was indifferent to women and had half-unconsciously looked upon his indifference as a mark of moral superiority over other men.

Bewildered by the sudden uprising of unsuspected forces in himself, he took refuge in his sulky scowl and began to walk back to the house so quickly that she had to run to keep pace with him.

"There's a whist-drive this evening, isn't there?" she said breathlessly. "I like whist-drives because you play with so many different people that no one has time to get really annoyed with you. I hate bridge because people get so cross when you make mistakes. You'll be at the whist-drive, won't you?"

"I don't play cards at all," he said shortly and without looking at her.

They had reached a side door of the house, and he plunged into it abruptly with a muttered excuse, lingering inside just long enough to know that she ran on to the front door, humming to herself. He found his aunt in the drawing-room, talking to Miss Nettleton, leaning over her in her favourite conversational attitude.

"And then, my dear," she was saying in her penetrating whisper, "when I've finished withdrawing into the silence I sit for a few minutes sending out happy thoughts. I like to think of my happy thoughts going all over the world, brightening dull lives, healing sickness, comforting sorrow. . . . Oh, here's Brian. Brian and I, of course, don't see quite eye to eye about such things yet. Brian is at present only on the first rung of the ladder leading to the Infinite. Institutional religion, you know."

Brian conquered his irritation as best he could, saying nonchalantly:

"Had a good expedition to-day, Miss Nettleton?"

Miss Nettleton turned her vague gaze upon him and spoke in her loud deep drawl.

"Dreadful!" she said. "The place was swept by a most icy draught, and one simply couldn't get away from it. It cut through one like a knife. Nothing to see, of course. Absolutely nothing. And I took the entire day getting there and back."

"I should think you've practically exhausted the resources of the neighbourhood by now, haven't you?"

He was talking simply to prevent his aunt's breaking in with the confidential but piercing whisper that he found so indescribably exasperating.

"Oh no," said Miss Nettleton wearily. "There's a Roman villa over at Hallowes, or rather the remains of a Roman villa. I think you can just trace out the foundation. It's sure to be horribly draughty. Roman villas always are. And I shall have to wait all morning for a 'bus to get to it and all afternoon and evening for a 'bus to get back. I'm beginning to take that for granted. That's the worst of coming to a place right off the beaten track like this. I think I'll try the Roman villa to-morrow."

"Surely someone will be going over in a car. Couldn't you get a lift?"

Miss Nettleton's face grew set and purposeful.

"I can't bear sight-seeing parties. I can't bear even one other person when I'm sight-seeing. I think that sight-seeing must be done alone if it's done at all."

His aunt, who had sat for the last few moments with her great fringed eyes fixed intently upon vacancy, seemed suddenly to return to a consciousness of her surroundings. She put her hand onto Miss Nettleton's arm again and moved her face close up to hers.

"Talking of happy thoughts, my dear," she hissed. "Do you know what I say every morning when I wake up? I say——"

The boy drew back from them, moving his chair slightly to be as aloof from them as possible.

The room was gradually filling. Cummings was in command, and the footmen were already hurrying to and fro with trays of tea. Mr. and Mrs. Standfield had joined forces with Mrs. Lewel and Mrs. Nightingale. Mrs. Lewel was knitting the charity-suggestive garment, Mrs. Nightingale was sleeping, and Mrs. Standfield was keeping up her usual monologue, occasionally appealing to her husband for confirmation.

"And we told them to send them to the garage where we always garage the car when we go in to shop. Then we went to several more shops. Where did we go, Humphrey?"

"To Melton's and the Creamery, I think, my dear."

"Yes, of course. Well, those were all small parcels, so we didn't have them sent, and then we fetched the car from the garage and went home. And it wasn't till we got home that we remembered that we'd never called at the garage office for the large parcels, and we had to go all the way back."

She laughed heartily at the conclusion of her narrative, Mrs. Lewel smiled wearily, Mrs. Nightingale nodded in her sleep.

Brian's gaze moved on round the room. He recognised the elderly man whom he had seen in the garden that afternoon, and the girl with the sloe-coloured eyes and reddened mouth. They were having tea with Miss Wingate. The three were, of course, the only unattached people in the party, so they had naturally gravitated together.

Miss Wingate was speaking in her clear precise voice, clipping her consonants, throwing out her vowels like sharp rattling little pebbles.

"We spent a most enjoyable holiday there. My friend was carrying out some investigations on Hadrian's Wall for a book on Roman Britain that she was writing. It's strange how many people are under the impression that Hadrian's Wall was a military work in the ordinary sense of the word. It was really intended as an obstacle against smugglers and raiding parties. It was quite unlike Agricola's forts in the same region."

There was a curious look in her eyes as she talked, a look that suggested she was listening to herself in helpless bewilderment and dismay. The man spoke occasionally in his pleasant cultured voice, but he was obviously not much interested. The girl did not even make a pretence of being interested. Her sharp sloe-like eyes darted from face to face of the people round her, furtively, restlessly. Beneath the table her thin hands folded the edge of the table-cloth into little patterns, unfolded it, folded it again.

A fresh couple had entered the room and were being shown by Cummings to two easy-chairs and a tea-table. The woman had a small, rather common face. The man's face was large, but his features seemed to be so crowded together in the middle of it as to leave an undue proportion of it unoccupied. He had a small dark moustache and wore eye-glasses.

As soon as they had taken their seats they opened a newspaper and began at once to discuss a cross-word puzzle upon which they had evidently been engaged during their journey.

"I don't see how it can be 'manual.' Anyway it's seven letters. ... You did pack the dictionary, by the way, didn't you, George?"

"Yes, it's in my bag."

"Sure?"

"Yes."

"Because I shall never forget that awful holiday at Brighton when you'd left it behind, and we didn't get a single one done—not *really* done—all the week."

The sound of conversation in the room rose and fell rhythmically. When it was noisiest it was a roar drowning all individual words. Then quite suddenly it would die away, and individual words and sentences would stand out clearly. It died away now, and through the half silence came Mr. Standfield's pleasant listless voice:

"I was very successful last year with dahlias, but my sweet peas were rather poor. It was the early drought, I think."

Brian Mallard threw a glance of angry scorn at him. Having heard that he intended to take Orders, Mr. Standfield had made tentative overtures of friendship, but Brian had rejected them brusquely. He had rejected them, as he rejected all overtures of friendship, in a sudden agony of shyness, but, on this occasion, he approved the brusqueness, instead of, as usual, enduring torments of regret. There was an almost fanatical light in his eyes now as he glared across the lounge at the unconscious clergyman, who was explaining the methods by which he obtained his success in dahlia culture. The boy, deciding suddenly against the strict silent Order, resolved to fling himself with all his energy of mind and soul and body into the work of a large slum parish in Manchester or Birmingham or somewhere like that. The parish would be deplorably under-staffed, and he would probably overwork to such an extent that he would succumb to an early death. (The idea of an early death had always appealed to him.) Certainly such things as dahlia culture would not enter into his life. He whipped up his angry scorn more vehemently, because to do so dulled a certain ceaseless nagging of his conscience that he shrank from facing.

Another sudden lull fell upon the conversation.

"But you don't spell it like that, surely," said the voice of the cross-word puzzle wife in a tone of almost passionate earnestness.

The sloe-black eyes of the girl opposite were still moving about the room. They found the boy and rested on him speculatively. Though he did not return her glance, he was hotly aware of it. His young face grew set and stern under its flush of embarrassment. He moved his chair so that he need not meet her eyes. This brought another corner of the room within his range of vision, and for the first time he noticed a couple sitting on one of the window seats—a stout overdressed woman with very large ankles and very small shoes, and a girl so like the girl he had met in the garden that his heart stopped, then raced unevenly. She had the same ash-blonde hair, light-blue eyes, delicate complexion, sweet childish mouth, and slight build. But something of the sparkle and vividness of the other was lacking, and he felt that he would have known them apart anywhere, though feature for feature they were identical.

Then slowly, determinedly, he turned to face that incessant nagging of his conscience. He remembered with shame and self-loathing the sudden impulse to take the girl in his arms, the thrilling imaginary foretaste of the sweetness of her lips. It had been definitely a Sin. The girl herself was definitely a Temptation. He had vowed to abjure all such enticements of the flesh. The voice of the fat woman reached him plainly in another momentary lull:

"And I can't eat cauliflower at all, it makes my stomach feel that puffed up."

The girl made a vague murmur of interest and sympathy.

It was his first real Temptation of that sort, thought the boy, tightening his lips. He mustn't give way to it, not for one second. He would set himself a penance for this afternoon. He would—the door opened, and they came in, the girl herself, a boy of about seventeen in plus-fours, a woman strikingly like her twin daughters, and a tall broad-shouldered handsome man with a face that was both humorous and determined. They were an exceptionally good-looking party—the men satisfactorily masculine in build and expression, the women ethereally feminine. The sister left the fat woman with a murmured apology and went to join them.

They sat down in the only unoccupied corner of the room, and the father ordered tea in that indefinable manner that marks out a man as experienced in dealing with waiters. An added agility, a slight servility even, informed the manner of the footman as he brought up another table. The new arrivals seemed suddenly to dominate the whole room. Conversation had died away, and everyone was watching them covertly. Everyone except the boy, who, though aware of them in every nerve, was staring glassily at the toe of his crossed leg as he moved it up and down, round and round. But the temptation to look at her was so irresistible that he knew he must succumb to it if he stayed there one moment longer. He rose abruptly and strode jerkily towards the door. To reach it he had to pass the new-comers. He meant to pass them without a glance, but somehow his eyes slid to them as if by their own volition. Angela looked up, met his gaze, and smiled, an eager friendly smile of recognition.

He stared at her for a moment without smiling, then strode on.

In the hall he stood still to recover his breath. He was trembling, his heart was racing, and he was more acutely miserable than he had ever been in his life before, but he felt that he had dealt Temptation an almost staggering blow.

Chapter Eight

MISS KIMBALL and Miss Lattimer took their places at one of the little tables arranged for the whist-drive. Miss Kimball wore a close-fitting dress of black velvet that emphasised the whiteness of her skin and the copper sheen of her hair. The girl wore green, with a sheaf of lilies of the valley pinned onto her shoulder. They were talking and smiling together, but all the girl's animation had vanished. Her smile was strained, and she watched the elder woman warily.

"Isn't that fireplace wonderful?" Judith was saying. "The eighteenth-century decoration seems to hit the happy mean between the Victorian—all cluttered up with irrelevancies—and the modern that's so bare it almost makes one's teeth chatter."

She was acting her friendliness so well that an ordinary observer would never have known it was not genuine. But Sidney knew, Sidney who responded like a sensitive instrument to Judith's subtlest shades of tone and manner. It had happened this afternoon, but Sidney still didn't know quite how or why, still felt bewildered by the sudden change from radiant kindness to this icy travesty of it. Judith's temper had been serene all yesterday evening and all this morning. Her sweetness had raised Sidney once more to that pinnacle of happiness to which only Judith's sweetness could raise her. They had walked over the common this morning, and Judith had been, as she always could be when she liked, the most charming of companions. When they returned for lunch Sidney had found a box, sent to her by post to Judith's order from a London florist, containing the spray of lilies of the valley for her to wear with her green dress to-night.

"Oh, *Judith*," she had gasped, "how lovely of you! I simply *adore* them."

And Judith had smiled tenderly and said:

"They're rather like you, you know. . . ."

They had set off for their drive this afternoon, still in that happy consciousness of unclouded friendship.

When they reached the highest part of the common, Judith had tapped on the glass for Bennet to stop.

"You must look at this glorious view, darling," she had said to Sidney. "You aren't paying enough attention to the landscape. After all, as Miss Nettleton would say, someone might ask you if you'd seen it. . . ."

It was only when Judith was in a very good temper that she made fun of the people they met. She generally treated them all alike with scornful indifference.

They both gazed at the undulating common that stretched away like a sea to the haze of the distant hills.

"Come along, lazy-bones," said Judith, opening the door of the car. "Let's go for a walk. . . ."

She turned her head in Bennet's direction and, without looking at him, said shortly, "We'll be back in about ten minutes."

They walked briskly over the resilient peaty ground. Despite the sunshine the air was crisp and keen, and the faint breeze carried a touch of ice in its caress. The bare branches of the silver birches stood out with the delicate vividness of an etching against the pale-blue sky. They startled a rabbit that scuttled in sudden panic across their path. Once a robin's song, and once a wren's, fell with silvery clearness through the still air.

When they returned to the car, the frost had whipped colour into their cheeks and brightness into their eyes.

"I'd love to bottle some of it and take it home, wouldn't you?" said Judith.

Her laughing voice changed abruptly to curtness as she gave Bennet the order to drive home, and again she merely threw a disdainful glance in his direction as though it were too much trouble to focus him properly.

The studied insolence of her tone and manner made Sidney feel hotly uncomfortable. One *couldn't* treat him like that. He was so nice. He'd been so kind to her that dreadful day they arrived. She turned to him on an impulse, anxious only to make amends for Judith's curtness.

"It's a lovely view, isn't it, Bennet?" she said.

He gave her once more that gentle reassuring smile. Don't worry, it seemed to say, I don't mind. And there was something more than reassurance in his smile, though Sidney couldn't have told what it was.

"It's lovely, miss," he agreed.

For an almost imperceptible moment they stood there smiling at each other, then she followed Judith into the car. The whole episode had only taken a few seconds, but it had raised up the wall of ice again between her and Judith. She realised it the moment she sat down, and her heart sank with a qualm of actual nausea at the realisation. When Judith next spoke she spoke quite pleasantly, commenting on the scenery and weather, but Sidney knew that the real Judith—miles and miles away behind the wall of ice—was angry and hostile, was probably already shaping weapons for her punishment. Right down at the bottom of Sidney's mind was a faint spark of resentment—the first spark of resentment that she had ever felt in these strange, one-sided quarrels that had troubled her relations with Judith at intervals ever since the beginning of their friendship. After all, what had she done? She had only said "Isn't it a lovely view, Bennet?" Surely *anyone* might have said that. But the spark of resentment was unconscious. All her conscious energy was absorbed in coping with the wall of ice, in making desperate efforts to win Judith back to good-humour, in steeling herself for the outburst—though outburst was hardly the word to describe the cold calm deliberateness of Judith's attacks—when it should come. But Judith's delusive pleasantness had lasted all through the afternoon and evening. She had gone into Sidney's room before dinner to pin the lilies of the valley carefully into their place on the frilly green shoulder.

"Well, what about this whist-drive?" she had said casually as she did it. "Are we going?"

Sidney hesitated.

It was Judith herself who had put their names down for the whist-drive on a list that hung in the hall. She had looked at the prizes, which were ranged on a table just underneath the list, and said: "I'll win the clock and you must win the saltcellars." She had even teased Sidney about her salt-cellars during their morning walk.

"We've put our names down for it," said Sidney tentatively. "I—I think it will be quite jolly."

Judith shrugged her beautiful shoulders.

"Of course, darling, if you're keen," she had replied in a voice that removed Sidney to immeasurable distances of childishness.

And here they were, sitting at a little table, waiting for the whist-drive to begin, and Judith was making polite conversation as if they had just been introduced to each other for the first time.

"And the ceilings," she was saying. "Just look at that cornice. I think good workmanship went out when machinery came in."

Sidney was relieved when Mr. Ellison sat down at their table and began to talk to Judith. She leant back in her chair and looked round the room.

It was almost full now. At the next table sat the girl who had arrived that morning—Miss Torrance, Sidney heard someone call her—with the black slanting eyes and red lips.

The Paynter twins had just come in. What darlings they were with their silver-gold curls and delicate flower-like faces! They looked so young and fresh and unspoilt that they made even Sidney feel maternal towards them—maternal and elderly, weighed down by care and experience. Their dresses were of white lace, reaching to the floor, made in Empire style with tiny high waists. One of them wore an apple-green ribbon sash, the other a blue one, tied in bows behind with long flowing ends. They reminded Sidney of two children dressed in their party frocks to come down to the drawing-room. It must be rather fun to have a sister, she thought wistfully. They were throwing bright friendly glances around. She would have liked to smile at them, but Judith hated her making friends with other people. Judith never seemed to want other people, although her beauty and poise always attracted them. At this moment she was showing Mr. Ellison quite plainly that she didn't care whether he stayed or went away.

The Christmas party was now complete. The last members of it—a man and two women—had arrived before dinner and were entering the room behind the Paynter twins. The man was of average height, but with a sort of finicky elegance of build that had in it a suggestion of effeminacy. His clothes were just too well tailored, his whole person just too well groomed. There was nothing effeminate, however, about his face. Its expression was dare-devil and debonair. Beneath a small moustache his mouth smiled—a gay, rather cruel little smile. He held himself upright and swaggered slightly as he walked. He didn't seem to belong to this century, thought Sidney, watching him. He should have been one of the rollicking rakes of the Restoration. The set of his head suggested a plumed hat, his swagger a cloak.

The woman who followed him bore an elusive resemblance to him that lay less in any particular feature—she was indeed plain where he was handsome—than in something of careless cynicism that lurked in the dark eyes and the curves of the faintly smiling lips.

One could hardly tell what the other woman's face had been like, so disfigured was it by the scars that ran across it, pulling the features completely out of shape. The mouth was twisted, the nose broken and bulbous. She moved in a stiff jerky way, and her face, for all its distortion, was expressionless.

"They're the Downings," Sidney heard a voice behind her saying. "You'd never guess that she'd been beautiful, would you? She was thrown from her horse against a wall when she was hunting this January. At first they didn't think she'd live. I just saw his sister for a minute in the hall. She said that her sister-in-law was rather self-conscious about her disfigurement, and they thought that a place like this would suit her better than an ordinary hotel."

Sidney threw another furtive glance at the woman. The expressionlessness of the distorted mask gave it a likeness to a battered broken doll that she had had when a child.

She looked away again with a shudder.

Chapter Nine

CELIA came into the room, looked smilingly round, then rang the little silver bell for the whist-drive to begin.

"Hearts are trumps," she called in her clear, brisk voice.

Miss Bella Torrance stubbed her cigarette, dropped the end into the small enamelled ash-tray, then put out her hand to draw for deal. Her slanting sloe-black eyes swept the room speculatively as she did so. A pretty dud-looking lot on the whole. . . . She wondered why on earth she'd come to the place. But, of course, she knew quite well in her heart why she'd come to the place. . . . She'd wanted to get among nice people and start fresh. And, duds or not, these were certainly nice people. Depressingly, appallingly nice. . . .

She glanced at her cards. Not a single heart. Futile sort of game, anyway. The wonder was that anyone played it out of the nursery. Even Auction seemed pretty tame nowadays. . . . It was Simon who had taught her Contract. . . . At the memory of Simon the red lips tightened. She mustn't let herself think of Simon. She'd sworn to forget him. She'd come here in order to forget him. He meant nothing to her—now. She was starting fresh, getting to know nice people. . . . She'd always secretly hankered after a quiet, respectable life among quiet, respectable people. It had been just a mistake that she'd lived the other sort of life for so long. She'd never really wanted to. Guy used to tease her about what he called her "respectability complex."

She had a sudden vision of Guy entering the room with his boyish mischievous smile, and calling, "Beulah, my sweet, where are you?" She'd never told Simon that her real name was Beulah, because she wanted to forget about Guy when she was with Simon, wanted to pretend to herself that there'd never been anyone but Simon. . . .

73

Her father was a Plymouth Brother and had called all his children by names taken from *Pilgrim's Progress*. Like many other men of weak character, he had gratified a secret lust for power by bullying and browbeating his family, using, in his case, his particular brand of religion as his weapon. His children had all left home as soon as they were old enough to support themselves, losing touch with both the home and each other. They had had the ideal of family love and duty dinned into them so incessantly from earliest childhood that it had lost its attraction for them. They had so frequently been forced to love each other and yield to each other and apologise to each other under threat of punishment that they had hated each other before they were in their teens. Well, those days were far enough away. . . . She did not know where any of her brothers and sisters were now. She herself had been lucky enough to get a job in an office the week after she ran away from home. She had rented a small room in Highgate and at first had been completely happy in the freedom from her father's blustering tyranny. . . .

"Sorry," her partner was saying cheerfully.

He was a good-looking boy of about seventeen, the brother of the pretty girls in the lace frocks. Already during dinner Bella had been watching them with smouldering resentment as they sat laughing and chattering together over their table. They were obviously the sort of people who not only had money but knew how to spend it. Those girls had had everything they needed from babyhood. One glance at them told you that. And not only money. . . . The mother looked sweet and gentle, the father's face wore a good-humoured smile. She remembered the angry scowl that was her own father's normal expression, and the sick terror she had felt of him before she was old enough to despise him. Those girls had never known anything like that. . . . They'd be horrified, of course, if they found out what she was, but—she wouldn't have been like that if she'd had their chances. If she'd had their chances Simon might have married her. . . . The pang that shot through her heart at that thought made her shut her eyes as at a stab of physical pain.

"Let's see . . . I move, don't I?" the boy was saying.

He stood up to move to the next chair, exchanging signs with his sisters across the room.

"Cicely's lost and Angela's won," he announced to Bella, and went on, as he sat down, "I can't play for nuts, you know. You're lucky that I didn't revoke. I did trump your ace, didn't I?"

"Only once," she replied.

The other two partners had arrived—the rather nice-looking clergyman and the appalling woman in the brown wig. Bella had noticed her at tea-time. Her wig had then shown a little fringe of white all round the edge, but it didn't now. It was tidier, too, and of a slightly different shade of brown. Her best wig that she only put on in the evenings, presumably. . . . She wore a black evening dress, obviously several years old, and a mangy fur necklet whose fastening had evidently lost its spring, as the end of it escaped the grasp of the hairless little head whenever she thrust it in. She thrust it in continually and absent-mindedly as she talked, and this gave the small creature the appearance of ineffectually worrying itself throughout the evening.

She at once began to ask the clergyman in a startlingly loud voice how to get to a Druids' circle that was somewhere in the neighbourhood.

"It's a very complicated journey," he replied, "and really there's nothing to see when you get there but a few big stones."

"I know," she said, "but I ought to see it."

Mrs. Beaton rang the little bell again and announced:

"Diamonds are trumps."

They took up their cards.

"Good egg!" said the boy. "Two aces! One of trumps, too!"

Somehow his tone reminded Bella suddenly of Guy. Guy used to call out "Good egg!" like that. Guy had been boyish and irresponsible, living in the present, never looking backward or forward. She'd met him first in a restaurant. She'd "picked him up," in fact—a thing that nice people never do, but she'd been so sick of going from the office to her dingy room, from her dingy room to the office. The first thrill of independence had faded, she had made no friends among her fellow-workers, she was feeling tired and lonely and unutterably depressed. And when Guy smiled at her across the crowded restaurant, she had smiled back. . . . He rose when she did and followed her into the street, and they went to the pictures together. After that they met regularly every evening. When they could afford it they went to dances and night clubs. He visited her in her room, and took her to his. Though he never tried to make love to her, she sometimes wondered if he meant eventually to propose to her. She hoped he wouldn't, because she didn't want to marry him—she didn't love him enough for that—and yet she hated the thought of losing his friendship.

The end—or rather the beginning—came quite suddenly. One night he returned with her to her room and stayed there. She supposed that they'd both had a little too much to drink during the evening. Anyway—it happened. And then—well, Guy wanted it to go on, and it seemed silly to make a fuss about it once it had actually happened. Like locking the stable door after the horse was stolen. Moreover, she liked him and felt grateful to him. He had been very kind to her, and had spent a good deal of money on her. He never told her much about himself. She knew that he worked in a stockbroker's office, but he never mentioned his family to her, and she did not even know whether his parents were alive, or if he had any brothers or sisters. At first she had felt unhappy about the situation, for her early home training had unconsciously taken deep root in her mind, but, oddly enough, it was her hatred of the father who had implanted that early training that had finally made her decide to go on living with Guy. She felt that the fact that she was a "harlot" (she had often heard her father use the word in connection with such women as she was now) punished him in some mysterious way for his cruelty to her in her childhood. So she went on living with Guy, and they were happy enough on the whole. Guy's high spirits were infectious. He liked to be always "on the go," so they went to pictures, night clubs, dances, and tore about the countryside all summer in his small sports car, bathing, picnicking, playing tennis. . . .

Then quite suddenly that, too, came to an end. She was in bed for a week with influenza, and as soon as the fear of infection was over she wrote to Guy asking him to come and see her the next evening, but he neither came nor sent a message. She rang him up but was told there was no reply. Thinking that he, too, might be ill, she went to his rooms and met him coming away from them with a girl. He looked, as usual, gay and debonair, and he was laughing down at the girl's face just as a few days ago he had laughed down at hers. Fortunately neither of them saw her, and she went quietly back to her room. She wasn't at all heart-broken. She had been fond of Guy, but she had never really loved him, and his restlessness had proved rather wearing. She thought that she would now be able to settle down happily to the old life. But she found that she couldn't. All the savour had gone from it. Guy seemed to have left some of his restlessness with her, and, though she still persisted to herself that she had not loved him, she missed him acutely. She disliked more than ever the clerks and typists with whom she worked. She felt lonely and nerve-racked. She walked about the streets by herself, noting speculatively the glances that men threw at her, half deciding that if she met one who reminded her of Guy she would accept his unspoken invitation.

"Splendid, Miss Torrance!" the clergyman was saying. "Ten tricks."

"I'm awfully sorry I revoked," the boy was apologising to his partner. "You see, the heart had got in among my diamonds, and I didn't notice it. . . ."

"*Quite* all right," said Miss Nettleton, but she spoke rather coldly, and the head of her little fur made a specially vicious grab at its tail, for the boy had simply thrown away trick after trick, besides the three that he'd lost by revoking. "After all, it's only a game."

"Yes, that's just what I think," agreed the boy heartily.

"We move, Miss Torrance," said Mr. Standfield.

Bella went to the next table.

That dreadful little woman who was a don at a college or something like that, was laying down the law there as usual in her irritatingly precise voice.

"The word trump is short for triumph, which was the name of the older game from which whist developed and——"

She saw Bella waiting and sprang up with an apology, her pursed lips slightly relaxed. Bella sat down.

The cross-word puzzle couple—Mr. and Mrs. Osmond—glanced at her abstractedly, then returned to the discussion of a disputed point.

"To begin with," Mr. Osmond was saying, "I don't think that Venus was the goddess of the moon."

"But it's the right number of letters," said his wife.

Miss Downing joined them, smiling faintly as though at some secret joke.

From the next table came Mrs. Standfield's voice: ". . . and the Vicar found that the gardener had been putting lime and soot on together, which is ridiculous, of course, because they counteract each other, as it were, and, of course, that explained why the vegetables had been so poor that year and——"

"Is Mr. Beaton here?" asked Miss Downing. "We only saw Mrs. Beaton when we arrived."

"Yes, he's over there playing bridge with the Fieldens and Mr. Ellison," said Mrs. Osmond. "He's that rather plain man with red hair."

In one of the window recesses the blind man was playing bridge with his wife, his host, and Mr. Ellison. His face was still set and grim, and it resembled more than ever the face of a prize-fighter at the most crucial moment of the fight. In a sudden lull their voices reached Bella.

"Two of hearts. . . . Seven. . . . Knave. . . ."

"They each name the card they put down," explained Mrs. Osmond. "Mr. Fielden has a marvellous memory and never forgets a single card that's gone. I was watching them just before dinner."

Mrs. Beaton's bell rang once more.

"Clubs are trumps," she announced, "and losers score double."

There was a buzz of excited discussion.

"You try to lose, you see. . . ."

"You try to win just the six tricks. . . ."

"We get up most successful little whist-drives in our parish,"

Mrs. Standfield's high-pitched voice announced through the clatter, "and we always make it a rule that——"

Bella made a quick, impatient movement. Damn them, damn the whole lot of them, damn everything and everybody! . . . Why had she come here? Why hadn't she stayed in town as Hugh had asked her to? Hugh wasn't Simon, but he'd known Simon; he'd been one of their set. He used to come and help them get ready for the parties they gave in their little studio. He had always admired her. Once Simon had said, "If I didn't know you loved me, I'd jolly well warn off old Hughie. You can see with half an eye that he'd like to be in my shoes. . . ."

"Oh, Simon, don't!" she had said, for the very idea of it then had been horrible.

She had thought from the beginning that Simon was going to marry her. He said that he wasn't earning enough to marry just yet, but that, as soon as he was, they would get married at once. Meantime, he wanted her to live with him. She had told him about Guy, and he had been very nice and understanding about it, and, though she would rather have waited to live with him till they were married, it seemed silly to hold out when he knew about Guy, and they were so passionately in love with each other.

Simon's friends accepted the situation quite naturally. They were mostly artists like Simon, doing any odd jobs in the way of book-jackets, posters, and advertisements that came their way, complaining always that it was impossible for an artist to make enough even to live on, and spending prodigally every penny that they earned. She went to live in Simon's studio with him. . . .

"Simon, darling," she said once, "why shouldn't we—I mean, what's the difference—why shouldn't we be married?"

He had smiled at her tenderly and said, "Darling, I'm not going to marry you till I can give you something more worthy of you than this."

They had been radiantly happy. He had painted her in every position and from every angle. Sometimes they would go into the country for the day, not flying along at seventy miles an hour in a sports car, as she had done with Guy, but wandering through the woods and lanes, revelling in their peace and loveliness, watching daylight fade to twilight and twilight into night. . . . Simon would bring his sketching-block, and she would prepare a picnic meal and set it out with great care, decorating the table-cloth with trails of ivy and little bunches of wild flowers. Simon used to tease her about her "fairy feasts," as he called them. Often in the evenings his friends would come to the studio, and they would have hilarious parties, dressing up in the "property" clothes, acting charades, cooking ridiculous dishes over the one little gas ring. . . . They had been happy, care-free, halcyon days, their most trivial happening made wonderful by her love for Simon.

Then—quite suddenly—that, too, had ended. One day, instead of coming home to her, Simon had sent her a note in which he said that he thought their affair had better finish now while all their memories of it were happy ones and before they had tired of each other. He said that he wasn't coming back to the studio and enclosed a cheque for £500.

That was the last she heard from him directly. Other news trickled through to her by way of his friends. He had been made a partner in his father's business. The position had apparently always been waiting for him, when he should tire of being an artist, and—well, now he had tired of it. He'd never meant to marry her. He'd been play-acting, and she was just part of the play—the artist's mistress, the finishing touch to the Bohemian atmosphere. However passionately he had loved her, she'd never been more to him than that. . . . A week after he left her she heard that he was engaged to a girl who was his sister's friend. At first she was distraught. It seemed literally impossible for her to go on living without him. And then Hugh had come to her and asked if he might take Simon's place. That had pulled her up sharply. She didn't want to be just something that one man could hand over to another as he tired of her. She saw suddenly the way she was going, and it frightened her. She'd never really meant to "go wrong." It had all been a sort of mistake. Deep down at the bottom of her heart was an inherited love of respectability, a secret longing for a home, a husband, children. . . .

"But how absurd!" said Mrs. Osmond. "We've lost, and we've doubled it, and *still* the other people have got more. I don't understand it. It's all very confusing."

"We've won, Miss Torrance," said Mr. Osmond, screwing up his tiny features into an ingratiating smile. "We played jolly well, eh? . . ."

She smiled with an effort and moved on to the next table. That awful woman with her hair all over her eyes was there, and the fat peroxided woman who tottered about on high heels as if she were on stilts, and one of the Paynter twins—the one with an apple-green sash. Bella's slanting eyes shot a quick glance at her, noting again her air of dewy innocence, of unsullied youth. Probably not much younger than she was herself. Her mouth hardened. I might have been like that if I'd had a decent chance, she thought again resentfully.

"Are you you or your sister?" said the fat woman, with a high-pitched giggle.

The girl smiled.

"I'm Angela. It was my sister Cicely you were talking to this afternoon."

"Well, now, you're as like as two peas, aren't you? . . . We got on together a treat, your sister and me. We found we'd a lot in common. . . . It's going to be ever such fun here, I think, don't you? . . . Though I thought I shouldn't be able to come last night. I'd got such a splitting headache——"

Mrs. Stephenson-Pollitt leaned forward and placed her hand on her arm.

"You hadn't," she said in her low, tense voice.

Mrs. Kellogg stared at her in amazement.

"Hadn't what?" she said.

"Hadn't got a headache," said Mrs. Stephenson-Pollitt, and added slowly, portentously: "There's no such thing in the world as a headache."

"'Ere," said Mrs. Kellogg, letting go some of her careful gentility of accent in her amazement. "'Oo're you gettin' at?"

"There's no such thing as pain of any sort. You only imagine it. . . ."

"Me?" said Mrs. Kellogg indignantly.

The girl smiled shyly across at Bella.

"Isn't it lovely country round here? Have you been out on the common?"

"Yes," said Bella shortly, and lit a cigarette.

Sweet and fresh and innocent and all that, but she'd bore you stiff if you got to know her. She wouldn't be able to talk about anything but herself and her family. She'd probably even tell you about the mistress she'd had a rave on at school and show you snapshots of her dogs. . . .

"Spades are trumps," called Mrs. Beaton.

Bella took up her cards languidly. She was bored, bored, bored. How on earth could she stand four days of it? Why on earth had she come at all? She answered herself quite frankly. It wasn't only that she wanted to start fresh. It was more than that. Right at the back of her mind, unacknowledged, had been the hope that she would meet here a man of the marrying sort who would fall in love with her, and that gradually she would learn to forget Simon that way. . . . She wanted to be married, to have a home of her own and children. . . . Well, she was pretty good at summing men up by now, and she'd realised at once that there was no chance of that here. Mr. Ellison was a bachelor of the old-maid type, and in any case he wouldn't be likely to fall for her, and the only other unmarried men were the two boys—that Paynter schoolboy, and that dreadful young prig who'd been having tea with the woman whose hair was all over her eyes. . . . She'd spent a lot of money on clothes for this visit (she had not obeyed her first impulse to send Simon his money back. On second thoughts she had come to the conclusion that he owed her that, at any rate), and it was all going to be wasted. . . .

Then suddenly she saw a man watching her across the room. She hadn't noticed him before. He had a small moustache and under it his lips were curved into a smile that was cynical, mocking, boldly appraising. His eyes moved over her with a slow, challenging, experienced stare. Her boredom vanished. She did not meet his gaze, but for the rest of the evening she was acutely and not unpleasurably conscious of it. . . .

Chapter Ten

THE blind man's brow contracted irritably behind his blue glasses. Damn that little bell they kept ringing! It was maddening having to play bridge in the room where the whist-drive was going on. And the fools jabbered like a zoo full of monkeys between the games. He could hardly hear his own table speak. . . . It was Beaton's lead.

"Ten of clubs——"

Nice voice the chap had—slow, pleasant, aristocratic. You could tell from it that nothing on earth would ever get him rattled. Sort of chap who'd stroll along the trench smoking a cigarette with shells bursting all round him. The last thing he had seen had been that—a chap strolling along the trench, smoking a cigarette, with shells bursting all round him. He'd seen it sixteen years ago. Sixteen long, slow, blasted years. . . .

It was his wife's lead now. She made a sort of clicking noise with her teeth, denoting indecision, that he always found unspeakably exasperating. He frowned again sharply behind his blue glasses. She put down a card.

"King of diamonds."

Her voice was a constant irritation to him. It was thin and high-pitched and monotonous. When it became querulous and tearful, as it often did, it goaded him to the verge of madness. . . . It still seemed strange and unnatural to him to be married to a woman he had never seen, though he supposed that it must have happened to thousands of men after the war. The stranger thing was that, though he could form a pretty clear idea of the appearance of other people from their voices, he had no clear idea of what his wife looked like. One thing he did know. She was as unlike as possible the description of herself she had given him before their marriage. . . . She was leading again.

"Ace of hearts."

What a fool he'd been! He might have known from her voice—even sixteen years ago—that she was a middle-aged woman. She'd told him that she was twenty-three. It wasn't till after their marriage that he discovered she was thirty-nine. He'd never forgiven her for that. It wasn't so much that she'd deceived him. He could have forgiven that. It was that she'd made a fool of him. Everyone must have been laughing at him—marrying a woman ten years older than himself and believing that she was a young girl. The thought of it used to turn him hot and cold with humiliation. She'd made a fool of him, tricked him, held him up to public mockery. He had always been over-sensitive about his blindness, looking upon quite innocent and well-meant offers of assistance as covert insults.

That darned little bell was ringing again, and the monkey jabber filled the whole room. People began to pass to and fro between the tables. A girl's voice, laughing and musical, just behind his chair, called out, "Cicely, we only got *one* trick! Wasn't it dreadful? How many did you get?"

Again behind his chair another girl's voice, sweet and low and rather breathless: "Judith, darling, you're looking so tired."

And a woman's voice, deep, assured, with a hint of disdain: "I am tired."

"Would it be all right if we just spoke to Mrs. Beaton and slipped away now? They could arrange it somehow, couldn't they?"

"Of course not."

They were settling down at last, thank heaven! That maddening little bell again, then silence. . . .

Maud was setting out the dummy: "Hearts—king, queen, ten, six. . . ." He listened carefully. It was his pride that no one ever had to tell him a card twice. He'd trained his memory assiduously since he lost his sight.

Four tricks . . . just his contract. . . . Good. The monkeys were beginning to jabber again, damn them! There was a woman somewhere who spoke in a sort of hissing whisper. He could hear her now. "I have psychic dreams, you know." Why on earth didn't someone wring her damned neck? Then there was another who spoke in a voice that could be heard at least a mile off. She was talking about a ruin she'd been to see and complaining that it had been draughty. Why didn't someone wring all their damned necks?

"I'm sorry," Beaton was saying, as if in reply to his quick scowl. "I'm afraid it's horribly noisy. We'll play in another room next time. It hardly seems worth while moving now. . . ."

"Oh, it's not so bad," said Ellison. "At least they're quiet while they're playing. I've played in noisier places."

Nice voice that chap had, too, thought the blind man. He could almost see him—tall, thin, well dressed. . . .

"Of *course* it's all right," put in Maud quickly.

He'd just been going to say it was all right himself, but Maud's chipping in like that put his back up, and he only set his lips more grimly and said nothing.

He knew that she didn't mean to irritate him as much as she did, and he sometimes tried, though without much success, to control his irritation. After all, he had been glad enough to turn to her when Betty threw him over. . . . Even now he shrank from remembering those days. When they told him after the operation that his sight was gone for ever, he had thought at first that he was going mad. He had clung for sanity to the thought of Betty. His whole world had crashed about him, but Betty was left. And then—he'd got Betty's letter throwing him over. It was a very sensible letter. She told him that, while he was away at the front, she had fallen in love with another man. She'd meant to tell him herself the first time he came home on leave. But he came home wounded, and so she had decided to wait till after his operation, and now that that was over she felt that the kindest and most straightforward thing was to write at once. She realised that it seemed cruel to break off the engagement just when he had lost his sight, but it would be far more cruel, she wrote, to go through with it, loving someone else.

It was Maud who had read the letter aloud to him, sitting by his bed in her nurse's uniform (he'd imagined her young and pretty and roguish-looking, like some of the V.A.D.'s he'd met in France), and it was Maud who had put her arms around him to comfort him at the end when he broke down and cried. . . . The blow had completed the shattering of his world. For days he had longed only for death. Then something of his fighting spirit had come back, but he was weak and helpless and bewildered. He had turned to Maud for everything, as if he had been a child. It was she who took him out, guiding his footsteps, describing the things and people they passed. They went to concerts together and had meals together in little unfrequented restaurants (he hated crowds since he was blind). He didn't actually fall in love with her, but he became so dependent on her that he literally could not contemplate life without her. He felt that no one else would ever know just how and when he needed help.

And she, on her side, was in love with him. He was a handsome man, even with his shattered eyes, and the fact that he belonged to a higher social class than hers shed a glamour about him. She encouraged his delusion as to her youth and prettiness. She lied deliberately about her age. She invented compliments that she said had been paid her by other patients ("You're far too pretty to be a nurse") or that she had overheard ("I say, she's a peach, isn't she?"). She let him see quite plainly that she was in love with him. She gave him several opportunities to propose, and in the end he took one. He never even pretended to be in love with her. That sort of thing's all over with Betty, he had told himself, but I must marry someone—especially now. She loves me, and I'm fond of her. We shall get on all right.

The buzz of conversation rose again.

"Eleven tricks!" screamed someone. "Just fancy! Eleven!"

"I say, I'm awfully sorry," said a boy's voice. "I didn't realise it was your king when I put my ace on."

"Isn't Ian *dreadful?*" said the girl's voice that he had heard before—a sweet laughing voice that reminded him of a waterfall. "I believe he's revoked every single game."

87

"No, I haven't," the boy assured her earnestly. "Honestly, I haven't. I didn't at this one, and I didn't at the last but two."

The bell rang, and there rose the stir of people passing to and fro between the tables. The buzz of conversation continued.

"Terribly disfigured, isn't she?" said a lowered voice just behind his chair. "It was a hunting accident at the beginning of this year."

He felt a quick bitter pang of sympathy with the unknown woman. Knocked out, like him, poor devil. . . . Then he grit his teeth together again. He wasn't knocked out. . . .

"Winners score double," announced Mrs. Beaton.

There followed little screams of excitement, then silence.

Ellison was putting down his dummy, naming the cards as he did so in his quiet voice.

"Diamonds—ten, five, two. . . ."

Maud cleared her throat—a nervous habit she had that always brought a sharp scowl of irritation into her husband's face. . . .

They'd got on all right at first. He was still completely dependent on her. He had been happy with her in those early days, as a child is happy with its nurse. She had read to him, fed him, dressed him. . . .

Then gradually he had begun to find his feet, to feel his way alone. He had set himself with a sort of dogged determination to win back his place in the world of normal men. He wouldn't remain a being apart—wouldn't meekly accept his handicap. . . . He began to resent his dependence on her; her attentions even when necessary began to irritate him. His affection for her died, killed finally by the discovery of her age, and his gratitude was poisoned at its heart by the bitterness of a discovery that seemed an insult to his manhood. He still needed her—needed her indeed to this day—but that very need of her formed strangely one of his secret grievances against her.

The thing he had most feared was that his blindness would make him deteriorate physically. He could no longer take part in games, but he could keep himself fit by exercise and diet, and he flung himself into the pursuit of physical fitness with the grim ferocity of a fighter. He worked under a trainer—running, boxing, exercising, swimming, jumping. His diet was a carefully thought-out, carefully balanced regimen. He kept himself at the acme of physical perfection, being overhauled by a doctor at regular intervals. Those exercises in which he could compete with normal men—running and swimming especially—were his greatest joy. He took unsparing pains to train his memory. He could remember not only facts but distances. Once he had felt his way from one object to another, he never forgot the distance, never took a step too few or too many.

Since his marriage he had managed a poultry farm in Sussex. He disliked both the place and the work, but with his wife's help he made it pay, and he had no other source of income. Once or twice a month he would go up to Town to his club, and no one, watching him moving about there and listening to his conversation, would have dreamed that he was blind. He went there simply in order to test himself, to assure himself that he was still holding his own. The knowledge that he was still holding his own brought him, not joy or satisfaction, but a sense of savage triumph over his adversary.

"Rubber to you, Fielden," said Ellison. "Shall we cut for another?"

"We have a Women's Institute, of course," shrilled a woman's voice near him. "Jam-making competitions and that sort of thing. So good for the women."

The blind man's hands made an angry movement, almost as if they were engaged in wringing the speaker's neck.

"You and I, Fielden," said Beaton.

As they changed places, Ellison said, "I suppose you read Braille? It's rather difficult to pick up, I believe, isn't it?"

"I don't read it," said Fielden curtly, and his grim mouth shut like a trap.

He avoided other blind men, and he refused to learn Braille. Both seemed somehow to emphasise the disability that he was determined to ignore, seemed to brand him as an exile from the normal world to which he was determined, in spite of everything, to belong.

Although the whist-players were in the middle of a game someone passed behind him, banging into his chair. He muttered an angry exclamation.

"Look where you're going, young man," said Ellison.

"I'm sorry," said a voice—a young voice, embarrassed, dignified, faintly aggressive.

The voice belonged to Brian Mallard. Having refused to come to the whist-drive, he had stayed up in his bedroom, trying to read Newman's *Apologia*. He had expected to find it absorbingly interesting, but he didn't. He kept thinking of Angela Paynter, and wondering where she was sitting, and whom she was playing with. Was she laughing that delicious silvery little laugh and chattering away with that childish spontaneity that was so indescribably attractive? She'd looked lovely at dinner in that white lace dress with the green sash, her silvery golden hair shining, her blue eyes alight. . . . He wished that he hadn't said he didn't play cards. After all, whist was hardly cards. . . .

Then, with a quick stern frown, he took himself in hand. He had decided only a few hours ago never to think of her again, and he must keep his resolution. He must not dally with temptation.

He made a gesture of dismissal with his hand, as if sweeping away from him a whole Venusburg, and returned to Newman:

"It was Dr. Hawkins, too, who taught me to anticipate that, before many years were over, there would be an attack made upon the books and canon of Scripture. I was brought to the same belief by the conversation of Mr. Blanco White, who also led me to have freer views on the subject of inspiration than were usual in the Church of England at the time."

Of course, it was frightfully interesting—it must be because he'd been told that it was—but somehow he couldn't really become interested in it. Not that he was thinking of her again, because he wasn't. He was most resolutely and determinedly *not* thinking of her. Still—he decided suddenly that it was his duty to take a greater interest in the events of the day than he did. He'd fetch the newspaper that his aunt had left in the drawing-room. The whist-drive was going on there, but he wouldn't disturb anyone. He'd merely fetch the paper. He wouldn't actually look at her, but, of course, it was just possible that he might catch a glimpse of her out of the corner of his eye as he walked through the room. He couldn't help it if that happened. It wouldn't be his fault.

He went downstairs and entered the drawing-room. Yes, there she was. He could see her quite plainly although he wasn't actually looking at her. How lovely she was! ... He plunged past the whist-tables and past a bridge-table, where some old fogies cursed him just because he happened to touch one of their chairs. He retrieved the newspaper from the window-seat at the further corner of the room, and made his way back. It was the end of the game, and everyone was beginning to talk.

"Aren't those Paynter twins exactly alike?" he heard someone saying. "I don't know how anyone ever manages to tell the difference between them."

A hot flame of indignation swept over him. Alike! Why, Angela was infinitely more beautiful than the other—infinitely superior in every way. He glared fiercely at the unconscious speaker. Then he went upstairs again, a warm glow of self-righteousness at his heart. He hadn't succumbed to temptation. He hadn't even looked at her. Not *really* looked at her. He'd merely gone down to the drawing-room to fetch the newspaper. ...

Chapter Eleven

FRIDAY EVENING *(continued)*

THERE was a burst of clapping as the names of the prize-winners were announced and the prizes brought in from the hall. The bridge-party still went on in the corner of the room, and the blind man's brow still contracted savagely at each fresh sound from the whist-players. The Paynter twins ran across the room to their brother.

"Ian, you've got the booby prize!"

He consulted his card with a faint attempt at dignity.

"Well, I had some quite decent scores," he said, "but, of course, ones and twos pull one down so."

Angela turned to Sidney, who was standing near.

"Ian's got the booby prize. I said he would. I bet him sixpence he would."

"Oh, well, I've scored anyway," grinned Ian. "The booby prize is jolly well worth more than sixpence."

"Show Miss Lattimer your card, Ian. He's got eleven ones."

"I had rotten cards," explained Ian, handing Sidney his scoring-card. They stood round her laughing as she examined it. She felt herself drawn into their circle of eager, light-hearted, hilarious youth. Suddenly she, too, began to feel light-hearted and youthful.

"Oh but *look*!" she said. "Here's a *six*!"

They all laughed again as if she had said something very witty.

"Are you ready, Sidney?"

She handed the card back to Ian quickly and with an odd sense of guilt. She hadn't known that Judith was standing just behind her.

"Yes."

"Shall we go up then?"

Sidney hesitated.

She would have liked to stay downstairs a little longer and watch the prize-giving and join in the cheers and laughter. Since she met Judith she had been trying so hard to be worthy of her friendship, to hide her youth and immaturity, to make herself poised and serious like Judith, that she had almost forgotten what it was to feel young and care-free as just for a few moments the Paynters had made her feel. And it wasn't only the Paynters. The memory of that kindly reassuring smile that Bennet had given her this afternoon had seemed to be hovering about her all evening, protecting her. She wished that Bennet could have been at the whist-drive. He would have looked so nice in a dress-suit. But that was absurd, of course. He probably had never worn a dress-suit in his life. . . .

"You didn't win the clock," she said to Judith as they went upstairs together.

"No, and you didn't win the salt-cellars," said Judith.

She smiled quite pleasantly as she spoke, but something in her voice made Sidney remember the smouldering moodiness that had darkened the earlier part of the day. The familiar feeling of wariness crept over her. Probably it was all right, but she must go very carefully. . . .

"It's been terrible, hasn't it?" said Judith, sitting down in the armchair by the hearthrug and putting her hands behind her head.

"Oh, Judith," said Sidney with a deprecating little smile, "I—I rather liked it."

"How dreadful of you, darling," smiled Judith. "I shouldn't have thought that even you could have got any pleasure out of such an impossible affair."

There was a barbed sting in the "even you," but she was smiling and her voice was still quite pleasant. Sidney laughed again rather nervously.

"I suppose it was a little dull," she said.

"Dull! It was appalling. Your first instinct about the whole thing was right, and mine was wrong. I apologise utterly and abjectly for bringing you here. 'Neither fish, flesh, nor good red herring,' you said, didn't you?"

Sidney smiled again the nervous little smile that made her look like a frightened child. She had a secret suspicion that it was because she had so obviously enjoyed the evening that Judith was depreciating it. Judith always hated her to enjoy things without her, and they had not met once during the whist-drive. She fought against the disloyalty of, the suspicion. She owed everything to Judith—even the clothes she wore. Judith had been wonderful to her from the moment they met.

A maid brought in a tray with two glasses of hot milk and a plate of biscuits.

As she closed the door they heard a loud burst of cheering. Sidney laughed, infected again by the sudden light-heartedness that had seized her downstairs.

"I'm sure that's Ian getting the booby prize," she said.

Slowly and in silence Judith removed a tiny piece of skin from the surface of her hot milk with a silver spoon. That done, she raised her delicate eyebrows and said "Ian"?

"Ian Paynter," explained Sidney. "You know, the twins' brother. He only got 70 all the evening."

Judith leant back in her chair and said "Really?" The tone should have warned Sidney, but it was drowned by the sound of loud laughter and cries of "Speech" from the drawing-room.

"Listen," she said, "I'm sure it's Ian. . . ." Then, in a burst of eagerness, because she wanted Judith to understand how nice the Paynters were, she went on: "They're so jolly, Judith. You've noticed them, haven't you?"

"Oh yes," said Judith, "I have noticed them. I thought them very noisy and badly behaved. The sort of people I've no use for at all, and the sort of people who don't do you any good." As if to make up for the words she leant forward and put a hand affectionately on Sidney's shoulder. "You know, dear, you're weak and easily led, and you've not had enough experience of the world to enable you to judge people properly. There's just a tiny part of you that I don't much care for, and noisy, rather vulgar people like these young Paynters bring it out. You see, darling, I'm very fond of you, otherwise I shouldn't bother to say this to you."

Only a day or two ago such a speech as this would have filled

Sidney's heart with a rush of passionate compunction and gratitude. She would have protested her love for Judith and sworn never to speak to or look at the Paynters again. After all, she had often met people she'd liked better than the Paynters and had gladly given up all idea of friendship because Judith had not cared for them.

She wanted to feel like that again. She tried to feel like that again. She didn't know why she couldn't. The Paynters were quite jolly, but she'd only known them for a day and they really counted for nothing in comparison with Judith.

Strangely enough it was the memory of something in Bennet's smile this morning that kept her silent, something that she hadn't noticed at the time. It lay behind the reassurance and kindness. It seemed to lei; in something of light and air into the stifling hothouse atmosphere of her relations with Judith. It seemed in some odd way that she couldn't have explained to give her back the individuality that she had surrendered so completely and so willingly to Judith. If it hadn't been for that strange elusive something in Bennet's smile she would have accepted Judith's estimate of the Paynters without question. As it was, she said slowly, her eyes fixed on the fire:

"I dare say they're a bit noisy, but, honestly, Judith, they aren't vulgar."

There was a silence. Sidney didn't realise till that silence what an unpardonable thing she had done in thus defending her new friends against Judith. She would have given anything in the world then to have taken the words back, to have uttered instead the familiar protestations of love and gratitude.

But it was too late. Her heart began to beat unevenly. Judith rose from her chair with a careless shrug.

"Perhaps not," she said. "After all, you ought to know."

She went over to the dressing-table, yawned, and began to undo the fastenings of the black velvet dress.

"Let me," said Sidney, and sprang to do it with unsteady fingers. There was over her that feeling of slight sickness that the fear of Judith's anger always brought. But Judith didn't seem angry. She seemed hard and poised and aloof, but not angry.

"Time we were both in bed," she said lightly. "You might put the glasses out, Sidney."

Sidney put the two glasses on the tray and carried them out to the table in the passage.

Then she went back to Judith's room. Judith still stood by the dressing-table.

"Good night, Judith," she said, and added, in a last desperate attempt to make amends for her fault and restore the situation to normality, "Your lilies smell so lovely. I must put them in water."

"Oh, I shouldn't trouble to do that," said Judith lightly. "Good night."

Sidney turned to the door with a sense of relief. The storm wasn't going to break, after all.

Then there came the sound of a scuffle on the passage outside, suppressed giggles, light footsteps running down the passage, a cry of "Angela, you wretch!" more giggles, more running, the sound of the banging of a door in the distance.

"Oh, Sidney," said Judith in her low suave voice.

Sidney turned. Judith had spoken quite casually, but her pallor had taken on its greyish tinge and her hazel eyes looked green. It was coming, then. Sidney braced herself for it.

"Yes?"

"I'm sorry to have to ask you a second time—I've already had to ask you once, you know—not to behave familiarly with my servants."

"I don't know what you mean," said Sidney breathlessly.

"You know perfectly well what I mean. I'm referring especially to your behaviour with Bennet this morning."

"Judith, I only——"

But Judith interrupted her. It was like a nightmare—that beautiful silky voice reminding Sidney that Judith was paying for this holiday, that Sidney had indeed been living on her charity for weeks, that she did not ask anything in return beyond ordinary standards of decent behaviour, but, if Sidney were going to begin flirting with the servants, their friendship must cease at once.

Sidney felt as if she were being buffeted by a raging sea, hurled against rocks, dragged over surf and shingle.

She tried to speak, but the words would not come. She could hardly see Judith for the mist that swam before her eyes. She felt sick and blinded. Her only desire was to get back to her own room before Judith spoke again. She couldn't bear any more. She turned and groped unseeingly for the door. But Judith was there before her—Judith, her eyes blazing in her white face.

"Sidney, I'm sorry," she panted. "I didn't mean a word of it. I swear I didn't. Forgive me. Sidney, don't look like that. I didn't know what I was saying. Darling, forgive me. . . ."

"Let me go, Judith."

But Judith still barred her way.

"No, I won't. . . . You shan't go till you've said you forgive me."

"But it's true."

"What's true?"

"I am living on your charity."

Judith was recovering her poise.

"What nonsense! I offered you the post of secretary, and that's no sinecure as any of the other secretaries I've had could tell you. You've had a fair amount of work already, and you'll have a lot more with the Hetherstone pageant when we get home. Sidney," her voice sank to a note of tender pleading, "you know that sometimes a devil takes me, and I don't know what I'm doing or saying. I don't even know what I said just now. What did I say?"

Sidney could only look at the floor in silence, with flaming cheeks and smarting eyes.

"Well?" said Judith.

It was funny how Judith always managed to put one in the wrong. Already Sidney felt that it was she who had behaved badly.

Judith pursued her advantage. She placed her hands on Sidney's shoulders and fixed her eyes on the flushed downcast face.

"Sidney, aren't you generous enough to make allowances? I told you right at the beginning that I'd got a devil's temper, didn't I? You know that I never mean anything I say when it takes hold of me. You know that I love you so much that I could never mean anything unkind to you whatever I said. Sidney, I thought we were more to each other than this. I thought you loved me enough to—understand."

In her low beautiful voice was that caressing note that could always break down Sidney's defences.

"I'm sorry, Judith," she said, and suddenly began to cry.

Judith's arms closed round her, and she sobbed luxuriously on Judith's shoulder, her hot cheek against the perfumed coolness of the sleek bronze hair.

"I'm sorry," she said again.

She had a vague idea that she'd been a beast to Judith, she didn't quite know how or why. The scene they'd passed through was like a confused nightmare. Her head was throbbing so unbearably that she couldn't remember quite what had happened.

Judith was smiling down at her.

"There, my sweet. Let's forget all about it."

Sidney put her hand to her head and shut her eyes as a sharp stab of pain shot through it.

"Does your head ache, darling?" said Judith solicitously.

"Yes."

"I'll give you some of my stuff—it will take it away—and then let's sit down and have a nice talk and forget everything horrid in the whole world—headaches and all."

Judith's "stuff" was something she took when she couldn't sleep or when she felt especially nervy. She had a difficulty in getting as much of it as she needed, because, as she explained to Sidney, though it wasn't exactly a drug, it came under the Drug Act, and doctors and chemists were rather awkward about it. She gave a dose to Sidney sometimes when she had a headache, and it always took the pain away at once. Sidney had never had a headache in her life before she met Judith, but lately she had had them frequently.

Judith gave her a dose now, and the headache vanished. They put on their dressing-gowns and sat by the fire far into the night, Judith in the armchair and Sidney on the hearth-rug, her head leaning against Judith's knee. They discussed their plans for the future. Judith was kinder than she had ever been before. A languorous happiness stole over Sidney, a happiness shut in on all sides by Judith's low sweet voice, by the subtle perfume that always hung about her. She and Judith must never quarrel again in all their lives. How stupid and silly and ordinary everyone else in the world seemed compared with Judith!

Chapter Twelve

THE Paynter twins chased each other up and down the stairs, the long blue and green sashes streaming out behind, and finally into their big bow-windowed bedroom, where they sank laughing upon the bed.

"I hope we didn't disturb anyone," panted Cicely. "Suppose someone had gone to bed early and we woke them up. . . ."

"They could go to sleep again," said Angela.

"Someone was just opening a door as we came along the passage. Perhaps they were coming out to tell us not to be so noisy. Did you see who it was?"

"Yes. It was Miss Lattimer. She was only putting out a tray with glasses on. Anyway, *she* wouldn't be coming out to tell us to make less noise. She's awfully nice. Perhaps she'd go for a walk with us sometime? D'you think she would?"

Cicely wrinkled her smooth white brows thoughtfully.

"I don't know. . . . I don't think Miss Kimball likes us."

"She doesn't look as if she liked anyone, but isn't she terribly, *terribly* beautiful? Wouldn't you love to be as beautiful as that?"

"We're quite pretty," said Cicely in a detached, judicial manner.

"Yes, but we're such an insipid type," said Angela. "I think our looks are almost grimly uninteresting—blue eyes and golden hair and that sort of thing. I've always longed to have red hair and green eyes like Miss Kimball. She's exactly my secret dream for myself."

Cicely laughed.

"I'd hate you with red hair and green eyes, Angel. It wouldn't suit you a bit."

"Well, it's no good worrying about it anyway," said Angela. "I could dye my hair, but I couldn't dye my eyes. I think anyone who discovered how to dye your eyes a different colour would make a fortune. One gets so tired of the colour of one's eyes."

"Idiot! And your hair would look awful dyed."

"Oh, I wasn't thinking of it seriously," said Angela. She went over to the dressing-table and, bending forward, peered at the reflection of her delicate flowerlike face, with its white pointed chin and frame of silvery golden curls. "No," she continued in a tone of resignation, "I shall bear my cross till death. But as soon as I'm dead I shall make definite arrangements to have red hair and green eyes in my next incarnation. Mrs. Stephenson-Pollitt believes in reincarnation. I heard her telling someone this evening that she was once a Babylonian queen."

"It always strikes me as so odd," said Cicely thoughtfully, "that people who've had former lives have never been anything but queens and kings and princesses and things like that. I mean, you never come across anyone who was a greengrocer or a plumber or a dustman in a former life. I suppose that those people weren't important enough to be reincarnated. I adore Mrs. Stephenson-Pollitt, don't you?"

"No, I think she's dreadful. I'm sorry for her poor nephew."

"Which is her nephew?"

"I don't suppose you've noticed him. He's not about much."

"Was he at the whist-drive?"

"No, he just came in for a paper and then went out again."

"Oh, that conceited, cross-looking boy. I didn't know he was her nephew. Yes, I saw him."

"I don't think he's *really* conceited or cross," said Angela slowly. "He's really rather nice, I think. He's the one I met when I was exploring this afternoon just after we got here."

"He *looks* conceited and cross."

"Perhaps he does," admitted Angela. "Yes, perhaps he does. But I'm sure it's only a *look*. I'm sure he's nice really. Anyway—you'd look cross if you had Mrs. Stephenson-Pollitt for an aunt."

"I might, but I jolly well wouldn't look conceited."

They both laughed.

"It's awfully late," went on Angela. "We ought to go to bed. Help me out of mine, and I'll help you out of yours."

They removed the lace frocks, flung them carelessly across a chair, and slipped into two silk kimonos—Cicely's pink and Angela's yellow.

"I think this is a marvellous place," said Angela, running the comb through her curls. "What shall we do to-morrow morning? Let's go for a walk, shall we?"

"Yes," agreed Cicely eagerly, then her face fell. "Oh, bother! I've promised to go out with Mrs. Kellogg."

"*Not* that terrible woman who caught you this afternoon?"

"Yes. ... She's rather pathetic, Angel. She was awfully fond of her husband, and he died just after last Christmas, and she has rheumatism and indigestion and gets awfully depressed."

"She sounds ghastly."

Cicely sighed.

"Yes, she is ... but she's pathetic, too."

"Oh, darling, you're *always* thinking dreadful people pathetic."

"I know, but they so often are."

"You'll have a hateful morning, tagging round with her."

"I know."

"She's got heels at least a foot high and ankles like balloons. I'd rather die than go for a walk with her. Couldn't you just forget? We could easily give her the slip."

Cicely considered the suggestion gravely, then shook her head.

"No, I couldn't. ... I'd be miserable if I did."

Angela, of course, realised that she couldn't. Other people could, but not Cicely—Cicely whose whole day could be spoilt by the memory of a sad or weary face glimpsed for a second in a passing crowd, Cicely who seemed doomed to be the victim of the boring and self-pitying and neurotic, Cicely who never could resist the claims of anyone who seemed to "need" her.

"Honestly, darling," said Angela, "you ought to try to be hard-hearteder than you are."

"It's harder hearted," corrected Cicely, and added meekly, "Yes, I know. I will try. But I must do it gradually. I mean, I can't just not go out with her after I've *promised*. That's too terribly unkind. I'd be much more unhappy not going and thinking she was hurt than going and just being bored."

"Why should you care whether she's hurt or not?"

"I don't know," sighed Cicely.

"It was just the same when we went to Newquay last summer. There was that dreadful woman there. And you never got a minute away from her the whole time."

"I know," said Cicely with her disarming air of meekness, "but she was awfully pathetic, too."

"Well, don't say I haven't warned you. This is going to be just the same if you aren't careful. It's not going to be any fun for you at all, and it will be your own fault. I should have thought you'd have learnt a lesson from Newquay."

"I did, darling," Cicely assured her pacifically, "but I must do it gradually. You see, she told me all about her husband and things like that this afternoon. It would be too cruel to drop her suddenly after that. I will do it, I promise, but I must do it gradually."

There came a loud knocking at the door. "That's Ian. . . . Come in."

Ian entered and closed the door behind him. His face wore its usual cheerful grin.

"I say, it's a fine penknife," he said, handing them his booby prize for inspection. "It's got a corkscrew and a thing to take stones out of horses' hooves."

They examined it appreciatively.

"It's super," said Angela handing it back, "and you're a *jolly* lucky booby. I always say that the next best thing to being really good at a thing is to be really bad. Have you only just come up?"

"Yeah. . . . I went to watch some men playing billiards, and then I had a bottle of ginger beer."

"Pig! Why didn't you ask us to have some with you?"

"I looked for you, but I couldn't find you."

"Parents gone to bed?"

"S'pose so. Didn't see 'em anywhere. . . . Not a bad place, is it?"

"Rather not. But poor old Cicely's got roped in by one of her curios already. Pretty grim, isn't it?"

"Serve her right for being a soppy idiot."

"Oh, I'm going to get rid of her," Cicely assured him earnestly. "Only, as I've explained to Angel, I must do it gradually."

"It's the barmaid with the balloon ankles," went on Angela, "and she's going for a walk with her to-morrow."

"Good Lord! What a fool the girl is, isn't she?"

Cicely tweaked his hair good-humouredly, and jeered "Booby!"

"What are you going to do to-morrow morning?" said Angela to Ian.

"Dunno. Golf, I think."

"The parents are golfing. They won't thank you for tagging on."

There was a sudden constrained silence, for what Angela had said went just a little too near the truth.

The three had long since realised that their father and mother were so completely sufficient to each other that on their rare short holidays (for Mr. Paynter was one of the busiest barristers in London) they did not care to be burdened overmuch by their children's company.

This did not prevent them from being kindly, indulgent, sympathetic parents. It made them perhaps more indulgent than are parents who take more pleasure in their children's society, for they always had a secret consciousness of guilt in this respect. With the fourth child, the three-year-old girl who had come to them late in life, it was different. She was the pivot of their existence, the consummation and completion of their love. Their idolisation of her was a joke among their friends.

The three older children felt no resentment. They, too, were fond of the sunny-tempered, curly-haired Jill, and they accepted their parents' disproportionate love for her and barely concealed indifference to themselves philosophically and without bitterness. Only it seemed to bind them together in a closer bond than that which usually unites brother and sister.

To cover her slip Angela snatched Ian's penknife from him and threw it to Cicely, crying:

"Keep it for him till he's a big boy. He'll only cut himself with it if he has it now."

The other two joined her in a rough-and-tumble scrimmage, eager also to drown the constraint that her remark had caused. In a moment they had forgotten both remark and constraint and were engaged in one of those childish romps that still frequently took place between them.

Ian had pinned Cicely into a corner and was trying to make her give up the penknife by tickling her, when there came a knock at the door.

Angela went to open it.

Miss Wingate stood on the threshold. She wore a red flannel dressing-gown, and her hair hung down her back in a long thin plait that narrowed till it seemed to consist of three meticulously woven hairs. She was a figure of vengeance—grim, outraged.

"My room is next door," she said in her clear precise voice, "and I cannot possibly get any sleep while this appalling noise is going on."

A stricken silence reigned within the room.

"I'm sorry," gasped Angela. "I'm frightfully sorry."

"I hope that I may count on quiet from now on at any rate."

"Yes ... yes, of course ... we're frightfully sorry."

With great dignity, Miss Wingate turned on her heel and left them. The interview was no novel one to her. The student whose bedroom adjoined hers at college received such visits almost nightly.

"How awful of us!" whispered Angela, closing the door. "Poor old thing! I say, we must go to bed now. Clear off, Ian."

"All right," whispered Ian, "but I'm frightfully hungry. Haven't you got anything to eat?"

"No." Angela considered for a minute then added. "Mummy may have. ... Let's go and see."

She felt that the suggestion somehow atoned for her unfortunate remark of a few moments ago.

"Come on, then," said Ian, and began to tiptoe across the room in a ridiculously exaggerated fashion, his finger at his lips. That made them giggle, and by the time they were at the end of the corridor Miss Wingate's visit had become, not a catastrophe, but a hilarious joke. Ian repeated the words she had said, pursing his lips and imitating her clipped precise voice till they held their sides with laughter.

"Oh, *do* stop," gasped Cicely. "Someone else will be coming out."

They scuffled up the stairs to the second floor, where Mr. and Mrs. Paynter's bedroom was.

"Suppose they're in bed?" said Ian.

"Then we'll beat a retreat, but they won't be."

They knocked at the door, heard a deep "Come in," and entered.

Mr. Paynter, in a Paisley dressing-gown, stood on the hearth-rug, leaning his tall finely proportioned figure against the mantelpiece. His wife lay back in an armchair by the fire.

She looked absurdly young and like her daughters, her complexion as clear and delicate as theirs, her silvery golden curls as bright and silky.

On the dressing-table stood a large framed photograph of Jill. She had none of her mother's delicate ethereal beauty. She was dark and solid-looking like her father, with a solemn determined mouth and level grey eyes.

"Come in, darlings," said the mother.

"Why this invasion?" demanded her husband, with raised eyebrows.

"We're hungry," said Angela. "Ian's starving. Have you anything to eat?"

"Good Lord!" said Mr. Paynter, with an air of helpless amazement. "Didn't you get enough to eat at dinner? You all ate your way steadily through seven courses if I remember rightly."

"That was hours ago, Daddy," explained Cicely. "We've been working awfully hard since then. Ian's won a booby prize."

There was an air of rosy languor about Mrs. Paynter as she lay back in her chair, wrapped in a filmy negligee, the soft glowing haze that hangs about a woman passionately desired, deeply beloved.

She turned her smiling eyes upon the children.

"You poor darlings! There's a box of chocolates in that drawer. Take as many as you like."

They found the box and sat round it on the floor, the three bright heads meeting.

"Those, my dear," expostulated her husband, "are the most expensive chocolates in London. I bought them especially for you. This rabble in any case probably prefers penny bars of chocolate cream or a packet of bull's-eyes."

"We don't."

"They're super," said Angela. "Do try one of those with little knobs on, Cicely."

She put one in Cicely's mouth, and Cicely sat back munching it.

"Lovely," she said, then, catching sight of a letter on her mother's knee, "You've had a letter. Lucky people."

"From Nanny," said her mother, handing it to her.

They fell upon it eagerly. Nanny's letters were a family joke.

"I'll read it aloud," said Angela. "We can none of us read it if you're going to fight for it." She opened it and began to read, spelling out the misspelt words.

"Dear Madam,
"Trusting these few lines will find you still procressing satisfactry and that you are having a nice and peacefull and also a restfull change. Our darling is lovely, she eats harty, frute after each meel and bowells well open, and she is really and truely happy and not freting and so intresting, not to speak of Heallthy and Bright which is every word the truth and I think all due to an apple a day keeps the doctor away, and also Regularity."

The man's eyes met his wife's over their heads, with a smile of whimsical protest. Her smile in reply was half reassuring, half pleading. It seemed to say: It's all right, they won't stay long. Don't make me send them away just yet.

He thrust his hands into the pockets of his dressing-gown to hide his impatience.

His strong face was lined and mobile like an actor's, as if ready to fall into almost any expression. Its normal expression was pleasant if somewhat arrogant, but it could lower ferociously when brow-beating a recalcitrant witness, and it could inspire stark terror in an opponent. Despite his virility he was a deeply uxorious man. Working to the limits of his strength in his profession, he found his chief rest and refreshment in his wife, while she on her side was still as completely dominated by his personality as she had been when she had married him.

It was she who had wanted children, but she always felt vaguely apologetic to him for them, anxious always to prove to him that their claims were as nothing in comparison with his.

Strangely enough it had been reserved for Jill, the late-born and at first unwanted, to rouse all their dormant parental love.

She met his eyes again, and this time obeyed the urgency of his glance.

"Children, it's time you went to bed. Take the chocolates with you."

"Oh, may we?"

"Yes. Good night."

They kissed her soft smooth cheek.

"Darlings," she said, "you looked so sweet in your lace frocks to-night."

Cicely, bending over her, saw the faint remorse and unhappiness in the blue eyes, as if she were saying: I'm sorry. Forgive me. Please forgive me.

There was an answering tenderness in Cicely's embrace. Don't worry, it seemed to reply. We understand.

They went to the door, and there it suddenly occurred to Cicely that the six of them stood in their two groups, mysteriously but irrevocably sundered, the father and mother with Jill's portrait at one end of the room, she and Angela and Ian at the other.

"Good night," said their father. "Don't come to us if you're sick in the night."

He spoke in the pleasant teasing tone he always used with them, but Cicely caught his sigh of impatient relief as the door closed.

Outside the corridor they divided the chocolates, then Ian went to his room, and the twins wandered back slowly down the staircase. They were rather silent. The scene in their parents' bedroom had been a normal, affectionate, happy family scene, yet it had left them both vaguely depressed. We were all pretending, thought Cicely. We were all pretending that they wanted us. . . .

"Let's go and see if Miss Lattimer's up and give her a chocolate," suggested Angela suddenly.

Their spirits rose at the suggestion, and they crept silently to her room. There they saw that the door was slightly ajar and the room in darkness.

A low murmur of voices came from the next room.

"She's with Miss Kimball."

"Let's go in and give them both some chocolates."

"Oh, we daren't. Not Miss Kimball."

"No, perhaps we daren't. Shall we leave some on her dressing-table?"

"I don't think we know her well enough."

"Perhaps we don't. . . . There's nothing to do then but to go to bed, is there?"

"No. . . . I expect everyone else has gone to bed."

They went back along the passage towards their rooms. On the way they met the blind man and Mr. Ellison coming upstairs together, and stood against the wall to let them pass. Mr. Ellison smiled and said "Good night," and the blind man threw his quick suspicious frown in their direction.

How charming they looked, thought Mr. Ellison, standing there so solemnly in their dressing-gowns like a couple of pretty children, munching chocolates.

"I'm sure everyone's gone to bed now," said Cicely.

Angela went to the banisters and gazed down into the well of the hall.

"No, there are two people standing by the fire talking."

"Who are they?"

Angela leant over further.

"One's Miss Torrance, and the other's the husband of the woman with the scarred face. I've forgotten his name."

Chapter Thirteen

THE Paynter twins entered the dining-room, saw Sidney breakfasting alone, and, after a slight hesitation, approached her table.

"We came to your room last night," said Angela, "to give you a chocolate, only you weren't there."

"That was very kind of you," said Sidney, but she spoke absently, almost distantly. There was about her none of that eager, care-free *camaraderie* of youth that had so attracted them the night before. She looked pale in the clear morning sunlight.

Cicely glanced at the empty place.

"Isn't Miss Kimball coming down to breakfast?"

"No. She's got a headache. I don't think she'll be getting up at all to-day."

Her voice was curt, her glance unsmiling, and she was glad when the two girls took the hint and moved on.

It was partly through them that the trouble had arisen, of course. The memory of Judith lying where she had just left her in the darkened room, her eyes looking like great bruises in her white face, her beautiful lips tight with pain, filled her with an aching tenderness, a passionate loyalty, a bitter self-reproach. It was last night's scene that had caused Judith's headache. Judith's nerves couldn't stand scenes. ... Well, thought Sidney, it's taught me a lesson. I'll never again try to make friends with people. What does anyone in the world matter, besides Judith? She glanced with dispassionate contempt at the young Paynters, chattering eagerly to each other over the breakfast-table. Noisy, crude, immature. ... How could she have set them even for a moment against Judith's exquisiteness? She was so stupid, so clumsy, so imperceptive. She must irritate Judith a hundred times a day. ... She'd try to make up for her last night's clumsiness, anyway.

About a fortnight ago Judith had sent her out to do some shopping, telling her carelessly to keep the change. The change had been seven shillings, and she still had it. She would go into Hunton (the neighbouring country town) this morning and spend it all on flowers and fruit for Judith.

She finished her breakfast and returned to Judith's room.

Judith still lay in bed, her closed eyes black circles against the pallor of her face. An untouched breakfast-tray stood on the small table by the bedside.

Sidney closed the door soundlessly.

"How are you, darling?" she whispered.

Judith answered without moving or opening her eyes. "Just the same. . . . Put the tray out, Sidney. The smell of that toast makes me feel sick."

"Won't you just have a cup of tea?"

"If I wanted one I'd have had it."

Sidney put the tray on the table in the passage, then returned to the bedroom, and stood irresolute, looking down at the beautiful, pain-racked face.

"Is there anything I can do, Judith?"

"You can go into Hunton and get a prescription made up for me. I daren't take any more of my stuff, but I know that the prescription will make my head better. . . . You'll find it in my dressing-case. You may take the car."

"I can easily walk."

"I said, take the car."

Half unconsciously Sidney realised that Judith wanted her to take the car in order to be sure of her being alone. If she walked, the Paynters or someone else might join her, but she would not dare to take anyone with her in the car. Even unconsciously, however, she did not resent this, so abased she was by self-reproach and love and pity.

She still hovered solicitously about the bed.

"Judith, you do look ill. I wish you'd see a doctor."

"Nonsense!"

"But, Judith——"

"Don't be tiresome, Sidney. Go away now, there's a good girl. And I may be able to sleep, so don't come back again till lunch-time."

Sidney went out, gave the order for the car, then put on her hat and coat. The car was standing at the front door when she came down again.

She said "Good morning, Bennet," as distantly as Judith herself could have said it, and stepped through the door the chauffeur held open for her into the spacious, luxurious interior. They drove to Hunton, where she had the prescription made up, and bought some roses and a bunch of hothouse grapes.

"That's all, Bennet," she said, as she returned to the car. "We'll go back now."

He glanced at the clock.

"It's a nice run back by Woodberry, miss," he said. "It takes you right over Woodberry Common."

"Very well," she said. "Let's go that way."

She felt rather ashamed of her distant manner to him, and moreover was finding it difficult to keep up. She gave him a tentative smile, but it was his turn now to be dignified.

"Very good, miss," he said, and returned to the wheel.

The road led them out of the little town and over the common that stretched for miles on every side. At the highest point Bennet stopped the car and opened the door.

"I thought you might like to get out here for a minute, miss," he said. "It's a very fine view."

She leapt out eagerly. It had been dull and stuffy and rather lonely in the big saloon car.

"Oh, isn't it glorious!" she said.

Golden bracken spread like a sea around them. In the distance the pale winter sunshine pricked out the colours of the trees on the hillside—the green of the fir-trees, the silver of the birches, the warm grey of the lichened beech. . . .

"Jolly, isn't it?" he said.

She breathed in the keen crisp air deeply.

"You ought to be riding on a day like this," he went on, "not sitting in a stuffy car."

"I know," she said. "Wouldn't it be a glorious! . . . Do you ride?"

"When I can get hold of a horse."

She took out her cigarette-case and handed it to him.

"Have a cigarette."

He shook his head.

"I'd better not, thanks. Someone might come along and report me to Miss Kimball, and then I'd get the sack."

The memory of Judith lying in the darkened room with pain-shadowed eyes came back to Sidney, but only as the memory of a faintly troubling dream. Even her love for Judith seemed to belong to that dim, uneasy dream. They couldn't exist in the same world as this bright sunshine, this clear keen air, and the laughing eyes of this rather impudent young man. She glanced up at him curiously.

"You're not an ordinary chauffeur, are you?"

His boyish grin flashed out.

"What do you think I am? The Prince of Wales in disguise?"

She laughed. All her depression had vanished. She felt young and care-free and happy again, ready to laugh at anything with anybody.

"Don't be silly! I mean—well, what school did you go to?"

"Marlborough."

"That's what I meant."

"Yes, but I'm not the rich young man of the movies proving that he can earn his own living. I took on this job because I hadn't a bean, and I didn't want to starve."

"Do tell me about yourself," she pleaded.

"I will if you'll tell me about yourself."

She hesitated a moment, then said, "All right . . . you first."

"Well, where do you want me to begin? My earliest memory is of getting completely covered with coal at the age of two."

"You can miss all that out," she said. "Begin where you left school."

"All right. When I left school I went to Cambridge, but my father died in my first term, and it turned out that he'd been speculating. Anyway, there wasn't anything except just enough for my mother to live on. A friend of my father's gave me a job in his firm. Quite a decent screw and quite interesting work. We lived in a nice old cottage at Hampstead—the mater and I—and we were awfully happy. Then the firm I was working for went bust, and for the life of me I couldn't get another job. There was the same tale everywhere—reduced staff and long lists of applicants. I hated living on my mother instead of helping her, so, after trying for months to get the sort of job I'd had before, I decided to be less particular and take what I could get. I went to a Servants' Agency to see if they had anything for a valet or footman or chauffeur—I could have managed any of them all right—and as it happened they'd just heard that Miss Kimball wanted a temporary chauffeur in a hurry, so they sent me along. . . . That's my story. Now what about yours?"

She considered his story thoughtfully.

"What's your Christian name?" she said at last.

"Richard."

"I'm sure nobody calls you Richard. Some people call you Dick, but most people call you Dickie. . . ."

"Right," he grinned. "Well, what about the story of your life?"

Something of her glow faded. She began rather hesitatingly.

"Well—mine's a bit like yours in a way. I mean, I was left on my own without any money or any sort of qualification for a decent job. I was brought up in a convent in Antwerp. My mother lived in London, but she didn't much want me, you see, and I never saw her even in the holidays. But I was awfully happy. . . . Then she died, and I came back to England. She hadn't any money of her own. Someone had left her an annuity, but she hadn't saved anything, and her things had to be sold to pay her debts. I wrote to my relations, but there weren't many of them, and none of them answered. I think that they hadn't approved of my mother and hadn't seen or heard anything of her for years. So I tried to get a job, and at last I got one in a school. It was a hateful, cheap little private boarding-school in Putney—the sort that oughtn't to be allowed to exist. The woman was common and mean and a bully, and there were only two assistants, and she made us do the house-work as well as the teaching and supervision and mending. She only paid us thirty pounds a year each, and she was nagging at us the whole time. Then the other girl broke down, and I had to try to carry on alone. The woman was a beast to me, and her husband began to follow me round and make love to me, and I was desperate when I got Judith's letter. She's a sort of distant cousin, you know, and I'd written to her with the others, but she hadn't answered. Then she wrote asking me to go and see her, and I went, and—oh, she was so sweet to me. It seemed like going straight to heaven from hell. She wouldn't even let me go back to the place for my things. She just sent them my term's salary and told them to keep my things. . . ."

He was watching her with narrowed eyes, all the laughter gone from his face.

"Why hadn't she answered your letter before?"

"I don't know. She's awfully busy. Why should she, anyway? It seemed like a dream at first. I couldn't believe it was real. Judith's lovely house . . . beautiful things around me . . . peace and quiet after the squalor and ugliness and that woman's hateful voice nagging all day long. . . . I hadn't had enough to eat, and I wasn't well, so we went away to the sea together, and—oh, I keep saying it was like heaven, but it was. It's the only word I can find for it. You see, I was awfully stupid. I hadn't met people or read books or anything like that. She was so patient with me. She took me round to old places and told me about architecture, and took me to concerts and plays and read aloud to me. It was like—no, I'm not going to say heaven again—honestly, I'm not—it was like finding wonderful new worlds that one hadn't known existed."

He still looked at her in silence. He could gauge the appeal that her fresh innocence, her eager receptivity, her quick responsiveness, would make to Judith Kimball's jaded senses.

"Well?" he said. "Go on. . . ."

"That's all . . . nearly all, I mean. . . . When we were away she had me taught riding, and we used to ride and bathe together every day. It was all—wonderful. Then, when we came back, I said that I must try to get some work again—I couldn't live on her—but it happened that her secretary had just left and she wanted another, so she said I could be her secretary. That's six weeks ago. I've been with her ever since."

"She pays you a salary, I suppose?"

Again she gave him her little nervous smile.

"No ... she buys me everything. She's bought me the most marvellous clothes. She's spent more on my clothes already than most people pay their secretaries in years. And I go everywhere with her."

"She doesn't actually give you much cash, then?"

"I don't need cash. I told you. She pays for everything,"

"I see ... What does she want a secretary for, anyway?"

"Oh, she does a lot of work. She's awfully artistic. She designs dresses for nearly all the pageants that are given by Society people. She's rich and doesn't need to work, but she enjoys it. She designs dresses for stage shows, too, sometimes. She could have as much work as she wanted, because she's frightfully clever, but she only takes what appeals to her. There's really quite a lot for me to do. I have to go to the British Museum and make notes on costumes, and often just answering letters takes me all morning. Honestly," she assured him earnestly, "I wouldn't stay if it were just charity."

"Is she easy to work for?"

Again she hesitated.

"Y-yes," she said at last, slowly. "I mean, she has wretched headaches sometimes, but generally she's terribly nice to me."

The glow of eager youth had faded from her as they spoke of Judith, and there had come over her that air of timidity and wariness that she so often wore when she was with Judith.

There was a short silence, then she said suddenly:

"You dislike her, don't you?"

He laughed shortly.

"That puts it mildly."

"Oh, you don't understand," she pleaded. "She's so sweet really. It's just her manner that—that seems hard. I know her better than anyone, and I *know* how wonderful she is. Just *think* what she's done for me. If it hadn't been for her I'd have died by now at that hateful school, I'm sure. I'm so grateful to her that sometimes I can hardly *hold* my gratitude. And—and people as highly strung and sensitive as Judith are always nervy at times. When she's her nicest self, she's—nicer than anyone else in the world ever could be. Sometimes I look back to the days when I didn't know her, and I can't think how I *lived*. ... She's been—a sort of angel to me. It's hateful of me even to discuss her with you——"

"All right, don't," he interrupted. He was smiling at her again. "Heaven knows I don't want to discuss her. Let's talk of something else."

"We ought to be going on, oughtn't we?"

"Need you be back till luncheon?"

"No."

"Well, let me take you a real drive. Off the beaten track. I know this country rather well. I once spent the school holidays with some people called Hatfield at a place near here called Ottary. I—by Jove!"

A young man who was cantering past them had reined in his horse suddenly.

"Dickie!" he said.

Dick Bennet's features fell into their familiar impudent grin.

"Hello, Tony! Talk of the devil!"

"This is luck! The last I heard of you you were something in the city."

"Now I'm one of the great submerged," said Dickie cheerfully. "I'm chauffeur to Miss Kimball, who's staying at Chedsy Place."

"Good for you!"

"This is Tony Hatfield. ... Miss Lattimer. ..."

"I'm Miss Kimball's secretary," put in Sidney quickly.

Somehow she was anxious to associate herself with Dickie as an employee of Judith's.

"Well, this is great," repeated the other. "Come over and see us, won't you? The mater often asks what happened to that nice boy who once stayed with us and climbed up onto the roof to rescue her parrot."

"Forgetting, I hope, that I also taught it some very undesirable expressions."

"She put that down to me, I'm afraid, though I always told her that it was entirely your doing. . . . You're still her favourite of all the young devils I used to bring home for the holidays. Seriously, do come over and see us."

"Can't, old man. I'm on duty."

"Surely you have some free time?"

"No, we're slave-driven, aren't we, Miss Lattimer? Honestly, there's really very little to do, but I've got to be on the spot in case I'm needed."

"Oh well, I shan't let you off. . . . Did you say you were at Chedsy Place?"

"Yes."

"I heard that the Beatons were holding some sort of Christmas jollification there. What is it exactly? Local rumour varies. Some say that he's turned the place into a lunatic asylum, and others that it's merely a rest home for the feeble-minded."

"It's a sort of mixture of paying guests and a hotel," smiled Sidney.

"Heaven help him!" said Tony. "I can't see old Beaton in a show of that sort."

"One doesn't see him very much," said Sidney, "but she's terribly capable. It's really beautifully run."

"Lackadaisical chaps like Beaton always marry efficient women. It's one of life's tragedies. . . . Oh well, it keeps the place going, I suppose, and that's something. I don't know how much longer the pater can keep up our place. To hear him talk you'd say not a day longer. . . . I say, Dickie, that's a becoming uniform. I believe that's the sole reason you took on the job. Well, you've not seen the last of me. I shall descend on you and defy Miss Kimball and carry you off with me. The mater will never forgive me if I don't. . . . Good-bye."

He waved to them, then cantered away over the springy turf.

"Nice chap," commented Dick. "Well, what about this drive?"

"I'd love it, but—you *will* be back by lunch time, won't you?"

"Yes. I promise. Are you coming in the front with me, or will you travel in the royal coach behind?"

She laughed happily. How absurd he was!

"I'm coming in front with you, of course," she said.

He continued to be absurd throughout the drive—a drive along winding country lanes with tall mossy banks on either side, past little slumbering villages with thatched roofs and squat grey churches, through a wood where the road was little more than a cart-track ("Good thing her ladyship can't see where I'm taking the car, isn't it?"), and where the sunshine threw down upon their path a delicate shadow tracery of the bare boughs above them.

Again and again her happy childish laughter rang out. . . .

It seemed all too short a time before he stopped the car and said, "We're rather near Chedsy Place now. I think perhaps you'd better get back into the royal coach."

Reluctantly she returned to the deep saloon. It seemed dark and gloomy after the outside seat, and the heavy, faintly aromatic scent that Judith used hung about it. The laughter died out of her eyes and heart.

The car drew up in front of Chedsy Place, and Bennet (he wasn't Dickie any longer) opened the door, looking at her with an impassive face.

Her arm full of Judith's flowers, she gave him her little nervous smile, then went quickly into the house.

Chapter Fourteen

SATURDAY MORNING *(continued)*

THE Paynter twins stood side by side on the terrace, looking out over the garden, their elbows resting on the stone balustrade. The clear morning sun revealed a myriad varying tints of grey and green and russet on the bare branches of the trees and on the sleeping grass of the lawn. Above them the sky was a pale windswept blue.

Through the still air came the sound of Mrs. Fielden's voice reading aloud to her husband. They were sitting on two basket chairs at the further end of the lawn, she muffled up in a fur coat and scarf, with a rug over her knees, he without overcoat, his collar open at the neck. Already before breakfast the twins had seen him running round the park, dressed in shorts and a singlet. A gardener had been with him the first time to show him when to turn the corners and to warn him of any obstacle in his path, but he had dismissed the man after the first round and on the second and third rounds had taken the corners and avoided the obstacles as well as if he actually saw them. Now he sat rigidly upright and motionless, and his face still wore its fighting look, for though only listening to the day's news, he was still fighting. He must be as well equipped as any man who could read and reread the paper at his leisure throughout the day. In no chance conversation that might arise must his adversary be able to take him at a disadvantage.

"You won't want this next paragraph, dear," said his wife plaintively. "It's something about agriculture in Abyssinia."

The trap-like mouth opened to shoot out "Read it," then relapsed into grimness.

Her voice took up its plaintive strain.

"Oh dear!" said Angela. "It must be dreadful for him."

"And for her," said Cicely.

Miss Nettleton came out of the side-door and strolled past them in her slow, apparently aimless fashion.

Her face looked wrinkled and yellow in the morning light, and her wig was more than usually awry under the battered felt hat. She carried a collection of guide-books and a packet of sandwiches.

"Good morning," she said in her deep drawl. "I'm off to spend the day waiting for 'buses as usual. I never can think why people built ruins in such inaccessible spots."

They watched her lank upright figure disappear down the drive.

"Isn't she a pet!" laughed Cicely.

"They're all pets," said Angela, "except that awful woman who roped you in last night. You aren't really going out with her this morning, are you?"

"I must, Angel," replied Cicely, suddenly serious. "I said I would."

"What a priceless ass you are, aren't you?" said Angela affectionately. "Look! Here are the parents."

Mr. and Mrs. Paynter came along the terrace, dressed for golf, carrying their clubs.

"Hello, children!" the father called carelessly as he passed.

The mother hesitated, as if she were going to stop, but her husband good-humouredly took her arm and drew her on with him.

"Come along," he said. "No time for gossip. The morning's too short as it is."

She looked back at them with that faintly unhappy smile they knew so well.

"Good-bye, darlings," she called. "Have a nice morning."

Poor sweet! thought Cicely. She *is* so pathetic. . . .

Miss Wingate scuttled past them, giving them that slight relaxation of her pursed mouth that did duty as a smile. She held a small brown-paper packet somewhat furtively under her arm.

"I wonder if I ought to go in and look for Mrs. Kellogg," said Cicely.

"No, you certainly oughtn't," replied Angela firmly. "We'll give her ten minutes more, and if she hasn't come for you by then I'm bagging you for the morning. Hello, kid."

Ian was approaching, his golf-clubs over his shoulder. He had evidently given his parents time to get well on their way to the golf course before he started. He was whistling jauntily, and beneath the jauntiness was a faint hint of defiance.

"Hello," he said, stopping by them. "Come up to the golf course, you lazy blighters."

"Can't. We're going for a walk, unless the barmaid runs this ass to earth within the next ten minutes. If she does I'll wander up and see how you're getting on. Hope you find someone to have a game with."

"If I don't, I'll have a knock round by myself. Quite good fun."

He went on, still whistling jauntily. He's pathetic too, thought Cicely. Oh dear, I must stop thinking people are pathetic. It's growing on me. It's a sort of vice. I suppose that really everyone's pathetic and the only thing is to try not to see it. . . .

"That's Miss Kimball's car at the door, isn't it?" Angela was saying. "Perhaps she's feeling better and is going out for a drive."

They stood with their backs against the balustrade, watching the drive. Miss Lattimer, looking very pale, came down and entered the car, the chauffeur arranged the rug over her knees, then sprang onto his seat, and the big luxurious Rolls set off smoothly down the drive.

"Their chauffeur looks rather jolly," commented Cicely, "but Miss Lattimer seems awfully worried, doesn't she?"

"Yes, I expect she's worried about Miss Kimball. It must be awfully worrying having someone ill in a hotel."

"She's—almost like two people, isn't she? Miss Lattimer, I mean. Sometimes young and jolly and sometimes terribly old."

"Yes. A sort of Miss Jekyll and Miss Hyde. Oh, darling, you're cornered, I'm afraid."

Mrs. Kellogg was waddling along the terrace, dressed in a fur coat, with a fashionable but wholly unsuitable green hat perched on the side of her large flaxen head. Her rubicund face was, as usual, heavily coated with white powder, which imparted a mauve tinge to it. She smiled roguishly as she came up to them.

"You weren't giving me the slip, love, were you?" she said, shaking a plump forefinger.

"Oh, of *course* not," said Cicely earnestly. "I was just waiting for you. I knew you'd come here for me."

"Would your sister like to come too?"

"Thanks so much," said Angela hastily, "but I've arranged to go up to meet my brother on the golf links."

"Oh well," wheezed Mrs. Kellogg, "after all, two's company and three's none, isn't it?"

Angela winked at her twin, and Cicely looked quickly away.

"We'd better be getting on, hadn't we, love?" said Mrs. Kellogg.

"Yes . . . good-bye, Angel."

"Good-bye, my pet."

The two set side by side off down the drive, Cicely vainly trying to accommodate her steps to her companion's erratic waddle.

"Nice place, isn't it?" said Mrs. Kellogg in her husky breathless voice. "Doesn't half cost a lot, but it's worth it, don't you think?"

Cicely murmured that she thought it was.

"I reckon it never pays to economise on a holiday," went on Mrs. Kellogg, warming to her theme, "not really it doesn't. Now there was the place I went to in the summer. Guest-house, it called itself, and the woman was for ever turning me out for meals. Telling me I ought to go for a little charabanc run to this place or the other and have my lunch or my tea there. Sheer robbery it was, considering I was paying her for my keep. And whenever I didn't go she got that sulky with me I wished I'd gone. Paid twice over, I did, for nearly all my meals in that place. She wouldn't have dared put on me like that if Bert had been alive. He'd never let me be put on, wouldn't Bert. But since he's been took—well"—she heaved a deep sigh—"I'd never thought before how many ways there was that a woman could be put on. From the milkman leaving milk *blue* with water to Scotland Yard."

"Scotland Yard?" repeated Cicely in surprise.

"Yes, love," said Mrs. Kellogg. "You wouldn't believe it, but it's true. Really it is. And it was an umbrella Bert gave me, to make it worse. Real ivory handle, it had, in the shape of a bird's face.

Bert would have made them give it up all right. He wouldn't stand no nonsense from anyone, wouldn't Bert."

"Yes, but what was it?" said Cicely, still more mystified.

"An umbrella, love. I've just told you. I left it in a 'bus, and I went to Scotland Yard for it. Of *course* they'd got it. If ever a man looked guilty that man that said they hadn't got it did. I could *see* they'd got it by the look in his eye. No, he said, it hadn't been brought in. Was taking it home to his wife that very afternoon, as like as not. I bet he'd have brought it out all right if Bert had been with me. He wouldn't have told Bert they hadn't got it."

"But perhaps they really hadn't," suggested Cicely mildly.

"Oh, they had, dearie. Why did they try to get me out of the place in such a hurry, if they hadn't something to hide? No, love, I'm as trusting by nature as anyone alive, but—well, a woman's got to be careful."

They had reached the end of the drive now. Opposite them on the other side of the road a path led up over a stile onto the common. Cicely looked at it wistfully. On the common one could perhaps forget this dreadful little creature who waddled by one's side.

"Shall we go up there?" she suggested.

Mrs. Kellogg shook her golden head.

"No, love. I must keep on the level. I'm short of breath, you know. It's with being on the fat side, I suppose. My Bert always said he couldn't stand a skinny woman. Let's just go down to the village and look at the shops, shall we? I don't suppose there'll be many, but I can always look at a shop, can't you, whatever it's like. I'm glad you and me have palled up like what we have. It's nice to have someone to go about with. You know, dearie, it's not safe for a woman to go anywhere alone in the country. You never know what'll happen. You've only got to read the papers to see that. I don't mean, of course, that it's any safer at the seaside. I went to some rooms in Brighton in September. Got the address out of a paper, and—believe me or not as you like, love—I only just escaped in time."

"In time for what?" said Cicely. "I mean, what did you escape from?"

"There's things worse than death," said Mrs. Kellogg mysteriously. "I got there, and I didn't like the look of the woman from the start. She gave me a meat pie and coffee for supper and—well—believe me or not—I've never tasted anything queerer than that coffee. It *looked* like coffee and it *smelt* like coffee, and she said it *was* coffee, but all I could say was that it didn't *taste* like coffee. Well, love, I've read enough about the White Slave Traffic and suchlike to put me on my guard, and I just walked straight upstairs and packed my bag and called out to her I was going, and went. And, as I told you, I only just got away in time. The next day"—she sank her voice to a sinister hiss—"would have been too late."

"But perhaps it was just too much chicory?" said Cicely.

"Oh no, it wasn't, love. The woman herself proved what it was all right. I never saw anyone so mad as what she was when I went off. Proper mad, she was. Oh no, there wasn't any doubt what *she* was up to. Drugged, that's what it was, love. Drugged."

"Did you feel drowsy or anything afterwards?"

"Oh no, love. I'd not taken enough for that. Only just enough to taste the stuff. I'd been very careful. Of course, my type's the sort they're always after. Pure blonde, you know. Bert used to say that my colouring struck him all of a heap the first time he set eyes on me. But beauty's often more of a curse than a blessing, especially when a woman's left unprotected like what I am."

It's dreadful, thought Cicely. I can't stand all the morning with her. To herself she practised saying, "Do you mind if I go back now? I've suddenly remembered that I have to write a letter this morning," or "I'm afraid I can't go on any further, I don't feel very well," but she knew that she wouldn't be able to say anything of the kind. She dragged her wandering attention back to the husky wheezy voice.

"And it's not only rheumatism, love. I suffer from corns and bunions something cruel. Bert was always proud of my feet. Threes I used to take, and p'raps I did ought to have taken fours, but he was that proud of me taking threes, it didn't seem right to disappoint him. Some days, of course, they're easier than others, but some days they're downright chronic. An' I'm not one to complain either. No one would guess what I suffer sometimes. Let's just sit down on this wall a minute, love, shall we, and have a rest."

Cicely sat down dejectedly on the low stone wall. Mrs. Kellogg opened her fur coat to display a very green *crêpe de Chine* dress.

"Pretty, isn't it?" she said complacently. "Bert always liked to see me turned out nice. He liked me in bright colours. When he was ill, he said, 'Now don't you go putting on black if I pass out, Emmy,' he said. 'The brighter the colours you wear, the better I'll be pleased, wherever I am.' And it was only a week after that he did pass out, too. Couldn't bear me away from his sight the two days before. Passed out quite peaceful, he did, holding my hand." Suddenly she broke down and began to sob, her fat shoulders heaving convulsively, the tears making little runnels down her powdered cheeks. "I can't bear goin' on living without him. I'm that lonely. . . ."

An agony of unbearable compassion surged over Cicely. She put her arm about the fat heaving shoulders.

"Don't," she said, "oh, don't. . . ."

Angela stayed for some moments alone on the terrace. What a shame that the old hag had caught Cicely after all! They might have had such a jolly morning together. Oh well, she'd go for a walk over the common and then join Ian on the golf course. She went down the drive, climbed the stile, and stood watching the road where she could see the incongruous figures of Mrs. Kellogg and Cicely in the distance—Mrs. Kellogg walking with the side-to-side movement of the very stout, Cicely making experimental attempts to accommodate her footsteps to it.

"Poor lamb," sighed Angela, then set off briskly over the springy upland turf.

Brian Mallard had come out onto the terrace. He was scowling gloomily. He'd resisted temptation again. All the time the two girls had been standing on the terrace he had been at his bedroom window, watching them furtively, longing to come down and talk to them—or rather to talk to Angela, for Cicely seemed to him only a pale colourless shadow of her twin. Sternly, grimly, he had resisted the impulse, forcing himself to see in the sleek golden head only a wile of the devil to entrap him. He had glared down at her unconscious figure, defying it to entrap him, excusing himself for continuing to fix his eyes on it by asserting that it was better to face temptation than to flee from it. There was a glow of self-righteousness in his heart. He had been so sorely tempted to come down and talk to her, especially when the other twin had gone and she was left alone. If he had yielded to temptation he might have been with her now. But he hadn't yielded to temptation. He had resisted temptation. He had stayed up in his room till the terrace was quite empty. He had seen her go down the drive, and—still with the idea of facing temptation instead of fleeing from it—he had leant out of his window to watch her through the trees as she climbed the stile and set off over the common.

He stood on the terrace, looking round uncertainly. He must do something. He couldn't hang about like this. His aunt might come down any minute, and it would be pretty grim if she collared him to spend the morning with her. The only thing to do was to start out for a walk at once before she appeared. And, of course, there was really nowhere to go to but the common. The fact that he'd seen Angela (he lingered over the name in his thoughts) set off in the direction of the common was nothing to him. He would either go a different way or, if he went the same way, he would merely raise his hat and pass her without speaking. There was nothing to be afraid of. He had just proved to himself that he could face and resist temptation. He felt quite secure. He went down the drive, walking more quickly than was his wont, crossed the stile, and strode on over the common. Yes, there she was ahead of him. A track led away from the path she was following, but the boy decided not to take it. Instead he would face and resist temptation again. It would be good practice in facing and resisting temptation. He hurried on after her. Suddenly she turned and stood waiting for him, smiling, screwing up her blue eyes in the sunshine.

"What a hurry you're in!" she laughed as he came up to her.

And immediately a flood of happiness engulfed the boy. He forgot his decision to face and overcome temptation. He even forgot that this slender figure with the laughing blue eyes and childish lips and flawless skin embodied temptation. What a darling she is, his soul sang, what a darling, what a darling! Sang and seemed to dance within him, so that, for the time being, his heavy burden of priggishness and premature age fell from him, making him feel almost light-headed with relief.

"I've been hurrying to catch you up," he said, and laughed in boyish high-spirits as if he had said something amusing.

She laughed too, as if she appreciated the joke, and their clear young laughter rang out over the moorland, light and buoyant and care-free like the song of the birds.

"Why did you want to catch me up?"

"I wanted to come for a walk with you."

He laughed again, and this time his laughter had a ring of defiance, as if he were saying to the deposed prig: You *did* want to go for a walk with her. All the time you did. You *know* you did.

"How nice of you! Come along then. I hate going for walks alone, don't you? And Cicely was captured by the old hag."

"I know. I saw. I was watching out of my window."

And again they laughed. The boy felt that he had to laugh in order to relieve the almost unbearable feeling of happiness that had seized him. (What a darling she is, what a darling, what a darling!)

"Poor pet," went on Angela. "She's got a kind heart, and it's fatal to have a kind heart. You're damned for life, you know, if you have a kind heart."

"Haven't you got a kind heart?"

"No, I'm terribly selfish. I do just what I want. I don't go out with old hags. I go out with you."

It seemed to the boy that she was the cleverest and most charming and most beautiful being in the whole world. He couldn't think how he'd lived all these years before he met her.

"Ah, but that *is* kind-hearted, to go out with me," he said.

She turned her sweet laughing face to him.

"Who's fishing?" she said.

This conversation did not seem crude or futile to the boy. On the contrary it seemed subtly and incomparably witty. His heart still sang with ecstasy. The whole world around was bathed in an unearthly glamour.

"Poor old Cicely!" said Angela and, adopting a waddling gait and a husky cockney voice and shaking a forefinger roguishly, went on, "You weren't giving me the slip, love, were you?"

The prig raised his head in shocked protest, but, laughing exultantly, the boy pushed him out of sight. (Get down, you old fool! Get down, will you?)

"Oh, look," said Angela suddenly. "There's Miss Wingate. What on earth is she doing?"

Miss Wingate was bending over the ground, poking it with her stick. She raised a flushed face as they approached, peered at them through her pince-nez, relaxed her pursed mouth very slightly, and spoke constrainedly.

"Good morning. I'm just examining the heath here. It's not in flower, but still one can tell a good deal from the plant. There are, of course, innumerable varieties of heaths."

"Are there?" said Angela. "I never knew that. But I know very little about flowers. I expect you know heaps."

"I'm interested in botany," said Miss Wingate, still looking rather embarrassed. "Well, I must be getting back. . . ."

She set off over the common again with her prim scuttling gait.

"She looked terribly guilty," said Angela. "I believe she's committed a murder and was burying the body. She's just the sort of person to do it. It's always the most respectable person in the book. Whom do you think she's murdered? It can't be the old hag, because she's out with Cicely. Can it be the clergyman's wife? The one who calls her husband the Vicar and was telling everyone last night in the drawing-room exactly how she decorated the pulpit for Harvest Thanksgiving?"

"Yes," laughed the boy. "I'm sure that's it. I don't wonder. I nearly did it myself. They're probably heads of rival gangs in disguise."

"Of course they are. Then the clergyman will kill Miss Wingate. He's the secret agent of a Balkan state double-crossing everyone."

"And, of course, the crown jewels are at the bottom of it all."

"Yes. The clergyman's wife had them, and that's why Miss Wingate murdered her."

By this time they felt as if they had known each other all their lives. They held hands, swinging their arms, as they strode along.

Miss Wingate scuttled on over the common back to the road. Really, it was very awkward. It seemed as if the absence of a hair-tidy were going to spoil her whole holiday. She'd been down to the village shop to try to get one yesterday evening, and they didn't seem even to know what she meant. They'd offered her nets and combs and curling-pins and things like that. So after breakfast she'd made all her combings up into a little parcel and had brought it out to bury. And it had taken nearly the whole morning, because, of course, she had to wait till no one was in sight, and always, just when the coast seemed clear and she was going to bury it, someone would come along, and she had to pretend that she was merely going for a walk. And then, when she was actually burying the thing, those two young people had come upon her and had made her practically tell a lie, though she prided herself on speaking the exact truth in all circumstances.

She crossed the road and went up the drive.

Mr. Ellison was sitting on the terrace in the sunshine reading. He looked up from his book as she passed. She peered at him short-sightedly through her pince-nez to make quite sure who he was, then unpursed her mouth slightly.

"A beautiful morning, is it not?" she said.

"It's almost incredible," he replied. "Sitting out of doors in December. Just think of it."

"Yes, indeed," said Miss Wingate and scuttled indoors.

She really could "mix" quite well, she assured herself. It had been absurd of her ever to have thought that she couldn't. There was an hour before lunch-time. She would light the gas fire in her bedroom and do an hour's solid reading. Then she would do another hour's solid reading this afternoon. She always made it a rule to do two hours' solid readings day in the holidays. She was enjoying this holiday very much indeed. She told herself so several times as she bustled about her bedroom, lighting the gas fire, taking out her books, and drawing the easy-chair up to the hearth.

Mr. Ellison continued to read. After a few minutes Miss Bella Torrance came out of the French windows of the drawing-room and strolled across the terrace to the stone balustrade. She wore a red-and-black knitted costume with her usual air of rather daring sophistication; her dark hair was sleekly groomed, her lips boldly coloured, but for all that her face looked pale and lined. She had had a wretched night. She had slept little, and whenever she had slept there had come to her tormenting dreams of Simon. She had awakened from the last one with a delirious hope that he might have written to her. She had dressed quickly and come downstairs. But there was no letter. She had known in her heart all the time that there would be no letter. As she stood by the stone balustrade she was wondering whether to write to him and ask him to meet her in Town. It would be useless, of course. He didn't want to meet her. If he had, he would have written himself to suggest it. Her thoughts went back to last Christmas Day. She and Simon had hung mistletoe all over the studio, and Simon had kissed her under each single sprig. Her thin lips twisted at the memory, and she drummed her fingers on the stone balustrade. . . . She mustn't think of that. She'd go mad if she let herself think of that. What was the matter with her? Yesterday she had thought that she was getting over it, and this morning it was as bad as it had ever been. It was that Downing man, of course. He wasn't like Simon in any single feature, and yet he reminded her of him. He looked at her as Simon used to look at her. It was a look that mocked and challenged and invited—a quizzical look that caressed her boldly and that held a faint hint of cruelty. He wouldn't care—just as Simon hadn't cared. He knew all the tricks of it. He'd wheedle her soul out of her body, and then, when he'd got all he wanted of her, he'd pass on, laughing at her and at himself, and never think of her again. Amoral . . .

where had she heard that word? That's what he was. Amoral—and as fascinating as sin. Oh well, it was lucky for her that she'd learnt her lesson. She wasn't likely to be taken in by the same tricks twice. Besides—she'd finished with that sort of thing. She was starting fresh. Suddenly she saw him coming round the corner of the house onto the terrace. Her heart missed a beat, but she set her lips firmly. She wouldn't turn round, wouldn't look at him. Slight, dapper, elegant, he came up and stood by her.

"Good morning, Miss Torrance."

He fixed his eyes on her with the boldly caressing smile that was so like Simon's. He knew, of course. He wouldn't look at her like that unless—he knew. She threw him a cold defiant glance.

"Good morning."

A thrill shot through her as she met his eyes. Stop it, she said to herself sternly. You're through with that sort of thing. . . .

"Are you going out for a walk this morning?" he asked.

"No, I'm not," she said, and turned away in an obvious desire to end the conversation.

"Oh, but you ought to," he said. "I'm going down to the river. Won't you take pity on my loneliness?"

Cheek! Laughing at her . . . making fun of her.

"I'm not going out," she said again shortly.

He raised his hat and passed on, unabashed, the smile still hovering on his lips.

Her heart was beating wildly. Thought he'd get her, probably. Well, he'd find out that he was mistaken for once. But the vague depression that had possessed her before he came had given place to a heady excitement. She summoned again the memory of his dark challenging gaze. Cheek! she said to herself again, but at the memory a thrill—sharp and poignant as a knife—shot through her. She braced herself. She wasn't going to falter in her chosen path just because she met a man who looked at her as Simon used to look. After all, it was the way they all looked at you. It meant only one thing, and she'd had enough of that. Why the hell couldn't they leave her alone when she was trying to go straight? They didn't give a girl a fair chance. She glanced round and saw Mr.

Ellison reading on the seat on the corner of the terrace. He looked safe and kind. On an impulse she went over and sat down beside him.

"What are you reading?" she said.

He handed her the book. She took it, grimaced, and handed it back.

"Foreign. What is it?"

"Italian. *Il Trionfo della Morte.*"

She glanced in the direction that the other man had taken. He was hanging about, looking back at her in shameless invitation, obviously waiting for her to join him. She pretended not to see, and bent her head low over the book. Her heart was hammering wildly.

"How funny it looks!" she said. She pointed out a line at random. "What's that in English?"

He translated slowly.

"'His past dragged behind it through time an immense dark net, all full of dead things.'"

She shuddered.

The other man was still waiting—still sure that she would join him. Well, she told herself again, he was going to learn his mistake. She'd just talk a little more to Mr. Ellison (why were nice men always so dull? and then she'd set off down the drive in the opposite direction.

"Have you been in Italy?"

"Yes."

"Tell me about it. What's it like?"

She'd wait till he'd finished telling her about Italy (she wasn't listening to a word he said), and then she'd get up and walk away quickly in the opposite direction, without looking back. That would show him all right. . . . Perhaps he'd leave her alone after that.

"You ought to go there in the spring, of course. Spring's the time for Italy. Though winter isn't bad either. I always used to spend Christmas in Rome in the old days. Cold nights, but often glorious days like this."

She rose.

"Well, I won't disturb you any longer. I must go for a walk like everyone else this lovely morning, mustn't I?"

"Of course you must. Only people of my age are allowed to be lazy. Where shall you go?"

She stood hesitating, a bright colour in her cheeks.

"Up on the common, I think."

She took a few steps in the direction of the drive, then hesitated again. "No, I won't. I'll try the other way. I've never been down to the river. Good-bye. I'll remember all you told me about Italy."

"Good-bye. Have a good walk."

There was no hesitation in her manner now as she set off to join the man who was still waiting for her at the end of the lawn.

Angela and Brian Mallard came up the drive together in silence. He looked sulky and morose. The prig was again in complete possession. He had leapt upon him and overpowered him as he climbed the stile into the road. He had returned in a fine frenzy of righteous indignation. He had in fact bludgeoned the boy unmercifully, and the boy had been absolutely defenceless, without justification or excuse. He couldn't even pretend that he hadn't yielded to temptation, yielded to it with hardly a show of resistance. He felt desperately ashamed. He had tried to atone for his fall by being as curt and aloof to the girl as he could ever since the prig had returned to possession.

"Mummy hated leaving the infant behind," Angela was saying, "and she is rather a darling. It's jolly to have an infant sister after all these years. Everyone makes fun of her, of course. Some people call her the Afterthought, and others call her the Accident."

He set his mouth in prim disapproval and said nothing.

"What's the matter?" Angela challenged him. "Why have you suddenly turned so sniffy?"

"Nothing's the matter," he said coldly. "I don't know what you mean."

They had reached the front door, and he bolted into it with a muttered "Good-bye," leaving her staring after him in amazement.

She entered the hall slowly and went into the drawing-room. It was empty except for the Osmonds, who sat side by side on one of the settees, their heads bent over a newspaper. They looked up at her, nodded vaguely, then returned to their cross-word puzzle.

She went to the window and stood looking out over the terrace, her small sweet mouth set tightly. Nobody had ever been so rude to her in all her life before. She wasn't going to be treated like that. She'd have nothing more to do with him, she assured herself vehemently. Nothing. Ever. She tried hard to be as angry as she knew she ought to be, but all she could feel was an aching compassion and tenderness, a longing to hold his head to her breast and comfort him.

"Yes, but what does occult *really* mean?" Mrs. Osmond was saying. "Let's look it out in the dictionary and make sure. I think it's something to do with fortune-telling."

Angela went slowly upstairs to her bedroom. Cicely was combing back her short fair curls before the looking-glass.

"Oh, darling," said Angela, "was it awful?"

"Worse than awful," replied Cicely. "She told me all about Bert's last illness, every minute of it. I feel as if I've been watching by Bert's deathbed for months. And she cried all over me. She said it did her good to have a good cry. I'm still damp. And she takes awful little steps that you can't keep in step with, and she asked what I was doing this afternoon, and I had the presence of mind to say I'd promised to go out with you."

"Darling, you *must* be firm."

"I know. I'm going to be."

"If you'd be really firm to her once or twice she'd stop bothering you."

"I know. Honestly I'm going to be." She sat on the window seat and looked down at the drive. "Mr. and Mrs. Fielden are coming back," she continued. "He just stalks on as if he were training for a Marathon race, without speaking a word, and she scurries along beside him, looking as if she were just going to cry. . . . Here's Miss Kimball's car back. Miss Lattimer's just getting out. She's got some lovely roses. An armful of them. And she looks her nice young self again. I'm so glad. She looked a hundred years old at breakfast, didn't she?"

Judith Kimball lay, pretending to be asleep, watching Sidney from beneath half-closed lids, as she moved noiselessly about the room, arranging the roses in vases and putting the grapes into a dish.

There was an air of glowing eager youth about her, and Judith feasted her tired eyes on the sight, postponing the moment when she should say: "Is that you, Sidney?" and the child would turn to her, eyes dark with adoration in the pale oval face. The adoration of a young girl was no new thing to Judith Kimball. She had always had it, always enjoyed it, had taken always a sadistic pleasure in inflicting a thousand little cruelties on her adorers. Even when her unkindness alienated them, it was so easy, so ridiculously easy, to win them back to her. Just a smile, a caress, a certain endearing inflexion in her voice, and the little fools were at her feet again. Then sooner or later she had always hurt them beyond healing, and they had left her, and she hadn't cared because there were hundreds of girls in the world, all waiting, as it seemed, to step into the empty place. But now suddenly it was different. She loved Sidney as she had never loved any of the others. This did not make her kinder, for that perverse desire to hurt where she loved was stronger in Sidney's case than ever before, but—she realised that she must be careful. She must not hurt Sidney beyond healing. She could not live now without Sidney's freshness and youth and adoration. It was more necessary to her than her drug. She was at the zenith of her beauty, her hard charm, her exquisiteness, but it wouldn't last much longer. She felt the beginnings of middle age in herself, though no signs as yet showed outwardly. She must have Sidney with her for her middle age, for her old age. She mustn't let Sidney go. It had been a mistake to come here, perhaps. It wasn't like an ordinary hotel where you could keep away from other visitors. She wouldn't share Sidney with anyone. Not with anyone. Ever.

She sat up in bed.

"Oh, my dear, what *lovely* flowers! How sweet of you!"

Sidney crossed the room to the bedside.

"How are you, darling?"

"I'm better. Much better. How perfectly *sweet* of you to get me those flowers."

"Oh, Judith, it wasn't. I'm so glad you're better."

"So well that I'm getting up after lunch. And we'll go for a drive, shall we?" She caught Sidney's hand and pressed it to her lips. "You spoil me, childie."

"Don't say things like that," said Sidney sharply. "I can't bear it—when I think of all you do for me."

"So you are just a teeny bit fond of me?" smiled Judith.

"I adore you. You know I do."

Out on the sunny upland Judith hadn't seemed to exist, but here in this scented, darkened room she seemed once more to be the only thing that did exist. There was a subtle enchantment about her. Always, when you were with her, nothing and no one else in the whole world mattered. Sidney gazed at the beautiful pale face, the sculptured lips, now smiling tenderly, the deep-set hazel eyes, the gleaming red-gold hair, and adoration swept over her afresh. This morning was a dream. It was some ghost of herself, not her real self, who had laughed and talked in the sunshine with Dickie Bennet.

"You know I do," she said again. "You know I do."

Chapter Fifteen

THE billiard room had, under Cummings's direction, been transformed into a ballroom. The billiard table had been moved out, and chairs, interspersed with tall palms, ranged along the wall. A small orchestra had taken its position in the window-recess and was already tuning up.

Several parties of strangers had come in from the neighbourhood for the dance. A tall, thin, middle-aged man had dined with the Paynters and was now standing with Mr. and Mrs. Paynter, throwing restless glances about the room as he did so. The three young Paynters stood together a short distance away. Angela and Ian were admonishing Cicely to display firmness if Mrs. Kellogg should attempt to appropriate her for the evening. Ian was holding a rehearsal, in which he impersonated, first Mrs. Kellogg attempting to appropriate Cicely, and then Cicely displaying firmness.

Suddenly they turned and saw Mrs. Kellogg in the doorway. She wore a lace-and-satin dress of a particularly virulent shade of purple that fitted her small plump figure like a glove. Paste ornaments sparkled in her massed hair and on her shelving bosom, and her fat little wrists were loaded with bracelets. As soon as her gaze fell on Cicely, she waddled across to her with a broad smile.

"There you are, love," she said. "I've been feeling that down, but I knew I'd be all right once I was with you." The music had struck up and a few couples were preparing to take the floor. "Let's sit down and watch a bit, shall we?"

"Yes, let's," said Cicely.

Ian was making urgent signs to her behind Mrs. Kellogg's back, but she ignored him.

"You're young, though, love," went on Mrs. Kellogg wistfully. "You won't want to waste your time with an old woman like me."

"Don't be silly. . . . Of *course* I want to sit with you," said Cicely, and, still ignoring Ian's grimaces, accompanied her to the sofa that stood against the wall by the fireplace.

"I did mean to dance myself," said Mrs. Kellogg, "but my feet are that chronic again to-night. . . . Somehow it doesn't seem right to Bert to let myself go just because he's not here to take a pride in me, but I never as near put on a pair of bedroom slippers to come downstairs in my life before."

"Oh, but why didn't you?" said Cicely. "Do! Let me fetch them. I'll slip them on for you, and no one will see. . . ."

"No, love. I always say it's a woman's lot to suffer, and it's no good fighting against it."

Mrs. Paynter, dancing with her guest, threw Cicely a smile as she passed.

"Sweet your mother looks, love," went on Mrs. Kellogg. "You've all the same colouring as me, haven't you? Like as two pins, you and me are, when one comes to think about it."

There was a slight stir as Judith Kimball and Sidney Lattimer entered and, without hesitating or even looking about the room, slid into each other's arms and began to dance. Judith moved with the sinuous grace of the born dancer. The heavy white eyelids drooped as she gazed down at Sidney, the red lips smiled faintly, there was a subtle insolence in the way she ignored everyone else in the room.

"Like it?" she said.

"Love it," said Sidney. "You're heavenly to dance with, Judith. You dance better than anyone else in the world."

There was indeed something almost of intoxication in following the lithe, rhythmic movements of the beautiful body.

"So I've been told before," said Judith, still smiling down at her. "It's quite a good orchestra, isn't it?"

"Yes. Oh, do look. There's Mrs. Kellogg. . . . Doesn't she look dreadful!"

A wry aloof amusement invaded the sweetness of Judith's smile.

"Darling, how *do* you remember the names of all these appalling people?"

Sidney laughed light-heartedly. An elusive sense of happiness had upheld her all evening. Suddenly she began to try to trace it to its source. It must be the drive with Judith this afternoon—Judith at her most charming, all traces of the headache gone. But no—oddly enough, it wasn't that. It was this morning. The realisation surprised her. It wasn't Judith. It was this morning. She saw herself standing by the car in the sunshine, talking to Bennet, and the wave of happiness surged over her again with redoubled force. She thought of his impudent blue eyes, of his long humorous mouth dented at the corners, of his lazy laughing voice, and she gave a funny little skip in the middle of the step from sheer lightness of heart.

"Darling," said Judith, "what *are* you doing?"

"Only dancing," laughed Sidney.

She hadn't told Judith about Bennet. When she came in she had had an impulse to pour it all out—the story of his father's death, his mother's struggle, and the reason why he had become a chauffeur—but she had stopped in time, remembering that it was dangerous to refer again to any subject, however innocent, that had once caused trouble between her and Judith.

The dance music died away, and they sat down.

"Had enough?" said Judith.

"Oh no! Do let's stay here just a little longer," pleaded Sidney.

"If you like."

A look of anxiety came into Sidney's face, and she glanced half fearfully at Judith, then drew a quick breath of relief, reassured by Judith's smile. It was all right. She wasn't annoyed. . . .

"The baby shan't leave the party before it wants to," went on Judith.

Sidney laughed again, responding automatically and with a skill born of long, and sometimes difficult, practice to Judith's slightest change of mood.

"Yes, the baby must always have its own way," she said.

The music for the second dance was beginning, and Mr. Ellison was coming across the room towards them, followed by the Paynters' guest. Judith gave them a faint smile of welcome.

"May I have the pleasure of this dance?" said Mr. Ellison to Judith with old-fashioned courtesy.

His companion, introduced as Mr. Grant, turned to Sidney.

"I hope you're free for this one?"

Judith shot him an approving glance. Satisfactorily middle-aged. Almost old. She wouldn't mind Sidney's dancing with him.

She smiled assent, and they joined the crowd of dancers.

"Lovely floor," said Philip Grant with mechanical brightness.

It was the opening gambit he had used at dances for thirty years. Sidney didn't answer. She was smiling at Ian and Angela, who were just passing. Her partner glanced down at her. She was certainly a peach. There was an eager glowing youth-fulness about her that stirred one's pulses. And beneath it there was a suggestion of responsibility, an adorable childish gravity.

He looked into a large Chinese mirror that hung on the wall. He'd kept his figure and his hair. No one would ever guess his age. . . . Tentatively he claimed kinship with her youth.

"I love these modern dances," he said. "I can't think how people used to put up with affairs like the lancers and the polkas in the old days."

She turned her clear ingenuous gaze upon him.

"But I suppose they seemed quite jolly to you, then," she said.

He stiffened. No, she wasn't really pretty, after all, he decided. Mouth too big. Not enough colour. Lacked charm. Not his type at all. . . .

Mrs. Paynter had rejoined her husband on one of the palm-sheltered couches.

"Oh, so you're not going to dance with him all night?" he greeted her.

"Darling, I *had* to have one with him. He's our guest."

"That's not my fault. I don't know why you must have every single member of your family over wherever we go."

She laughed.

"Don't be so absurd. He lives just near here. He knew we were coming. I didn't tell him, but I suppose someone did. He wrote to ask if he could come over, so what could I do?"

"Say no, of course."

"I *couldn't*, Hugh. He's my cousin, and his mother died only this spring, you know. He's very lonely."

"So am I when you go off and dance with him. Now listen, woman——"

"I had to give him one dance, Hugh."

"Don't interrupt. I hardly see you when we're at home—you know I don't—and then when I try to take you away by yourself you must needs bring a cartload of children——"

"Darling, we *couldn't* have come away without the children at Christmas."

"Of course we could—and collect all your family from miles around. . . ."

"Don't be so ridiculous," she laughed.

He pulled her abruptly to her feet, slipped an arm about her waist, and began to pilot her skilfully round the room.

Downstairs in the basement Robert Beaton sat in Mrs. Hubbard's room, puffing at his pipe in silence, and gazing into the fire. He was aware that he ought to be doing his duty—dancing or playing bridge—upstairs.

"I'll just look in on old Mother Hubbard," he had said to Celia, "and then I'll come along and give you a hand."

But he felt strangely reluctant to leave the refuge of this small familiar room. For it was a refuge. The rest of the house seemed to have cast off his love, to have become hostile and alien. Only in this room did he feel at home. And—a still stranger thing—only with Mrs. Hubbard did he now feel wholly at his ease. He felt oddly ill at ease with Celia. He didn't know what to say to her. He avoided being left alone with her. On the rare occasions when they were alone together, she would praise the house to him, remembering how in the old days he had loved to talk about it, not realising that to him Chedsy Place didn't exist any longer. It was nothing to him now but a memory. Unwillingly he admired the energy with which she flung herself into this new venture, but, like the house, she seemed to have changed, to have become alien, hostile. He was almost grateful to the endless claims that separated her from him. With the old woman opposite he felt different. The bond that united them was strengthened by the alien house in which they lived. Sometimes, sitting together in this small dark room, they seemed to him like two sailors shipwrecked upon a raft. . . .

He roused himself from his reverie and looked at his watch.

"Well, I suppose I ought to be going upstairs."

"Mrs. Beaton will be tired after this, I'm afraid. She's had a lot to do."

She was pleading with him for Celia: Don't be hard on her even in your thoughts. She doesn't mean to spoil things. . . .

"Of course. . . . Good night, Mother Hubbard."

He kissed her lined old brow and went out.

As soon as he had gone Kathleen entered with a box of coals.

She knelt on the hearth-rug, putting the coal on the fire, piece by piece. As she put on the last, she heaved a deep sigh of ecstasy.

"Isn't it lovely, ma'am?" she said.

"Isn't what lovely, Kathleen?"

"Everything, ma'am. I never thought I'd ever come to be in a place like this."

"Like what?"

"Full of posh people an' something going on all the time."

"There's certainly plenty going on," agreed Mrs. Hubbard, rather dryly.

"It's just like a dream," continued Kathleen rapturously. "And their *clothes*! That dress Miss Kimball's got on to-night! Oo, it's a treat. Did you see it, ma'am? She's beautiful, isn't she?"

"Very," agreed Mrs. Hubbard.

"She's one of them Society beauties one reads about, I shouldn't be surprised. Queens it in spacious halls in London's palaces of luxury."

"You've been to the pictures again, Kathleen," said Mrs. Hubbard severely.

Kathleen looked guilty.

"Well, ma'am, I did go, over at Hunton . . . but they were very *good* pictures. There was one all scenery. Ever so improving." She rose, hesitated a moment, then went on eagerly: "May I go and water the hyacinths in Miss Kimball's bedroom, ma'am?"

"I think they've been watered, Kathleen."

"May I just go and make sure?"

"Very well . . . but don't touch any of her things."

"No, of course not, ma'am."

In Miss Kimball's bedroom Kathleen stood for a moment surveying herself in the glass and seeing, not a rosy-cheeked dumpy little person in a cap and apron, but a tall sinuous figure in black velvet with white skin and red-gold hair. She spoke over her shoulders in a voice of affected gentility.

"How did you enjoy the duchess's ball, deah? I was tarribly boahed, weren't you? . . . So many people there that weren't no clahse at all. What was the prince saying to you just befoah we came away?"

Robert Beaton ascended the basement steps and went through the green-baize door into the hall. The quarter of an hour that he had spent with Mrs. Hubbard had soothed his irritation. He felt calmer, more able to cope with things.

Suddenly Mrs. Stephenson-Pollitt, wearing a purple velvet dress with a Medici collar of lace and a long train, swept out of the library. Her great lustrous eyes peered at him from behind a bush of hair.

"It's Mr. Beaton, isn't it?" she said. "The window of my bedroom seems a little stiff, Mr. Beaton. I'd be so glad if you'd see to it."

She swept on towards the stairs.

He stood staring after her. The colour had flooded his fair freckled face. He couldn't get used to the way these people treated him, as if he were a servant, in his own house. It outraged something in him. He lacked a sense of humour, of course. When it happened to Celia, as it frequently did, she was merely amused. He tried to feel amused now, curving his long mouth into a grim smile. He couldn't imagine the woman in the house at all in his uncle's time except perhaps as a visitor to the servants' hall. I'm a snob, that's what it is, he thought. He was surprised and amused by the discovery. We're both snobs, he went on, both Mother Hubbard and I. We're a couple of mouldy survivals. Well, then, *don't* be a snob, he adjured himself. Try to be modern and up to date. Try to move with the times, you prehistoric old stick. . . .

He entered the big drawing-room, where the dancing was going on, and stood watching in the doorway. It was an interval between the dances. The clergyman and his wife were sitting near the door. The clergyman was gazing round the room, while his wife talked to Mrs. Lewel, who sat near her. She was engaged on one of those rambling recitals that seemed to have neither beginning nor end.

"Well, we'd taken our tea with us because we'd meant to picnic. The Vicar had put off his confirmation class especially for it. But half-way there it began to rain so heavily that we decided to go home. . . ."

The band struck up for the next dance. Miss Kimball and Miss Lattimer were sitting side by side on the sofa against the wall. Someone obviously ought to be dancing with them. . . . He walked across to Miss Kimball.

"May I have this one?"

She smiled and rose. He was just slipping his arm round her when Ian Paynter came sliding up and made an exaggerated bow in front of Miss Lattimer.

"Wiltest thou hop this one *avec je*, fair dame?" he said.

Both of them laughed.

"I wiltest," she said, and was just rising, when Miss Kimball put her hand to her head.

"Sidney," she said, "I feel rather faint. . . . I'm afraid I shall have to go upstairs."

"Oh, *darling*," said the girl solicitously. "I'll come with you. . . . I'm so sorry. . . . I ought to have seen . . ."

He watched them go from the room. Rather odd that the woman had felt faint. Her colour hadn't faded in the slightest, and she looked perfectly well. He shrugged and turned towards the door. He'd see if he was wanted for bridge. The blind man would be playing in the small drawing-room. One of the dancing couples slipped out of the door in front of him and went across the hall to the library. It was Mr. Downing and Miss Torrance. . . .

He stood for another moment, looking round the room. Mrs. Downing sat alone, stiffly upright in a small chair at the further end of the room. Her eyes, in her twisted, expressionless face, were fixed glassily on the door. He wondered whether he ought to go and speak to her, decided not to, and instead crossed the hall to the little drawing-room.

Mr. Standfield was hardly conscious of his wife's voice that still kept up its unceasing monologue beside him. His eyes followed Angela Paynter round and round the room. He couldn't get used to it. When first he saw her the shock had been so great that, had it been possible, he would have made some excuse to go home at once. He felt that he couldn't live for five days with this ghost of Alice before his eyes. For she was Alice, as Alice had been thirty years ago, radiantly lovely, dainty, slender, and shy. This girl wasn't shy, of course. She was hard and modern and sophisticated. It was her appearance only that brought back Alice to him with this heart-stirring vividness. Alice, too, had had silvery golden curls (dragged back into a "bun" at her neck in her case), forget-me-not blue eyes, and a short upper lip that lifted adorably when she smiled, to show the small, regular teeth. He hadn't thought of her for years. He had made up his mind to forget her when he married Lucy, and he had honestly believed that he had succeeded. It was terrible that a chance likeness should set his pulses racing in this way. He remembered the last time he had seen Alice, her blue eyes full of desolation and a reproach that was wholly devoid of anger, the corners of her pretty mouth drooping disconsolately.

He had met her in his first curacy and had fallen in love with her at sight. And—he was sure of it, though no word of love had ever passed between them—she had fallen in love with him. Whenever their eyes met, hers had told him so quite plainly before they had time to veil themselves beneath their black lashes. After a few weeks he decided to propose. He could hear himself now saying: "May I walk home with you to-night, Miss Alice, after the parish social? There is something I wish to say to you." And she had said "Yes" tremulously, her fair cheeks suddenly suffused with blushes, her sweet eyes already giving him their answer.

And that very afternoon Lucy's eldest sister had sent for him. Even now the memory of that interview made him go hot and cold in turns. He could see her, grim, unsmiling, with her small tight mouth. Her young sister, Lucy, had fallen in love with him, she said. What was he going to do about it? She did not accuse him of encouraging the girl, but she was afraid that if he could not bring himself at least to give her some hope her health would suffer seriously. She was, the sister assured him, suitable in every way to fill the position of a clergyman's wife. She had been trained in rigid economy from her childhood. She was methodical, conscientious, and capable. The whole scene was like a nightmare. He was under the impression when he left her that he had stipulated for time to consider the matter, but the news of his engagement was all over the town by the evening. Everyone who met him congratulated him. Alice did not attend the parish social that night. . . . There had been a painful scene with Lucy. She was desperately in love with him, but ashamed of her sister's manœuvre. Sobbing, she clung to him and offered him his freedom. Both of them knew, however, that her sister would never let him go. He had committed himself by tacitly accepting the congratulations. Lucy was not pretty, but she was rather appealing in her devotion to him and her fear of the sister who had dominated her from childhood. Alice, in any case, would not accept him after this. He had bowed to what had seemed the inevitable, trying to tear the love for Alice out of his heart. He only saw her once again—an accidental meeting in the street, when she had looked at him, her blue eyes full of anguish and reproach. After that her parents took her away to Switzerland for a holiday, and when they returned he had moved on to another curacy.

Some years later he heard that she was unhappily married. A few years later still he heard that she was dead.

Once freed from her elder sister's rule, Lucy had quickly lost her timidity, becoming opinionated, dogmatic, stubborn. It had been strange to watch her growing more and more like her sister as the years went on. He glanced at her now, and, with the memory of Alice fresh in his mind, her likeness to her sister startled him.

He felt himself again a bewildered youth being told by that small, determined mouth that Lucy was in love with him, being asked grimly what he was going to do about it. . . .

He hadn't realised that she was gradually dominating him as her sister had dominated her till it was too late to resist. There was a strain of weakness in him. He liked to live in peace with those around him. So few things seemed worth fighting for. . . . And she had made him a good wife, looking after his creature comforts with almost embarrassing assiduity, "cosseting" him, arranging his work for him, guarding him from claims that she considered too exacting. He had long ago given up the struggle to keep any part of his life private from her. She invaded every sphere of it, managing, arranging, domineering. She ran the parish entirely, under a pretence of sparing him unnecessary work. He had taken the line of least resistance, sinking, as it were, into the rut she made for him—a rut of creature comfort, petty interests, narrow outlook. Generally he considered himself to be a very fortunate man, with an adequate income, a good wife, and a comfortable home. But now, seeing Alice's face again so vividly through the years, he caught a glimpse with it of all the grace and beauty and vision that his life had missed. . . .

"Wasn't she, Humphrey?" said his wife rather sharply.

He turned to her vaguely.

"What, my dear?"

"I was telling Mrs. Lewel how insolent Mrs. Burden was because we wouldn't help her grandfather from the Sick and Poor Fund when he hadn't been to church for over two years. . . ."

"Yes, my dear. Yes, yes," he said soothingly.

He remembered that he had tried to persuade her to give the poor old man some help, but she had set her small tight mouth and said, "No, Humphrey, this fund is for churchgoers. And for *regular* churchgoers, as long as I have any say in it."

She knew, of course, that she had all the say in it and always would have.

She shot him a keen glance.

"You're not looking well, Humphrey. I think I'll have that tonic made up again."

Chapter Sixteen

MRS. DOWNING'S eyes were still fixed on the door through which her husband had disappeared with Miss Torrance.

She sat motionless, except that the fingers of her clasped hands moved incessantly, twitching, writhing, straining together in her lap. . . .

She had deliberately taken her place where she could see herself in the Chinese mirror on the wall whenever she turned her head. She turned it now and faced her reflection with an effort. Even after all these months she could not accustom herself to the fact that this twisted, distorted mask was herself. This was what Ralph saw when he looked at her. Her first thought when she regained consciousness after the accident had been of Ralph: If my face is smashed up, I've lost him. And the agony of that thought had been sharper than the physical pain.

There had always been something precarious about his love. She had taken a deliberate risk when she married him. She had known even then that there was something lacking in him that should not be lacking in one's husband. Beneath his charm he was utterly, unashamedly selfish. It almost amounted to a yellow streak. And he was quite frank about it. He made no pretences. He had no need to make pretences. There was in him a subtle animal magnetism that carried him triumphantly through life, despite his obvious faults. She had yielded to it at once, falling passionately in love with him on their first meeting. Yet, as early as that, she had sensed the yellow streak, had known, half unconsciously, that he would fail her, gaily, irresponsibly, with never a scruple or an afterthought, if ever it should serve his purpose. He loved her, but only because she was the most beautiful and charming woman he knew. If ever he met anyone more beautiful, more charming, he would disown his loyalty.

From its beginning her married life had been a struggle to hold him. Each day the battle had to be fought afresh. She could never rest for an hour on her laurels. She had to continue unremittingly to be the most attractive woman he knew. And the amazing thing was that for five years she had succeeded. So well, indeed, had she succeeded that she had almost begun to hope she was forging chains that would bind even his will-o'-the-wisp fickleness.

Then came her accident. The irony of the situation was that she disliked hunting and only took part in it because her particular type of beauty looked its best in riding habit, and she knew that the sight of her on horseback always roused his admiration.

As she lay in bed in the nursing home, her face swathed in bandages, her body racked with pain, her thoughts had dwelt unceasingly on her husband. Through the long feverish nights she had tried to picture what would happen when she returned to him. Sometimes she imagined a final rupture between them; sometimes, less vividly, she imagined his love's proving triumphant over her loss of beauty.

Neither of these happened. He received her on her return with a fairly good imitation of his old devotion, though his first glance told her—what she knew already in her heart—that his love for her was dead. They continued to inhabit the same house. The accident had left her too lame to ride, walk, or play games with him. Often she did not see him for days except at meals, but whenever he was with her he behaved with courtesy and affability. He never paid attention to another woman in her presence. Often she tried to discuss their relationship, to come to some definite understanding with him, but she could not break down the wall of suave imperturbability that he had built up around him since her accident. There was something almost elfin in his elusiveness, just as there was in his charm. The most tragic part of the whole situation was that his charm still held her. She still loved him so passionately that she felt a fierce jealousy of every other woman to whom he spoke—a jealousy that she had never known in the days of her beauty.

She kept herself well in hand, building up defences of iron self-repression, hardly trusting herself sometimes even to speak to him. She became silent, abrupt in her manner, stiff and poker-like in her movements, ceasing every attempt to make herself attractive to him, brushing back her hair in a way that emphasised her broken features, dressing as plainly as possible, refusing the doctor's suggestion of another facial operation, scorning to undertake a losing battle.

Before her accident she had disliked her sister-in-law, but now she welcomed her presence. It helped to keep at bay the almost uncontrollable emotion that seized her whenever she was alone with her husband.

Her eyes moved again to the door by which he had gone out with the girl, and again her thin fingers twisted together in her lap.

Her jealousy was like a fire consuming her whole body. She sat, every muscle tense, trying to fight it down. Knowing Ralph as she did, she was certain that he was not faithful to her, but she hid the certainty away, refusing to look at it, to acknowledge its existence. As long as she could prevent herself from looking at it, it was all right; but if ever she *had* to look at it, if ever she should find actual proof of his unfaithfulness, it would be the end. She would no longer be able to control this seething fire within her.

Her sister-in-law, who had been dancing with Philip Grant, came across the room and sat by her.

"Dull show, Helen, isn't it?" she said.

"Isn't it," agreed Mrs. Downing, and added after a slight pause, "Do you know where Ralph is?"

Eleanor Downing shot a quick glance round the room.

"Playing bridge, I think," she said.

"What's that girl called he was dancing with just now?"

"Miss Torrance."

"Oh yes," said Mrs. Downing, as if without interest. "Miss Torrance."

Upstairs in his room Brian Mallard sat studying Hebrew. He disliked the language intensely and found his books of instruction so confusing as to be almost unintelligible. In fact, though he had been studying them at intervals now for several months, he felt that he knew no more than when he began. He was studying to-night as a penance. He had indubitably succumbed to temptation this afternoon. Once more he saw Angela Paynter as a complete Venusburg and shrank in horror from the very thought of her. True, he had only laughed and talked and rambled over the moors with her, but that was the beginning of the downward path. "*Facilis descensus Averno.*" he quoted sternly to himself, and felt slightly cheered by the fact that he was able to parse *Averno* correctly as a Local Dative used in poetry to denote Place Whither.

Fragments of dance music floated up from the billiard room. He put his fingers into his ears resolutely in order to drown the strains and closed his eyes to shut out the vision of Angela dancing in someone else's arms. . . .

Robert had found Celia playing cards with Mr. and Mrs. Fielden and Mr. Osmond. Mrs. Osmond sat knitting before the fire. She and her husband had spent the afternoon doing the cross-word puzzles in three newspapers, and they were now enjoying a well-earned rest.

Celia smiled at him as he entered.

"Oh, there you are, darling," she said. "Carry on for me, will you? We've just finished a rubber. . . . I want to go into the drawing-room."

Her generous loving smile warmed his heart, making him ashamed of his secret disloyalty to her. She took his hand for a moment as she passed him, and he gave hers a quick furtive pressure. He felt happier, less lonely, as he sat down at the table.

Mr. Fielden wore his grimmest expression. Mrs. Fielden looked flushed and peevish. Mr. Osmond kept up a desultory conversation with his wife over his shoulder while he played, occasionally asking what were trumps, and making the most elementary mistakes in his play. He looked, as usual, extremely pleased with himself.

"Little game like this does one good," he said cheerfully to Robert. "Clears away the cobwebs."

It was obvious that he took the little game no more seriously than he would have taken a game of Snap.

"I always feel a bit fagged after one or two cross-word puzzles," he went on expansively, "and a relaxation like this is just what one needs. . . . What did you say trumps were?"

"Hearts," rasped the blind man's voice.

There was a faint note of triumph behind his irritation. The man was a fool, and it always gave him a malicious pleasure to come across sighted fools. It seemed perceptibly to decrease his handicap.

Celia went into the drawing-room and stood for a moment watching the dancers. It all seemed to be going on very well. The thought made her realise suddenly how tired she was. Instinctively she thrust the realisation aside, keying herself up for further effort.

Mrs. Lewel was coming towards the door, her mother on her arm.

"I'm just taking mother upstairs," she said. "She has so enjoyed watching the dancing."

The old lady nodded and smiled radiantly.

"Good night, Joyce darling," she said to Celia. "It's been so kind of you to ask me. Your girls look so sweet, but then they would, wouldn't they?"

She patted Celia's cheek with a touch as light as a butterfly's wing, and passed on, nodding and smiling.

Celia went down the room to where Mrs. Downing sat, rigidly upright, beside her sister-in-law.

"Wouldn't you be more comfortable on the sofa, Mrs. Downing?" she said.

Mrs. Downing turned her expressionless face to her.

"No, thank you," she said. "I'm very comfortable here."

The music for the next dance was striking up. Mr. Downing and Miss Torrance entered the room.

Philip Grant claimed Miss Torrance, and they slid at once into the steps of the foxtrot.

Mr. Downing walked across the room, with his slight swagger, to where his wife sat.

"You all right, darling?" he said in a tone of easy, half-mocking affection.

"Yes, quite. . . ."

"Won't you try this one with me?"

"No, thank you. You know I never dance now."

"Will you, Eleanor?"

"Very well."

The other two watched them in silence for some minutes.

"How well your sister-in-law dances!" said Celia at last.

"Yes," agreed Mrs. Downing, but she wasn't watching Eleanor. She was watching Bella Torrance, with her slanting eyes and reddened mouth and the slender graceful body, every line of which was revealed by the tightly swathed red satin dress. She was conscious, not of anger or jealousy, but of an odd bewildering helplessness. It was as if she were exerting every atom of her power to keep some wild beast in check.

Philip Grant's thin face wore a restless wistful expression. He was, as usual, hovering between the two camps of youth and middle age, spurned by the one, refusing to join the other.

He had lived alone with his mother till this spring. To her he had always remained the delicate little boy who had needed constant care and attention to bring him safely through his ailing childhood. Their friends secretly made fun of her mollycoddling of him, but Philip himself never resented it. He had always been a "mother's boy," and up to the time of her death had been almost as dependent on her as if he were still a child. He had indeed felt himself still a child with her. But now she had gone, leaving him, to his terror and surprise, face to face with middle age.

"Mr. and Mrs. Paynter aren't dancing now, are they?" said Miss Torrance.

"No. They said that three dances were as much as they could stand nowadays. . . ."

"I'm feeling dead myself."

"Nonsense! You and I are both young enough to dance the shoes off our feet yet."

He gave her a hesitating smile, hoping that she wouldn't take his reference to his youth as a joke, but ready to join in it wryly if she did.

She didn't even seem to hear. She was straining every nerve not to meet the eyes of the man who was watching her across the room.

Her heart was still racing at the memory of that moment in the library when he had slipped his arm around her. She had broken away from him at once, but her body even now seemed on fire where he had touched it.

I won't have anything more to do with him, she was saying to herself. I won't look at him or speak to him again. Not once. All the time I'm here. If only he didn't remind me so of Simon. . . .

Cicely Paynter was dancing with Mr. Ellison.

"You've escaped, darling," whispered Angela, passing with Ian. "Don't go back to her."

"No, of course I won't," smiled Cicely.

But the small blue eyes beneath the towering flaxen coiffure followed her wistfully round the room, and there seemed to be something unbearably pathetic about the stout, isolated, magnificently clad figure, waiting so obviously for Cicely to return to it. . . . At the end of the dance Cicely returned to it. It greeted her with a beaming smile of welcome.

"You dance lovely, pet. You do for sure. . . . It's been a treat watching you. I'd have a go with you myself if it wasn't for my feet. I used to dance like a fairy, my Bert said."

The band struck up "God Save the King."

"Well, it's time we all went to bye-byes. Just come up with me, love, won't you? I always feel that nervous going into my bedroom in a strange place."

Cicely hesitated, then yielded to the pleading of the small blue eyes.

"All right. . . ."

"I've been that lonely since Bert was took," said Mrs. Kellogg expansively, as they went upstairs together. "I can't tell you what it means to me to find a friend like you. So much in common we've got, you and me, haven't we, love? Believe me or not, I used to wake up in the morning wondering how I was going to get through the day, but now I think of you—so kind and friendly and all that—and I feel that just meeting you again's something to get up for."

It's no use, thought Cicely despairingly. I shall have to give in to it. This holiday's spoilt now, anyway, because I shall feel hateful even if I do choke her off. . . . I'll start fresh the next time we go away. I'll be really firm and standoffish with people. . . .

Mrs. Kellogg opened her bedroom door.

"Look, love," she said, pointing to a photograph on the mantelpiece. "This is Bert." It showed the face of a small, common-looking man with protruding teeth and a waxed moustache. "It doesn't do him justice," she went on. "It doesn't show his smile, for one thing. He'd got a beautiful smile."

"It's—it's awfully nice," faltered Cicely.

"I never go nowhere without it," sighed Mrs. Kellogg, "though a photo's cold comfort, to be sure. I'd be that grateful if you'd just look under the bed for me, dearie. I find it so hard to bend in these corsets. . . ."

"Under the bed?" repeated Cicely, mystified.

Mrs. Kellogg grew serious and lowered her voice.

"I always look under the bed, love. Especially since Bert was took. A woman without a husband's placed so awkward. I always leave the door open, too, while I look under the bed."

"Are you frightened of burglars?" said Cicely.

"Well"—Mrs. Kellogg coughed discreetly—"them and other things."

"No, there's nothing under the bed," said Cicely after investigation.

Mrs. Kellogg proceeded to look in the wardrobe and behind the drawn window curtains.

"That's all right," she said.

"Have you ever found anyone?" said Cicely with interest.

"Not yet, love," replied Mrs. Kellogg, "but one never knows, and a woman can't be too careful living alone. . . . Look, dearie, isn't this a pretty nightie? I don't hold with women wearing pyjamas, do you, love? I think it's so unwomanly. It was my womanliness that first made Bert take to me. He often said so."

She proceeded to take her underclothing from the drawers and display it to Cicely—elaborate garments of embroidered lace-trimmed *crêpe de Chine*. A smell of stale scent filled the air as she shook them out.

"Bert always liked me to look nice underneath," she said, "and I'm sure he wouldn't like me to let myself go because he's been took. . . . He always fancied me in blue. 'Blue's your colour, Emmy,' he used to say. 'You stick to blue an' you won't go far wrong.' Look"—she spread out a bright blue, lace-trimmed negligee—"I'd got that new just before he was took, and he was ever so fond of it. 'You look just like a queen in that, Emmy,' he'd say. I've got a very white skin, you see, love, and he liked plenty of lace about my undies. 'You've no need to go covering yourself up, Emmy,' he'd say. 'Leave a bit of you showing through somewhere, anyway.'" She gave another discreet cough. "Of course, Bert wasn't as refined as what I am, but I never minded that. I mean, I always think it's the woman's job to be refined, and it doesn't matter so much about the man. . . . Don't you agree, dearie? Look, this chemise is pretty, isn't it? I'm ever so fond of ecru (she pronounced it eecru) lace. . . ."

Cicely watched her, stout, florid, forlorn, spreading out the meretricious mixtures of silk and lace that had embellished her in the eyes of the common little man who had loved her—and a lump started suddenly to her throat. She wanted to escape at once from the stuffy frowsty room and her own unbearable pity.

"I must go . . ." she said breathlessly.

"Yes, love," sighed Mrs. Kellogg. "I suppose it's time we both went to bed . . . though there seems little enough to go to bed for nowadays. . . . Still, one must just keep on keeping on. Bert was fond of saying that. Very cheery, Bert always was. 'Mustn't grumble,' he'd say. 'There's others worse off than we.' He was ever so amusing, too. He could sing comic songs a treat. Fit to make you split your sides with laughing. Some of them really weren't very refined, of course. Still, I never could help laughing. In some ways I wasn't *quite* as refined when Bert was alive as what I am now. I always think it's easier to be refined when you're feeling down in the mouth than when you're feeling perky, don't you, dearie? Yes, yes"—in answer to Cicely's movement towards the door—"I know it's time we both went to bed. I've so enjoyed this evening with you. It's cheered me up no end. . . ."

She went to the door and tried the key in the lock, shaking her head doubtfully.

"I never trust these locks," she said. "I wish there was a bolt on the inside. It's so easy to get skeleton keys and suchlike. I never feel really safe in a room where there isn't a bolt on the inside. Of course, this *seems* a very respectable place, but, as I said before, one never knows, and a woman can't be too careful."

Angela leant over the balusters, calling "Good night" to Ian, who was in the hall. She kept up an unnecessarily long and loud conversation, because she was just outside Brian Mallard's room, and she wanted him to come out and join her.

"Ian, pet, you don't know how funny your face looks upside down. Even funnier than the right way up."

He'd been so jolly this morning till just the end, and then he'd changed—quite suddenly. He *was* so nice when, he was jolly. . . .

"Don't insult me, wench," said Ian, striking an attitude in the hall below.

"I like the way your hair grows upside down. Like a cocoanut's top-knot."

All evening she had been hoping that he would come in to the dance. Perhaps she'd only imagined that he'd changed so suddenly this morning. . . .

"I'll start telling you what *you* look like in a minute," grinned Ian.

"Go on. Start," she challenged.

She didn't see how anything she'd said could possibly have

offended him. If he was still sniffy when she met him again, she'd ask him straight out what was the matter. The dance would have been much nicer if he'd been there. She'd have *made* him dance with her. . . .

A door behind opened, and she turned eagerly.

But it was only Miss Wingate, wearing a dressing-gown, with a shawl wrapped tightly round her head.

"I *wonder*," she said in her chill, clipped, precise tones, "if you'd be kind enough to go down to talk to whoever you're talking to. It would be so much less disturbing. I'm trying to go to sleep. . . ."

"Sorry," gasped Angela, as she turned to flee.

Inside his room Brian sat, his eyes fixed unseeingly on his Hebrew book, his mouth set tightly. He seemed to be fighting some actual physical force that was drawing him to the door to join her. Then suddenly he was saved by Miss Wingate.

"Damned old fool!" he muttered savagely to his Hebrew book.

There was silence now in the corridor outside. The temptation was over. He had not succumbed. But he did not feel that glow of happy victory that he expected and that he considered his due. He felt instead an utter desolation of loneliness, even a strange load of guilt, as if, instead of resisting temptation, he had been deliberately unkind, which, of course, was ridiculous. . . .

Life, he decided, with a sigh, was very complicated. . . .

Chapter Seventeen

CHRISTMAS EVE and Sunday. There was an air of quiet over everything—a sort of lull before the crescendo of Christmas Day. The women shed their brightly coloured country woollies and appeared in town-tailored clothes, the men in dark suits.

In the morning Judith had ordered the car to take her and Sidney to church.

"It's a lovely morning. Why not walk?" Sidney had said tentatively.

Judith glanced down at the Chanel dress of navy blue that she wore for the first time that morning. (When she saw it, Sidney had thought: Whatever colour you see Judith wear, you think it's just her colour and that she ought never to wear any other.)

"I'm not dressed for walking, darling. Besides it will keep Bennet up to the mark. I've used the car very little since we came here. It won't do him any harm to be on duty this morning. He can have this afternoon off. . . ."

A feeling of guilt swept over Sidney whenever Judith mentioned Bennet. Standing with him, laughing and talking, by the car on the common, driving with him through the sun-flecked lanes. . . . She felt bitterly ashamed of the memory. It had been the basest treachery to Judith. She avoided his eyes as she followed Judith into the car, and, as she took her place beside her, felt a sudden hysterical desire to confess the whole episode there and then. Judith would be furious, of course. She would dismiss Bennet at once, but that would perhaps be the best thing that could happen. Till Bennet had gone she couldn't be quite sure of herself or her loyalty to Judith.

"You aren't looking well, Sidney," said Judith suddenly. "Did you sleep all right?"

"Like a top," said Sidney with mechanical cheerfulness.

But she hadn't slept well. She hardly ever slept well nowadays. It was strange that when she had been at the school in Putney, overworked, bullied, and underfed, she had slept soundly and awakened refreshed each morning, but, now that she lived in luxury with Judith, her nights were uneasy and broken, tormented by dreams of Judith angry, Judith alienated, Judith speaking in that cold hard voice that hurt more than physical blows. Even when Judith had been kind all day those dreams troubled her at night.

The car had drawn up at the little Norman church.

"Be back for us at half-past twelve," said Judith to Bennet, speaking so curtly that Sidney could not resist throwing him a reassuring, faintly unhappy smile. His answering glance—it was hardly a smile—swept away all her vague fears and depression as if they were cobwebs, restored to her in a moment her youth and confidence. She followed Judith into church with a firmer tread, a more upright carriage.

Festoons of flowers and holly twined round the pillars and covered the little pulpit and font. On the wall the text "Unto us a Child is Born" had been pricked out crudely in holly berries on a background of cotton wool by unskilled loving fingers.

The strains of "While shepherds watched . . ." rang out loudly from the small organ. The congregation—mostly country people—sang with untrained heartiness. It was very different from the austere services in the convent chapel at Antwerp, yet something in the obvious sincerity and unaffected piety of it took her back to those days, and tears started suddenly to her eyes. Dismayed, she bent her head low over her hymn-book so that Judith should not notice. Lately she had begun to cry like this for no reason at all. Sometimes just a quick frown or an impatient tone from Judith would bring this hateful fluttering to her throat, these stinging tears to her eyes.

The service was over soon after quarter-past twelve.

Judith stood outside the church, tapping her foot impatiently, and looking up and down the road. At twenty-five-past twelve Bennet appeared, and the car drew up beside them.

"We've been waiting for nearly ten minutes," said Judith sharply. "I'd be glad if you'd try to be a little more punctual in future."

"I'm sorry, madam," he said, but he didn't look sorry. The dents at the corners of his long mouth looked rather grim, and there was a pugnacious gleam in his blue eyes.

Judith got into the car with tightened lips.

"*Insolent!*" she said angrily, when he had closed the door. "I shall tell the agency when I get back that he's thoroughly unsatisfactory."

"But, Judith, you said half-past," protested Sidney.

Judith waved aside the protest.

"He's the type of servant I detest more than any other," she went on, "the type that's managed to acquire a sort of veneer of his employers' speech and manners. He probably won a scholarship from some unspeakable board school to some still more unspeakable county school and considers himself the equal of anyone who employs him."

"But, Judith," protested Sidney again, "you did say half-past. You——"

She stopped. Judith's white skin had lost its transparency.

"Will you kindly not interfere in things that are not your concern," she said in a tone that sent the colour flaming into Sidney's cheeks and set her heart racing wildly.

Judith leant her head against the back of the car. Sharp, jagged pains were shooting through her temples, and the blind desire to hurt that always accompanied her headaches was strong upon her. Only a short time ago she would have vented this desire mercilessly upon her companion, but now—she'd somehow got the impression that she must go rather carefully with Sidney. Just for the present, at any rate. . . . She glanced at the girl's averted head.

"Darling," she said, "I'm hateful. I've got a beastly head, and you know it always makes me hateful. Say you forgive me."

She slipped an arm round Sidney, and Sidney leant back against the fragrant softness of her.

"Say you forgive me," she repeated.

"Of *course*, Judith."

But somehow the spell hadn't quite worked. It had roused all Sidney's love and loyalty as usual, but for the first time it hadn't quite conquered her pride. Her pride stood apart, urging, exhorting: Don't let her see how much you cared ... don't let her see how much she can hurt you.

She swallowed the lump in her throat and, fixing her eyes on Bennet's back, smiled stiffly.

"I'm so stupid, Judith. I always say the wrong thing, don't I?"

There was something wanting in the reconciliation. Even Judith felt that. The young form was relaxed against her shoulder, but in its very relaxation there was a hint of aloofness. The tearful apologies, the passionate protestations of devotion, were lacking.

Judith stared out of the window, frowning as another quick stab shot through her temples. She must keep Sidney away from her till this headache was over and while she was possessed of the devil it always brought with it. She'd take a stiff dose of her sleeping-draught and lie down till tea-time—no, till it was time to dress for dinner. She was generally her best in the evening. ...

"Darling," she said when they went up to her room after lunch, "I'm going to lie down and try to get rid of my headache. If I want tea I'll ring for it, but don't come in to me till about seven." She took Sidney's face between her long white hands and smiled down at it. "You don't quite hate me, do you?"

Now that there wasn't Bennet's curly head and strong square jaw to look at, the familiar spell conquered her wholly, conquered every bit of her, even her pride.

"You know I love you, Judith. You know I'll always love you. Nothing will ever make any difference."

"Sure?"

"Sure, sure, sure."

Judith opened a drawer and took out a square leather case.

"Look, I hadn't meant to give you this till to-morrow, but I can't wait. It's your Christmas present."

Sidney opened the case and held up the soft gleaming string.

"Pearls!" she gasped. "Oh, but Judith—they're lovely—they're *real*."

"Of course they're real, you little silly," smiled Judith. "Do you think I'd give you a string from Woolworth's?"

"But, Judith," the girl gasped, "they're—they must have cost——"

"If you like them that's all I want."

"I *love* them. I simply can't thank you——"

"Don't, then. Let me put them on for you."

She began to fasten them round the slender young neck. Sidney thought of her own present for Judith—a night-dress case that she had sat up every night for the last month to embroider in secret. Absurd, futile, beside this. She'd be ashamed to give it. Pearls ... little white shining links of a chain.

"There! Do you really like them?"

"Oh, *Judith*!"

It *was* a chain, of course. When one accepted an expensive present—the sort that one couldn't possibly give in return—one paid for it by a tiny bit of one's self. One had to. One belonged to oneself just a little less afterwards. One was just a little less free to think one's own thoughts, choose one's own actions.

Judith kissed her again, still smiling tenderly.

"Now don't say another word about it," she said. "You know I love giving you things."

There was a knock at the door, and a parlourmaid entered.

"Please, madam, the chauffeur wants to know if you'll need the car this afternoon and what time."

Judith set her lips, angry at the interruption.

"What a *fool* the man is! I said quite definitely he could have this afternoon off."

"You didn't tell him so, Judith," put in Sidney rather timidly. "You only said so to me."

"Oh well." She turned to the parlourmaid. "All right, you can go. You'd better tell him yourself, Sidney, and then I shall be sure of not being disturbed again. Good-bye, darling—and don't come back before seven. I shall have had a good sleep by then and be all freshened up. Good-bye, my sweet."

Sidney ran downstairs, an odd sense of escape at her heart.

The three Paynters, dressed for a walk, were just setting off from the front door as she reached it.

"We're a rescue party," said Ian. "We've rescued Cicely from the Kellogg hag. We're taking her off for the afternoon—what's left of her."

"Oh, *hush*!" said Cicely, laughing but looking anxiously round. "She might be somewhere near."

"Quick then or she'll be on you!" said Ian, and the three of them set off at a run, turning round to wave to Sidney at the bend in the drive.

She hurried on to the garage. As she approached it Bennet came out, holding a spanner in one hand and a grease rag in the other. He greeted her with his impudent grin.

"This is one of the tricks of the trade," he explained, "the first rule of chauffeurdom, in fact. As you sit in the garage reading your newspaper or detective novel, you always have a spanner and a grease rag ready to hand, and at the sound of your employer's footsteps you hastily snatch them up and sally forth to the garage door, wearing the expression of one disturbed in the middle of a vital piece of work on the car."

She tried to look dignified, then laughed.

"How silly you always are!" she said. "Miss Kimball sent me to say that you could have this afternoon off."

"I wanted to find out about that. That's why I sent the message. Have you got the afternoon off too, or are you on duty?"

She gave up finally the attempt at dignity.

"Judith's got a headache. She's lying down till this evening."

"I like the way your nose wrinkles up when you laugh," he said. "Like a rabbit. A rather nice rabbit."

She laughed again, then grew serious. She felt a half-ashamed compunction at the thought that Judith was going to give him a bad report at the agency. Perhaps she ought to warn him. She fingered the string of pearls round her neck nervously.

"W-would," she said with a sudden shy little stammer, "would it make a very great difference if Judith crabbed you to the people she got you from? She"—she sought for words to explain and excuse Judith—"she—takes rather sudden dislikes."

He smiled grimly.

"Well, this dislike's mutual if that's of any interest to her. No, as a matter of fact I don't think it would. I heard from an uncle last night, and he says that he may possibly be able to get me a job in a firm that belongs to a friend of his. A decent job in a decent firm with good prospects. Sorry to disappoint Miss Kimball, but I don't think it'll ruin my career permanently however many lies she tells about me."

"Oh, I'm *so* glad about the job, but"—her smile faded—"I wish you weren't so horrid about Judith. She's—not like that really. You don't understand."

"I understand all right. Better than you do probably." The grimness returned to his smile, but vanished as suddenly. "Never mind her. It's you I want to talk about. I was going to manage to see you by hook or by crook this afternoon. Tony Hatfield came here this morning. You remember him, don't you?"

"Yes, of course."

"He wanted us both to go over this afternoon to ride on the common with him and his sister."

She gasped.

"Oh, I *couldn't*."

"Why not? It's all right. His mother's expecting us."

"But—I've no things."

"He said his sister could lend you things. She's a jolly girl. I remember her. They aren't a bit sticky. You'll like them."

"Oh, I couldn't do it. You *know* I couldn't."

"Why not? Miss Kimball's made it all so gloriously simple. When you came along I was racking my brains, wondering how on earth I was going to arrange it, and now providence has arranged it for us. You can't throw a perfectly good gift of providence back in its face like that."

"What did you say to Tony?"

"I just said I'd do my best to fix it and I'd ring him up by three if I found I couldn't. Come on, Sidney, be a sport."

"Judith would be furious."

"Judith be damned!" he said impatiently. "She'll never find out. She can't kill you even if she does." He caught hold of her hand. "Come along, Sidney. Don't spoil the chance of a glorious day like this."

"It wouldn't spoil it," she said breathlessly. "You could go alone."

"I don't want to go alone. I might just as well not go if you won't go."

"I can't go. You know I can't."

"You mean you daren't."

She nodded.

"Don't be a little coward," he said. "I tell you, she'll never know."

"She might."

"Has she got you as cowed as all that?"

"She's not got me cowed at all," she flashed.

"Come to Tony's with me, then. Sidney, think of riding over the common on a day like this. What are you made of, child, that you don't thrill at the very thought?"

"Oh, I do."

"Think of it, *think* of it!"

She thought of it . . . riding over the moorland through the winter sunshine, with Dickie and Tony and Tony's sister, the springy turf beneath and the cold air whipping her cheeks. And suddenly all her fear dropped from her. She felt gloriously, irresponsibly young. She laughed aloud from sheer lightness of heart.

"Yes, I'll come. I'll just get my hat. I won't be two minutes."

It was his turn to be cautious.

"We can't set off together. Look here, we'll meet in the wood. Go through the park, then across the road to the field path that leads through the wood. I'll be in the wood."

"All right," she said. Her compunction gone, she was as eagerly excited as a child. "Let's hurry. It's too glorious an afternoon to miss a minute of."

She arrived at the wood panting a few minutes after him.

"I told you I wouldn't be long," she said triumphantly. "Which way is it? Tell me all about them quickly before we get there. What's Mrs. Hatfield like?"

He described the Hatfields and the holidays he had spent with them, and she laughed delightedly as he told her of the pranks that he and Tony had played in those days.

The sight of the house, however, slightly overawed her.

"Oh dear!" she said, drawing nearer to him. "It's rather terribly grand, isn't it?"

"*They* aren't a bit grand," he reassured her. "They're darlings."

Mrs. Hatfield came out into the hall to greet them and kissed Dickie affectionately.

"I remember you so well, dear," she said. "Tony's told me what you're doing, and I think it's splendid of you. Is this Miss Lattimer? How do you do, my dear? Sheila's going to lend you some riding things, isn't she? I'm afraid they'll be very shabby. She's such a tomboy. Now don't let these children tire you out. They're very rough."

Sheila was a solid girl of about sixteen, pleasant, unaffected, her round good-natured face tanned by the open-air life she so evidently led. She walked with a loose stride like a boy. Both she and Tony accepted Sidney quite simply as a friend of Dickie's. They showed little curiosity about, or even interest in, Chedsy Place. They lived completely in their own world and were anxious to show the visitors as much of it as possible in the short time their visit allowed. They took them to the stables and the kennels, where the brother and sister kept up a sort of duet, introducing the pets and relating their histories, and finally to the shabby old schoolroom, which was now their joint sitting-room, where Sheila offered them marzipan that tasted like soap, telling them proudly that she had made it herself.

Then she took Sidney to her bedroom—an austere schoolgirl's bedroom—and helped her to change into a rather battered pair of breeches and a washed-out sweater.

"They're falling to pieces, like everything else we've got," she laughed, "but I like shabby things, don't you? They're so friendly."

Downstairs the horses were ready for them, and they mounted

quickly and cantered down the drive, along the lane, and up onto the common.

"Whoopee!" shouted Dickie, galloping on ahead.

The others echoed "Whoopee!" and galloped after him.

It's heavenly, heavenly, heavenly, sang Sidney to herself. It's the loveliest thing that's ever happened to me. Her youth, starved and repressed for so long, surged up in a gay irresistible flood. She laughed exultantly as she raced the others over the springy turf.

"It *has* been fun," said Sheila, when they had returned and Sidney was slipping off sweater and breeches from her slender body, and putting on again her fawn jumper suit.

"It's gone too quickly," said Sidney regretfully. "It's hardly begun and now it's over."

"You'll come again, won't you?"

Something of Sidney's glow faded.

"I don't know whether I can. We're only here for a day or two, you know."

A tea of hot scones, Devonshire cookies, and home-made cakes, was waiting for them in the hall, where Mrs. Hatfield was just pouring boiling water into the teapot from a brass kettle. The hall was panelled in oak, and a log fire burned brightly in the open fireplace beneath the heavily carved overmantel. The furniture seemed to consist chiefly of shabby oak chests, littered with golf-clubs, hockey-sticks, and other sports implements. A spaniel sat on the rug in front of the fire, a red setter lay by the door, and Mrs. Hatfield's Pekinese lorded it disdainfully on the settee next its mistress. In a cage by the window was the identical parrot that the schoolboy Dickie had rescued, and Mrs. Hatfield persisted that she saw a light of recognition in its eye when she took Dickie up to it to be reintroduced.

It was a noisy hilarious tea-party, the two boys ragging Sheila and each other incessantly. Sidney watched and listened rather wistfully. It must be lovely to have a home like this, she thought. Dickie takes it all for granted, because he's had one. . . .

As soon as they had finished tea Mr. Hatfield entered—a thick-set figure with white hair and a ruddy weather-beaten face. He carried a gun, and two spaniels followed at his heels. He greeted the visitors heartily, apologised for his muddy gaiters, put his gun in a corner, and proceeded to eat an enormous tea. In the intervals of eating, he held forth on the ruin of agriculture and the impossibility of making an estate pay, but he looked all the time so full of health and cheerfulness that it was difficult to take his jeremiad seriously.

When finally Sidney and Dickie departed, the whole family stood at the door to see them off. Mrs. Hatfield kissed them both.

"Come again soon," she called after them. "We like young people."

They walked down the drive in silence. Sidney tried to retain the gay care-free mood of the afternoon's ride, but already it was fading, and a weight of heavy anxiety was beginning to drag at her heart.

"Dickie, I didn't say anything—I somehow couldn't explain—but they mustn't come to Chedsy Place. It would be dreadful if Judith found out about this afternoon. I oughtn't to have come."

"Why are you so frightened of her? I've asked you that before, haven't I?"

"It's not that. . . . It's—she's so good to me. . . . Look." She turned to him in the dusk and put her hand up to the string of pearls. "She gave me those to-day. . . ."

He examined them with a frown.

"Are they real?"

"Yes. They must have cost a tremendous lot. She's so generous."

"But she won't give you a salary. Surely you'd rather have a regular salary than take presents like this from her."

She set her lips and began to walk on quickly. "You don't understand."

He smiled.

"Try to explain to me then. Don't hurry so, anyway. We needn't be back till half-past six. Stop here a minute. I love the view over the valley from here. Even now when it's almost dark."

She stood by him, leaning against a field gate, gazing over the dusk-enshrouded valley.

"Sidney, I wish you'd leave her," he said suddenly.

She turned her head away and spoke unsteadily. "You don't

know anything about either her or me. You've only been with us for three days, and you'll only be with us two days more. I've told you what she's done for me, and if that means nothing to you I can't explain any more. I don't know why you should care anything about it in any case."

"Well, I do care, and I think you know why I care. She's killing you, for one thing. You're all nerves. You jump when she speaks to you. Your eyes look as if you never had a good night's rest. You're on the rack half the time. She's very clever at keeping people on the rack."

Through the trees in the valley she could see the chimneys of Chedsy Place. They seemed to bring Judith very near, and an intolerable sense of disloyalty swept over her.

"You know nothing about Judith," she said in a quick breathless voice.

"I probably know a good deal more than you do about women like Judith Kimball," he replied slowly. "They end in lunatic asylums, but they've time to do the hell of a lot of harm before they get there."

She shrank away from him. Suddenly the whole episode seemed shameful—taking advantage of Judith's headache to go off for the afternoon with her chauffeur. It was cheap, sordid, furtive.

"She's a she-devil," he went on.

"*Don't!*" she said hysterically, putting her fingers into her ears. "I won't listen to you. I wish I hadn't come."

He laid his hand on her arm reassuringly, but she shook it off, her breath coming in quick sobbing gasps. "Leave me alone. I never want to speak to you again."

Then she turned and ran down the road from him in the darkness.

Chapter Eighteen

THE drawing-room seemed fuller than usual at tea-time, as none of the guests had gone for expeditions. Even Miss Nettleton had taken advantage of the fact that it was Sunday to spend the afternoon lying on her bed. She had salved her conscience by reading a guide-book and reminding herself that during the morning service in church she had studied, as well as she could through their trappings of holly and ivy, the Early English pillars and the Norman font.

She was the first to invade the afternoon emptiness of the drawing-room, pausing, as she entered, calmly to straighten her wig in front of the mirror on the wall. After that she shut all the windows and settled down in front of the fire with her guidebooks.

Cummings next appeared, marshalling his forces for the serving of tea, and then the young Paynters burst in hilariously, appropriating their corner of the room.

"We'll have tea here," said Angela, "and you must sit here, Cicely, with your back to the room so that you can't possibly see anyone but me. And then, even if she comes in and wanders round looking for you, she won't be able to catch your eye. Get two more chairs for the parents, Ian. They'll be in any minute. They were just going upstairs as I came down."

After a few moments Mrs. Paynter entered and approached them with her faint apologetic smile.

"Darlings, don't wait tea for us. Daddy and I are going to have it in the library because he wants to write letters directly afterwards. Have you had a nice walk?"

"Awfully nice."

"Well, have a good tea," went on Mrs. Paynter, still hovering

174

apologetically over them, "and if they don't bring you enough to eat send for more."

"And more and more and more," said Ian, extending his eyes ravenously.

"Don't you worry, darling," said Angela. "We'll be all right. We'll behave very nicely and make Ian say his grace properly and wash his hands when he's finished."

Mrs. Paynter smiled again vaguely and left them.

"Thin," commented Ian, when she had gone. "Distinctly thin. What's to stop the old boy writing letters in here after tea? There are three writing-tables."

"Shut up, Ian," said Angela.

A footman placed a tray of tea on the table in front of them. Ian inspected it critically.

"We shall want more toast," he said, "more toast and more cake and more jam."

Brian Mallard sat with his aunt at the other side of the room. She was talking animatedly to Miss Nettleton, not because she found her a sympathetic listener, but because she was the only person near enough to be talked to. Miss Nettleton interrupted her occasionally to complain bitterly of the stuffiness of the room, forgetting apparently that it was she who had closed all the windows.

"I've been busy writing this afternoon," said Mrs. Stephenson-Pollitt, pushing the bands of towsled hair from over her eyes as she spoke.

"I thought you always went into quarantine in the afternoons," remarked Miss Nettleton.

"I retire into the silence if that's what you mean," said Mrs. Stephenson-Pollitt distantly.

"Oh yes," said Miss Nettleton, "I meant that. I'd just forgotten the word you used for it. . . . You could cut this air with a knife. Simply cut it with a knife."

"I've written nearly a whole chapter of my new book," continued Mrs. Stephenson-Pollitt.

"What's it about?" said Miss Nettleton, inspecting the plate of cakes with interest. "I hate seed cake, don't you?"

"It deals with reincarnation," said Mrs. Stephenson-Pollitt. "I mean, the two chief characters meet in various civilisations through history. I draw from memories of my own reincarnations, of course, supplemented by information I get from the British Museum. I'm not taking the story quite as far back as my own memories go." She fixed her dark piercing gaze upon Miss Nettleton, who, having finished her tea, was settling herself for a doze. "My first memory is of being a princess in Atlantis. . . ."

Brian Mallard edged further away from her. Everyone in the room could hear the old fool. What must people think of her? What must *she* think of her? He tried not to look at *her*. She was sitting in a corner, facing her sister and the room. He tried to fix his eyes where he could just see a blur of her without looking at her directly, but his eyes slid to hers, and they looked at each other for a second or two, then he turned away, his face flaming, and fixed his gaze upon Mrs. Osmond, who had propped up a knitting paper on the table in front of her and was engaged in the creation of a pea-green jumper. Glancing up, she was amazed to find the boy glaring at her ferociously. His face flamed afresh, and he moved his eyes to the cornice of the ceiling and kept them there resolutely.

Mrs. Standfield was talking to Mrs. Lewel, and as usual her husband sat next to her, listening to her voice, but not hearing anything she said. His eyes kept straying to the young Paynters, who were laughing together uproariously over their tea.

"How does anyone tell the difference between those twins?" he heard someone say near him, but, like Brian Mallard, he saw scarcely any resemblance between them. Cicely was like a pool of still water, clear, placid, serene. Angela was like running water, with her quick movements, brightly glancing blue eyes, and the tremulous smile that hovered always on her sensitive lips. It was Angela who brought back the ghost of Alice from the grave—the ghost of Alice and the ghost of himself, with his youth and enthusiasms fresh upon him. Cynical, disillusioned, beaten, he looked at the ghost. . . . He had meant to do so much. He could have done so much with Alice to help him. But instead he had sunk into a drowsy stupor of physical well-being, guarded and looked after by his wife, as if he were a child and she his nurse. The best of his physical and mental effort was now given to the cultivation of his garden, so far had he gone from the eager young visionary who had loved Alice. He stole another glance at the girl. She was watching Brian Mallard, and in her eyes was the same look he had once seen in Alice's. . . . So she loved the intolerable young prig. But perhaps he wouldn't be an intolerable young prig any longer if he learnt to love her.

His weary wistful eyes rested on the boy's face. Marry her, you young fool, he was saying. She's too good for you, but marry her. Your life will be sweet and gracious if you marry her. It will be barren and futile if you don't. . . .

Bella Torrance entered the room and looked idly round.

Everyone sat with their own parties except Mr. Ellison and Miss Wingate, who had drawn their chairs near each other so as to combine their lonely forces. The Downings had not come in yet. She lingered hesitating on the threshold. She could join Mr. Ellison and Miss Wingate again (there was an unoccupied chair at their table) or go and sit alone at the further end of the room. She hated being alone. She would rather be with anyone, however uncongenial, than alone.

She advanced to the table where Mr. Ellison and Miss Wingate sat.

"May I join you?" she said in her assured, rather defiant voice.

Mr. Ellison stood up with his old-fashioned courteous bow.

"Delighted," he said.

"*Do*," said Miss Wingate, relaxing her pursed mouth in welcome.

They were certainly nice people, decided Bella again dispassionately, as she took the unoccupied seat. If she was out for nice people she'd found them all right. Courteous, cultured, well-bred, and all the rest of it. Mr. Ellison wouldn't slip his arm round you and try to kiss you the minute he found himself alone in a room with you. Miss Wingate wouldn't pinch your man from you when you were down with 'flu. But, hell, weren't they dull! Or were they? Was it that she'd got Simon so on the brain that everyone who didn't remind her of him seemed dull? She set her lips. She'd come here to get over Simon, and she was jolly well going to. Thank heaven that Downing man wasn't in the room anyway.

"Tea, please," she said to the footman.

"Miss Wingate's a great botany expert," Mr. Ellison was saying. "I've just been asking her if she's found any fresh specimens of heath here, but, of course, it's not a very good time of the year for plant-hunting."

"Oh no, I'm not an expert at all," said Miss Wingate, looking rather embarrassed.

It was really too ridiculous that this stupid rumour about her botany expeditions had got round. It was all the fault of that wretched hair-tidy. This morning she'd had to walk for miles before she'd found an opportunity to bury her little parcel of combings without anyone's seeing her.

Bella leant back, watching the room. Gods, what a crew! That half-wit boy and his quarter-wit aunt. That dud clergyman and his unspeakable wife. That ghastly cross-word couple. She was knitting now, and he was proudly contemplating the cross-word puzzles they had solved that morning. Those Paynters, laughing together at some private joke. Thinking no end of themselves, no doubt, and never realising that other people would have been just as good as they were if they'd had their chances. She wished, after all, that Ralph Downing had been in the room. She wouldn't have given him any encouragement, not even by looking at him, but—just to know he was there would have taken away this deadly boredom that was like a physical ache. She tried to listen to what Mr. Ellison and Miss Wingate were saying.

"But surely," Mr. Ellison was saying, "there is no unchanging standard of beauty in art. A work of art that expresses and satisfies the best trend of opinion of the age is good, one that fails to do so is bad. And, of course, no work of art makes the same appeal to two different people. Association, subconscious memories, play their part. I suppose that no two people actually see the same thing when they look at a picture. . . ."

"On the contrary," said Miss Wingate, "I believe in an unchanging standard, a Platonic ideal."

Bella, who was in the act of stifling a yawn, stopped, arrested by the word Platonic. So they were going to talk about something interesting at last. Platonic meant a love affair that hadn't come off. "Quite Platonic," people said when they meant that there really wasn't anything in it. But the rest of their conversation failed to fulfil the promise of the word. It wandered off into incomprehensible terms such as *a priori, transcendental, metaphysical exposition*, and *postulate of empirical thought*. She released the stifled yawn.

"I'm afraid we're boring Miss Torrance," smiled Mr. Ellison.

"No, I'm loving it," drawled Bella. "Do go on. It's a subject I'm awfully interested in. I was thinking of it only this morning in bed."

Might as well do the thing in style if you did it at all.

Miss Wingate's clear, precise, clipped voice filled the room as if it were a lecture-hall. She was in fact delivering her favourite lecture on the Philosophers of the Eighteenth Century. And she was listening to herself in growing panic. Somehow she *had* to talk like that. She couldn't stop. Couldn't stop talking and couldn't stop talking like that. She hadn't got out of her rut, after all. She'd just brought her rut along with her. Stop it, stop it, she cried to herself frantically. But the voice refused to obey her. It went on and on and on. ...

Mrs. Kellogg entered the room, a package under her arm, looked about wistfully, and finally went up to the table where the Paynters sat. She wore a short dress of bright blue silk that revealed her thick ankles and fawn kid high-heeled shoes.

"I don't want to interrupt, love," she said to Cicely, "but you know you said you'd like to see those photos of Bert and I at Clacton, so I've brought them along."

"Oh, how kind of you!" said Cicely nervously. "Do sit down."

Ian rose with alacrity.

"Take my chair," he said. "I'm just going."

"So am I," said Angela.

Mrs. Kellogg sat down in Angela's chair.

"Thanks, love." She opened the packet. "Look, that was all of us at the boarding house. That's Bert in front on the bottom step and me just behind him. Of course, he doesn't look as nice-looking there as what he really was. The sun's in his eyes."

Angela hesitated a minute, then went across to Brian.

"I'm going to walk over to Hunton to-morrow afternoon," she said. "Would you like to come too?"

Taken by surprise, the prig fled, leaving the boy in complete possession.

"I'd love it," he said eagerly. "Thanks awfully."

"We'll start directly after lunch," she said, then went quickly from the room.

The prig returned to remonstrate indignantly with the boy. The boy defended himself hotly. Well, I ought to try to get to know her, to influence her for good, he said. One must try to help people. I only want to try to help her.

Robert Beaton entered the drawing-room and went over to the window, where he stood looking out onto the darkening terrace. He couldn't get over his feeling of indignation at the sight of these strangers sitting about in his home. He must have it out with Celia some time. She was so busy now, hurrying from one duty to another, that it was almost impossible to get a word with her. Of course he had let slip his opportunity. He should have said something definite the first night. He thought with desperate longing of his farm, its quiet, its calmness, its ordered simplicity. It had seemed the perfect setting for Celia, but he knew now that it had not been the perfect setting for her. She was far more at home and in her element directing and managing this place than she had ever been at the farm. He swerved away from the fear that was growing in his heart, the fear he dare not face or reckon with. He listened dully to the babble of conversation round him. Mrs. Osmond had discovered a misprint in her knitting instruction book.

"Such a *shame*," she was saying indignantly in her shrill voice. "I mean, you trust the directions absolutely. It's *scandalous*. It's thrown me *rows* wrong."

"My clearest memory," Mrs. Stephenson-Pollitt was saying, "is of being a priestess in Egypt. I can walk through the Egyptian section in the British Museum and simply *recognise* everything there."

Mrs. Kellogg's voice joined the chorus.

"And this is of me on the pier took by Bert. It was his favourite. 'The others don't do you justice, Emmy,' he used to say, 'but that one does. It brings out your charm.'"

"Well," Mrs. Standfield was saying, "the next time we went there the place had changed hands, and they were charging sixpence for a cup of tea. *Sixpence*. I told them straight out what I thought. I said——"

"Of course, Hegel followed Kant in maintaining a distinction between the world of appearance and the world of reality, but in his philosophy the word reality has a different meaning."

"Bert's favourite place was Margate. He didn't like wild places. I mean, places without piers and proms and that sort of thing."

"My memory of Rome under Nero is dimmer, but still quite clear."

"Stuffy simply isn't the word. You could cut it with a knife."

"I've a good mind to write to the editor. I mean, you naturally *trust* it when it's printed in black and white. I think it's a shame. *Rows* wrong, it's thrown me."

He made a movement of uncontrollable irritation and strode from the room. Bella Torrance's narrowed eyes followed him. Not her sort exactly, but not bad-looking and a decent figure. Quite nice if you liked that sort. She pretended that she liked that sort and imagined his arms about her, his freckled face bent down, his lips pressed upon hers. Then she pulled herself up sharply. Nice girls didn't think of things like that when they looked at men. What the hell *did* they think of, then, she asked herself despairingly.

He went out into the hall. Celia was crossing it, a pile of toilet linen on her arm. She smiled at him.

"Hello, my sweet. Be an angel and tell someone to bring in some more logs from the stable."

She blew him a kiss with her free hand and passed on.

He went out by the front door. A girl was coming in almost at a run. She was breathing fast, her cheeks were flushed, and she looked as if she had been crying. She ran past him and up the stairs. He glanced after her, puzzled. She was one of the girls who were staying there, of course. He'd seen her before, but had forgotten who she was. He went to the stables, gave orders for logs to be sent up to the house, then worked for some time at the sawing-horse. The exercise relieved the hot anger he still felt at the thought of the horde of aliens who were in possession of his home. On his way back to the house he glanced in at the garage. The good-looking young chauffeur with the blunt nose, blue eyes, and long impudent mouth, was polishing the bonnet of his car. He was polishing it with a sort of restrained fury, as if he too were working off his feelings.

He looked up, and Robert saw that the laughter was gone from his eyes and that the long mouth was grimly set.

"Nice evening," said Robert pleasantly.

"Yes, sir," said the boy, and returned to his work.

Celia knocked at Mrs. Fielden's door and, receiving no answer, went in with her armful of toilet linen. Mrs. Fielden was lying on the bed sobbing.

"Oh, I'm sorry," gasped Celia. "I was just bringing you a clean face-towel."

Mrs. Fielden arose, mopped her eyes, and straightened her disordered hair.

"Don't go," she said unsteadily. "Do come in. I'm all right. There isn't anything the matter. I—it's just that—sometimes I feel I can't go on with it."

"I'm so sorry," repeated Celia. To herself she was saying: Bother her, bother her, bother her! I can't stay here and listen to her troubles. I'm busy.

"He's so selfish," went on Mrs. Fielden. Her voice broke suddenly, and she began to cry again.

Celia sat down and put an arm about her.

"You're just tired," she said in mechanical comfort.

"I'm always tired. I get so sick of reading to him and waiting on him and going about with him. I have to help him all the time, and he isn't even grateful. I wouldn't mind if he was grateful. He takes it all for granted. He doesn't even pretend to love me."

"Do you love him?" said Celia curiously.

"I used to. I don't now. I can't. How can you love a person who doesn't even pretend to love you?"

"He's had a very hard time, you know."

"So have I. I've done my duty by him. I never have a minute to myself. He's gone out for a run now, but he'd be furious if I wasn't waiting for him when he came back, and yet he hates me because he needs me to be waiting for him. Oh, I'm so sick of it all. I wish I'd never married him."

"Why did you marry him, then?"

"I thought it was going to be so different."

"Why don't you leave him if you feel like this?"

"I can't. I haven't any money. I couldn't get any work. I'm too old. I'm—older than I look. No, it's just got to go on till one of us dies. Please forgive me for talking in this way. . . . It's just—day after day. I can't explain. I get so *tired* of it. I didn't know it was going to be like this. I thought it was all going to be so different. . . ."

She went to the looking-glass, combed back her dyed hair, and powdered her yellow sagging cheeks.

"He's coming," she whispered.

The door opened, and the massive figure with the set grim face appeared on the threshold.

"Oh, there you are," said Mrs. Fielden in her plaintive voice.

Celia slipped out.

Sidney went to her room and sat down till she had stopped trembling. Then she washed her face and tidied her hair, studying her reflection in the glass. Judith mustn't guess that she had been crying. She didn't know how she was going to face Judith with this terrible weight of guilt at her heart. She must have been mad. Once more the impulse came to her to confess, but she seemed to see the clear white skin turn opaque, the hazel eyes green, the lovely mouth settle into a thin cruel line, and trembling seized her afresh. No, she daren't tell Judith—but she'd never speak to him or look at him again. After all, there were only two more days. She wished they were over and she and Judith safely back in London, certain of never seeing him again. She powdered her face carefully to hide all traces of her tears, then, after standing motionless in the middle of the room for a few moments as if to brace up her courage, went to knock at Judith's door.

"Come in."

The voice reassured her. It was without the faint edginess that always betrayed a "mood."

She opened the door, entered, and closed it quickly behind her. Judith had changed and was sitting in the armchair by the fire, smoking a cigarette and reading a novel.

As she raised her head and smiled at Sidney, she looked so beautiful that the girl caught her breath.

"There you are, darling," said Judith. "Come and talk to me and tell me all you've done."

Sidney approached her slowly.

"How's your headache?"

"Quite gone. I'm my nice self."

She moved the black lace draperies of her dress from the floor at her feet.

"Come and sit down."

She was in that rare mood of languorous serenity that sometimes possessed her when she awoke from a drugged sleep.

"I woke up soon after five and had tea up here. I'd have sent for you, childie, but I thought I might as well dress first."

There was a laughing apology in her voice. She had imagined Sidney hanging about disconsolately downstairs, longing to be summoned to her, not daring to come before the appointed time.

"Why are you staring at me like that, you funny child?"

"You're so beautiful."

Judith's eyes still smiled in tender amusement.

"You sound as if you'd only just noticed it. . . . Come and tell me what you've been doing. Did you go out this afternoon?"

Sidney sank down on the hearth-rug, turning to the fire so that Judith should not see her face.

"Yes. . . ."

She had had tea in a lovely, shabby, oak-panelled hall with a crowd of merry young people, laughing and chaffing each other. But only in a dream. . . .

Judith leant down and fingered the slender chain of pearls around Sidney's neck.

"They suit you, darling. What are you going to put on to-night?"

"I don't know. There's nothing happening after dinner, is there?"

"No. Only a Sabbath calm and carol singers. The village choir, probably—hearty and unmelodious. But you must wear something nice, because you're all I've got to look at across the table. Put on your blue dress."

"Oh, Judith, isn't it too grand for just a Sunday night?"

"No. I love you in it, anyway. It's—just you. The minute I set eyes on it, I said to myself, 'That's Sidney,' and I knew I'd have no peace till I'd seen you in it. I couldn't have endured the thought of anyone else in the world having that dress."

"Oh, but you shouldn't have paid so much for it," said Sidney.

There was a faintly unhappy note of remonstrance in her voice. She had been amazed and aghast when she had heard how much Judith had paid for the dress. It was of filmy powder-blue chiffon with long sleeves and a long full-gathered skirt trimmed with tiny flounces.

"It was so like you, darling," went on Judith. "Shy and demure and young and rather sweet. It looked at me and said, 'I'm Sidney, Judith. Don't you recognise me?'"

"Oh, darling," Sidney laughed, but there was an unsteady note in her laughter.

After a few moments she spoke again jerkily, her face still turned away.

"Judith. . . ."

"Yes?"

"Judith, I—it's hard to say it properly—you've been so awfully good to me, but—I hate you buying me expensive things."

"And I love buying you expensive things," said Judith with her low sweet laugh.

"But—I mean—I'd honestly rather you'd—pay me a sort of salary for my work—and I'd—just buy the things I could afford with it."

Judith's good-humour was impregnable to-night.

"What sort of a salary?" she smiled.

"The sort of salary a secretary like me would get ordinarily."

"Have you any idea what salary a secretary like you would get ordinarily?"

"No—but I'd like to—manage on it. I could, Judith. Honestly—I'd rather."

Judith bent down and dropped a kiss on her hair.

"Darling, how I'd hate you in Oxford Street clothes!"

"Judith, do try to understand. You've done so much for me. It makes me feel—I can't explain. And I can do so little back for you."

"You do everything for me by just being yourself."

"That's different. I—you see, you've given me these pearls for Christmas, and all I've got you is a wretched little nightdress-case."

"So that's the trouble, is it?" smiled Judith. "I'll adore it. You know I will."

Sidney bit her lip. Somehow Judith seemed able to reduce everything to personalities. She thought now that Sidney was merely piqued because she could not give her an expensive Christmas present.

She made another attempt to explain.

"It's not—only that. It's—oh, I just want to have the money I *earn* and no more."

"Does it want a little more pocket-money, then?" teased Judith affectionately. "How much money have you got, poppet?"

"I haven't got any," said Sidney, "but it's not that. It's——"

Judith reached out a careless arm for a small bead bag, took a ten-shilling note from it, and dropped it into Sidney's lap.

"There's its Saturday penny," she said, still smiling.

Sidney's cheeks flamed. She hesitated, then put the note into the pocket of her jumper suit. Judith was evidently determined not to pay her a salary. She would buy her expensive things and give her a few shillings occasionally as a treat, not very often because she didn't want her to be too independent, but she wouldn't give her a salary or a regular allowance. Suddenly Judith leant forward and laid her cheek on Sidney's hair, slipping her hands down the girl's thin arms.

"Don't be ungenerous, Sidney," she whispered. "Don't grudge me the pleasure of giving you things. You know how I love it. You know you're all I've got."

The deep caressing note in her voice broke down Sidney's last defences.

She leant her head back against Judith's slender knees.

"Oh, Judith," she said, "I didn't mean—I'm sorry. You're so *good* to me. . . ."

Chapter Nineteen

THE long mahogany table was gay with flowers and holly and pyramids of crackers.

Robert sat at the head, Celia at the foot, the guests between them.

Dim portraits of freckled, red-headed men gazed down upon the scene from the walls. It filled Celia with pride to watch Robert sitting there at the head of the table beneath the portraits of his ancestors. She could not know, of course, that Robert himself felt, not pride, but a deep shame, that in three days she had destroyed for ever the glamour that had sweetened his childhood, youth, and later years. He fulfilled his duties as host, however, meticulously, entertaining his guests with his shy, half-indolent courtesy. Most of them looked with a new interest at the quiet, red-haired master of the house who had kept so much in the background till now.

At first the atmosphere was one of constraint. The diners, ousted from their small island tables and planted down at the vast mainland of mahogany, felt somewhat self-conscious, but gradually the barriers were broken down, and the conversation became general and lively.

Mrs. Fielden looked unusually serene, and there was a slightly relaxed look about her husband's grim mouth. Since tea she had been reading Jorrocks aloud to him in their bedroom, and both of them had laughed till they could hardly speak. The spirit of comradeship this had engendered still lingered with them, forming one of those periodic truces that marked their strange secret warfare.

Angela Paynter's bright glancing eyes were soft and radiant, her lips curved into a dreamy smile. She and Brian had been for a walk that afternoon, a long free tramp over the common, and the memory of it filled her even now with a soaring happiness that made her want to get up from her seat and dance round the table. She looked at him. ... He was sitting between his aunt and Miss Nettleton, wearing that aggressive scowl that was his defence against life in general and his aunt in particular. Only a few hours ago they had been drinking mugs of cider on a bench outside a little country pub, laughing at the antics of a puppy who was worrying a stone in the road.

"I'm dying of thirst," she had said. "Let's call here and have a drink. Isn't it a darling little place? Cider. We must have cider here. Cider in mugs."

He had grown serious for a moment.

"Oh, we'd better not. ..."

She had taken him by the hand and tried to pull him with her.

"Come along, you stupid ... of course you must."

He had laughingly resisted her attempts to pull him in. They had scuffled like a pair of children in the road. Then she had broken loose and run into the little inn, pursued by him. Everything had been gloriously silly and ridiculous. They had taken a short cut home through a churchyard and she had read out on a tombstone the legend:

> Our auntie has left us, our tears they fast flow,
> And we long for the beautiful land she's gone to.

Gusts of laughter shook them at the memory all the way home.

When they parted he had promised to come down to dance with her to-night.

"But you'll hate it," he had protested. "I'm a rotten dancer. I am, honestly. I've never been able to dance."

"You'll be able to dance with me," she assured him. "You will come, won't you?"

"Of course I will."

She tried to catch his eye now, but his dreadful aunt, who wore a dress of white velvet embroidered in green, with a green girdle at the waist, kept leaning across the table to talk to Miss Nettleton.

Mrs. Kellogg, too, had got herself up gallantly for the occasion, in a yellow satin dress, elaborately made and fitting closely to her ample figure. Several pearl necklaces and a paste brooch as big as a turnip glittered on her bosom. Enormous earrings swung on either side of her highly coloured, heavily powdered face. She was looking round the room and thinking: Bert would be proper proud if he saw me now in a swell place like this and dressed as nice as any of them.

She was torn between a desire to appreciate to the full the good things that lay before her, and a feeling that her thoughts ought to be set solely on the fact that this time last year she had had Bert with her.

Oh well, she said to herself at last, Bert always used to say that if you've paid for a thing you ought to try to enjoy it. He never liked to see good money wasted, didn't Bert.

Reassured by this reflection, she surrendered herself to the enjoyment of the excellent boiled turbot and lobster sauce. When she had finished it she bent forward in order to exchange greetings with Cicely Paynter further down the table. But Cicely was looking the other way.

"I'd like to have been with the infant to-day," her father had just said to her mother. "Its reactions to Christmas must have been rather attractive. . . ."

"I know," her mother had said with a little sigh. "I've been wanting it all day, too."

And Cicely was trying not to think: You haven't wanted us.

Bella Torrance was drinking her third glass of wine, and as always, when she had been drinking wine, there came over her a warm, happy conviction that everything was going to be all right; more than that, that something wonderful was going to happen to her. She seemed to be floating away on a radiant tide to some distant but attainable goal of happiness. She didn't know why she had let herself get so depressed and worried. Everything was going to be all right. . . . Everything was going to be quite all right. . . .

Mr. Fielden and Mr. Ellison were discussing the situation in the Far East. Mr. Fielden spoke vehemently and wore his most grimly fighting expression. He was evidently excellently informed on every aspect of the question. A casual listener would have gathered that it was a subject in which he was deeply interested, but he was, in fact, totally uninterested in it. It was merely News of the Day—one of the weapons he used in his struggle against his handicap. His blind eyes seemed to gleam triumphantly behind the blue glasses as he confuted the other man's arguments, referring to facts he was ignorant of or had forgotten.

By the time dessert was reached the barriers had completely broken down, and the gathering had become a large family party. Mrs. Nightingale emphasised this aspect of it by addressing her neighbours affectionately and familiarly by Christian names that did not belong to them.

"You cheeky boy!" she said delightedly to Ian Paynter. "Calling your old granny Mrs. Nightingale!"

When the guests had drunk the health of the King and of Mr. and Mrs. Beaton, Mrs. Nightingale rose and solemnly proposed the health of "Dear Charlie and Kitty in foreign lands, who I am sure are with us in spirit this day."

The whole table rose to drink the toast, and Mrs. Lewel explained in a whisper that Charlie and Kitty had gone out to Australia in 1892 and had both died more than twenty years ago.

The band in the billiard room struck up as soon as the first few couples drifted in. Again a number of people had come in from the neighbourhood for the dance. Philip Grant, who had fished in vain for an invitation to dinner, had arrived immediately afterwards and had at once attached himself to Bella Torrance. He had decided quite suddenly to marry, and to marry a young girl. He couldn't hide from himself any longer the fact that his youth had slipped away, and he dreaded old age with an odd sick terror that he could not have explained. He had a firm if illogical conviction that a young wife would restore his youth to him. Not, of course, any of the girls who had grown up around him, girls whose mothers had danced with him in their girlhood, and who therefore would never believe that he was still young, that actual years had nothing to do with it. . . .

He held Bella's soft firm body closely to him as they danced.

"It's luck," he said, "terrific luck for me meeting you like this. . . ."

"Do you think so?" she said in her slow indifferent voice.

She was passing Ralph Downing, who sat with his wife and sister. She passed him with downcast eyes and faintly smiling lips.

Mr. Ellison was smoking a cigar and lazily watching the room. A handful of almost painfully ordinary people taking part in a decorous Christmas party, but probably a dozen secret dramas were enacting themselves among them, if only one knew. Once he would have been desperately interested in them all, trying to probe beneath the surface, to separate these people's real selves from the selves they showed to the world, but now he didn't care. He was old and tired.

Mrs. Lewel came in and took the empty seat beside him.

"I've just been putting mother to bed," she said.

"I hope she hasn't found it all too much for her," he said in his pleasant, courteous voice.

"No. . . . She's loved it. She's very happy, you know. People are so sorry for her. They say it's so sad. But it isn't. It's the only happiness left to most of us—to forget. . . . I wonder why Christmas makes one's memories so unbearable. . . ."

He nodded.

"I know."

She was silent for a few moments, then said in a quiet unemotional tone:

"You see, I hurt the man I loved very terribly and unjustly, and I never saw him again. He was killed in the war."

He nodded again as if he understood.

"It was my husband," she went on. "I was jealous, and we had a very bitter quarrel, and he went back to the front without seeing me again or saying good-bye. And then he was killed. Before he'd had time to write. While he was still angry. And the worst of it was that I knew in my heart all the time that I'd no reason to be jealous."

"Yes," he said slowly. "That's the way it so often happens."

"And to go on for the rest of one's life, remembering, remembering. Sometimes it seems more than I can bear."

"Time helps," he said. "In the end one wins through to forgetfulness."

She glanced at him.

"Have you won through to forgetfulness?"

"I think so."

But he hadn't. Already the ghost of a Christmas twenty years ago was stealing back from the past to torment him. He sat for a moment, his fingers tightly clenched, then rose with an abrupt movement and went out by the French window.

The brightly lit dance-room was a festive sight now. The dancers wore their paper hats, streamers were thrown, balloons released. Ian Paynter had come down in a jumper suit of Cicely's and had constituted himself the comedian of the evening, coyly accepting partners among the men, pretending to flirt with them, dancing with exaggeratedly mincing steps.

Brian Mallard entered and stood in the doorway, awkward, coltish, wearing his aggressive scowl.

Angela Paynter came up to him. She looked very lovely and ethereal in her dress of white flounced tulle.

"How late you are!" she said. "Isn't Ian a priceless ass? I'm engaged to Cousin Philip for this one, but I'll cut him. Come along. . . ."

He slipped an arm round her waist. To touch her slender body like this made him feel almost dizzy.

"Why, you dance quite well," she said.

"I don't," he stammered.

He wanted to tell her that she was the most beautiful thing he had ever seen in his life, that he loved her with all his heart and soul and mind and body. Her loveliness and sweetness had put the prig completely to flight. All evening he had been wrestling with the prig, holding the door of his mind shut against him, but hearing him battering on it outside. He knew exactly what the prig wanted to say to him. He knew that the prig was furious about this afternoon. . . . Sitting in a public-house, drinking with a woman (the prig always referred to the girl as a woman), behaving with unseemly levity and frivolity in a public highway, laughing at sacred subjects such as verses on tombstones. . . . But that light in Angela's blue eyes extinguished the prig completely. How beautifully she danced! How sweet, how dear she was!

"No one could help dancing well with you," he said, and added hastily, "I don't mean I'm not dancing rottenly, but—you—you dance adorably."

His young cheeks flamed in sudden embarrassment at his daring.

"Silly boy!" she laughed happily.

The dance music came to an end.

"I'm so hot," she said. "Let's go out, shall we? It's quite a warm night."

They slipped out onto the terrace. Light from the long windows cut across the darkness at intervals, leaving black squares between. They slid into one of the black squares and stood close together, leaning over the stone balustrade, looking at the violet sky.

"Isn't it lovely?" she said, then suddenly found herself in his arms. He held her closely to him, pressing his lips upon the yielding softness of hers. She clung to him, their bodies strained together in the darkness.

Then he threw her from him abruptly, his face white and set.

"What's the matter?" she gasped.

"I'm a beast," he said, "a *beast*!"

"What do you mean?"

"I wanted to keep clear of this sort of thing, and—I'm only a beast, after all."

"A beast. . ." she repeated slowly. Her face was as white as his. "What do you mean by 'this sort of thing'?"

It was the prig who looked at her out of his eyes, looked at her with loathing and disgust.

"I mean you."

She shrank back.

"*Oh!*" she breathed.

He swung on his heel and left her.

She stood there, staring into space, her eyes blank. She knew what he meant by "this sort of thing." He meant beastliness, sin, sordid intrigue. And it was with that he classed the love she brought him, the love that was clear and innocent and unsullied, the love that had upon it all the dew and freshness of her own bright youth.

At the knowledge, shame swept over her like a flood, engulfing her whole body in wave upon wave of fire. The look of sick disgust he had given her seemed to sully and besmirch her so that she would never be clean again. She put her hands to her face and began to run down the terrace, as if to escape from it. Slender, light-footed, her white tulle floating out behind her, she looked like a ghost flitting through the darkness. She stumbled suddenly and would have fallen if a man, standing by the balustrade, had not put out his hand to steady her.

She looked up at him with a little gasp.

"Oh ... it's Mr. Ellison."

"Yes ... where are you running off to?"

She gave a strangled sob.

"I'm so unhappy. ... I can't bear it," she said.

He put a hand on her shoulder.

"*'On n'est jamais si malheureux qu'on s'imagine,'*" he quoted dreamily, as if speaking more to himself than her.

"That doesn't help ... that doesn't help," she wailed, and broke from him to run back into the house. ...

"Let's sit this out, shall we?" said Philip Grant. Bella Torrance gave a slight nod of assent and went with him across the hall to the empty library. There he took his seat near her—but not too near her—on the large leather sofa.

"A cigarette?"

"Thanks."

As he lit it she saw the admiration in his eyes—the respectful, protective admiration that a man of his type gives to the woman he wishes to marry. Well, this was what she'd wanted. Or, rather, this was what she'd thought she wanted. But suddenly she knew that she didn't. Simon had spoilt her for it. She didn't belong here. She didn't belong anywhere. ... She'd just go on drifting. Simon.

... She imagined herself returning home after this visit and finding a letter from him saying that he had discovered he did not love his wife and asking her to go to him. His wife would divorce him and they could be married. . . . Her heart began to beat unevenly.

"I'm a very lonely man," Philip Grant was saying. "Since my mother died this spring the house has seemed very empty. . . ."

It was as good as a proposal. It was, at any rate, the definite promise of a proposal. Here's your chance, something prudent cried out in her. Take it before it's too late. Here's your chance of money, safety, a home, a husband, and children. It may never come again. But all she could think of was last Christmas and Simon kissing her under every sprig of mistletoe in the studio. She shivered suddenly, feeling the ghosts of Simon's kisses on her lips.

"You're cold," said the man beside her.

"No, I'm not."

"Sure?"

"Quite."

"I'd so much like to see more of you. I wonder if we could meet sometimes in Town. . . ."

Listen to him, screamed that prudent something in her. Don't think of Simon. Think of what he's saying. *Think* of it. . . . She tried to think of it, but somehow she couldn't think of anything but Simon. . . .

She shrugged.

"Oh, I don't know," she said vaguely. "I'm generally pretty full up."

His thin face flushed. It was a rebuff, and she knew that such men do not take rebuffs easily. He would not risk a second one. Fool, fool, fool, cried her prudent self. But it's not too late. Say something nice to him. Flatter him. Men like that are so easy to flatter. . . .

But she couldn't. Last Christmas, after their friends had gone, Simon had carried her into the bedroom and undressed her, kneeling down on the floor to take off her shoes and stockings, holding her bare feet to his heart and kissing them. His moods of tenderness had been so rare that the memory of each one was precious.

The man beside her stirred restlessly. This girl had wounded his self-esteem, and he wanted to get away from her as quickly as possible.

"Well, the music's begun again," he said.

She rose languidly.

"I suppose we'd better go back."

She walked with him in silence across the hall to the dance-room. Ralph Downing was waiting for her in the doorway.

"This is ours, isn't it?" he said.

The other man bowed and left her. She danced without speaking, her eyes downcast, not daring to look up to meet the smile that was so like Simon's. Simon kissing her feet ... a year ago to-day. ... Her lips tightened into a tense line.

"Don't look so sad," he said.

"Enough to make anyone look sad, the way you're holding me," she bandied mechanically. "I can hardly breathe."

He laughed, but did not relax his hold. His wife's expressionless eyes followed them round and round the room. The music died away, and they went into the hall, standing by the great log fire.

"I like these fires," she said idly. "They're too hot, but they look so cheerful."

A girl in white ran across the hall and plunged up the stairs, colliding with another girl who was coming down, wearing a fur coat over her evening dress.

The girl in the fur coat looked back.

"That was Miss Paynter, wasn't it?" she said, joining them before the fire. "I wonder if anything's the matter."

"They're probably playing hide-and-seek or blindman's-buff," said Miss Torrance contemptuously. "They're a set of noisy kids. ... Seem to think the place is a kindergarten. ... You going out, Miss Lattimer?"

"Yes," said Sidney, dismissing the memory of that white anguished child's face and horror-filled blue eyes.

"Yes—I—" she broke off as if embarrassed, then went on jerkily, "the house is—so hot. ... I thought I'd like a walk," and hurried out of the front door.

"Come into the library," pleaded the man when she had gone. "There's no one there."

"No. ... I'm tired and I'm bored," said Miss Torrance. "I'm going to bed."

"Your bedroom's on the same floor as mine, isn't it?"

She raised her indolent eyes to him and drawled:

"What the hell does it matter to you where my bedroom is?"

He laughed.

"I might want to come in and kiss you goodnight."

"Try it," she said. "You'll find the door locked."

Their eyes met, and they looked at each other in silence for a few moments. Then hers slid away.

He knew that he would not find the door locked.

Sidney ran into the garage where Dick Bennet was waiting for her.

"I got your note," she whispered breathlessly. "I can only stay a second. Judith thinks I've gone to my own room to pack. What is it?"

"I had to see you," he said, speaking in a quick urgent voice. "I heard to-day from my uncle. He's definitely got me that job. I'm to start next week. ... Sidney ... Sidney, I love you so. I——"

She was in his arms, clinging to him while he kissed her eyes and lips and cold white cheeks.

"Sidney, you do love me?"

"Oh yes, yes, yes!"

From the first moment she saw him she had been fighting against her love for him. Yesterday she had made her final desperate effort. Now she surrendered. ...

"I loved you all the time. ..."

"You're crying, Sidney."

"Only because I love you so."

"Sidney, I want to take you away with me. Now. To my mother. Then we'll be married as soon as it can be fixed up. I'm—frightened for you as long as you're with that woman. She'll never let you go."

"Judith? Of course she will. She'll have to."

"Come away with me, Sidney. Let's elope in her damned car. Now. This minute. You trust me, don't you?"

"Of course. But—Dickie, be sensible. We couldn't go to-night." He sighed.

"I suppose we couldn't, blast it! But—come with me to-morrow. Don't tell her. Just come. Let's go off together directly after breakfast."

"Dickie, I can't go like that. It would be—cruel. I must tell Judith. I'll explain everything to her. She may be a bit annoyed at first, because I've deceived her, but—she'll get over it. Dickie, after all she's done for me, I can't—just run away from her. It would be hateful."

He held her face in his hands and looked down at it.

"I wish you'd believe me. It may seem cruel and unfair, but it's the only way. Once she knows—it's all over. I shall never get you. She'll stop it somehow. She'll stoop to any vile trick to keep you. . . ."

"Oh, but why *should* she?"

"You don't realise what you're up against, Sidney. I've only known her for three days, but I've got her sized up all right. You haven't. . . . You keep talking about what she's done for you. Don't you see that that's the way she's trying to get you? She's—*buying* you. . . . She wants to feed on your youth. And she loves hurting you. She was one of those children who like to tear the wings off butterflies, to watch them quiver and slowly die."

"Oh, *Dickie*!" she breathed. "How you misjudge her! I'd be furious with you if I didn't love you so much that I can't be."

He took her in his arms again.

"Sidney," he pleaded, "do this for me. Come away with me to-morrow without telling her. Just trust me. Believe me, that it's the only way. Once you tell her—it's all over. She's too damnably clever for us. She wants you too desperately. She's a witch, a vampire. She's slowly killing you." He looked at the smooth white throat. "There ought to be a tiny red mark here where she sucks your blood." He pressed his lips into the small, rounded hollow under her chin. "Oh, darling, how sweet you are! How I love you! I can't give you up. Promise me that you'll come with me to-morrow and not tell her. All our happiness hangs on it. If only you'd understand. . . ."

She pushed her face away gently, half laughing, half serious, holding it between her hands.

"Dickie, don't be such a darling idiot. Don't you see that I can't start my life with you by doing a thing like that? I'd feel mean and hateful and ungrateful always afterwards. It would spoil everything. You've got a sort of obsession about Judith. She's nervy, I know, but she's sweet and kind at the bottom, and she only wants my happiness. She's often told me so. It would be the cruellest thing in the world to run away from her like that after all she's done for me."

"If you say 'after all she's done for me' once more, I'll strangle you."

"Idiot!" she laughed. "But, seriously, darling, I will tell her to-morrow morning. I can't to-night. She's just a little tired, and her headache's beginning to come back. But I *will* tell her to-morrow morning."

"And then come straight away with me? Let me take you to my mother?"

"Oh, *Dickie*, how absurd you are! Why on earth do I love you so? Listen, darling. . . . If she's nice about it, of course I can't go to your mother's except for an ordinary visit. It would be too ridiculous for words. If she's nice about it, and wants me to be married from her house, of course I must be. . . . I want to be. No, I'm not going to say it again, but, Dickie, she *has* been so generous to me. . . . And I must go now. I've stayed longer than I ought to have done. Good night, darling."

He took her in his arms and looked down at her, his face serious.

"Sidney, my sweet—just this last time—won't you promise to come away with me?"

She shook her head.

"I've tried to explain, Dickie. I tell you, I can't start my life with you by doing something mean. Oh, my darling, don't be so unreasonable. And, good night, good night, good night."

Cicely Paynter had found her sister outstretched on her bed sobbing desolately. She sat now holding the slender form protectively in her arms, rocking it to and fro soothingly as she would have done a child. The golden hair was disordered, the blue eyes red rimmed, the soft tulle flounces creased and tumbled.

"Thanks for being so sweet to me, Cicely," said Angela unsteadily, as she wiped the tears from her flushed cheeks. "I'm all right now. ... I'm sorry I've been such a fool. ..."

"Darling ... but if he's like that, you know, Angel, he must be hateful."

"He *is* like that, but he isn't hateful, somehow. And I love him."

"He's been a pig to you, darling."

"I know. That's the funny part of it. ... I still can't help loving him. He's all the things you say he is, but—somehow he's nice in spite of it, and—well, I love him. I love every little thing about him. Even the way he wriggles his foot about when he's sitting down with his legs crossed. So it's no use talking about it any more."

"We're going home to-morrow, darling, and you'll soon forget."

"No, I shan't. I shall never forget ... but I don't want to worry you. You've been awfully sweet. Listen, they're playing 'God Save the King.' It's the end of the dance. ... Let's go to bed, shall we?"

Ian knocked at the door and burst in, still dressed in Cicely's jumper suit, crying "Whoopee!"

"I've come to give you back your togs. I say, hasn't it been super!"

Angela turned to him with a watery smile.

"Yes, hasn't it!" she said. "I've got a beastly cold in my head. It's come on quite suddenly."

"Clear out, Ian," said Cicely.

Ian went out very quietly.

The strains of "God Save the King" had died away, and most of the guests had gone to bed.

Helen and Eleanor Downing went slowly upstairs and along the corridor to Mrs. Downing's bedroom. As they passed one of the doors Miss Downing threw her sister-in-law a quick glance, but there was no change of expression on the blank distorted face. She hasn't heard, she thought. Thank God for that. But what a fool Ralph is!

"I saw Ralph going off to the library about a minute ago," she said casually.

"Yes," replied her sister-in-law.

In the bedroom Miss Downing switched on the light and stood hesitating.

"Can I do anything for you before I go, Helen?" she said.

"No, thank you. . . ."

"Well . . . good night."

Miss Downing still seemed uneasy, unwilling to go. . . . Helen hadn't heard, but—she might so easily have done. What a *fool* the man was!

"I'm next door if you want anything, remember."

"Yes. Thank you. . . . I shan't want anything. Good night."

"Good night."

Miss Downing went to her own room. Her sister-in-law waited till she heard her door close, then opened her own very slightly, turned off the light, and stood in the far shadow of the room, watching. She seemed still to hear the well-known laugh—low and mocking—that had come from behind the closed bedroom door. He was in there with that girl. She was not conscious of anger or jealousy, only of a despairing knowledge that she couldn't keep the wild beast in check any longer. It was the end. . . . Her whole body was strained and rigid in her struggle. But it wasn't any use. She knew that it wasn't any use.

At last the door on the corridor opened, and she saw her husband slip furtively out of it. The light fell upon the slender dapper figure. She saw the smile beneath his trim moustache. He put his hands in his pockets and, whistling nonchalantly, descended the stairs.

She waited till he had disappeared, then went along the corridor to the room he had just come from, walking with her stiff dragging gait. She opened the door and entered. The girl, who was lying on the bed wrapped in a pale pink negligee, started up in terror. She had only time to give a strangled cry before the woman's hands closed round her throat, pressing, shaking, the wild beast unchained at last. . . .

Eleanor Downing had been waiting and listening uneasily in her bedroom. Helen *must* have heard. He had laughed aloud, and surely, if anyone in the world knew that low mocking laugh, Helen did. . . . Then she had heard the girl's scream. It was so faint that it might have been anything, but she started up at once and sped unerringly to the room, flinging open the door without knocking.

"Helen, are you *mad*!"

She pulled the tense quivering hands away from the girl's throat.

Helen Downing stood, swaying slightly, staring in front of her with dilated eyes. Eleanor glanced at the girl to make sure that she was not really hurt, then led her sister-in-law unresisting back to her room. There, Helen gazed about her with an odd bewilderment in her eyes.

"I haven't killed her, have I?"

"No, she isn't hurt."

She limped across to the dressing-table and began to study her reflection, examining minutely, curiously, the scars that disfigured her face, the distorted mouth and nose. It was the first time since her accident that she had looked at herself in a glass without a conscious effort. Her sister-in-law stood watching her in silence, struggling with the inarticulateness that had always been a barrier between them.

"Helen," she said at last. "I'm so sorry——"

"Because of this?" said Helen, touching the seamed face with her fingers.

"No. Because you love Ralph. I'm Ralph's sister, and I'm fond of him, but I can't imagine a worse hell for any woman than to love him. He isn't worth it. You've always known that in your heart."

"Yes."

She turned her gaze from the mirror to glance round the room. It looked strange and new, as if she had never been in it before. Everything about her seemed strange. The wild beast had escaped at last. It had gone and left a sort of emptiness behind it—an emptiness, she realised suddenly, that she could fill as she liked. She thought of the things she could fill it with. There were books, friendship, music, there was the beauty of the countryside, ploughed fields, woods, the sunset over the hills. . . . Ralph? She felt as if Ralph were someone she had known many, many years ago and forgotten. He had gone with the wild beast.

She looked at her reflection in the glass again and felt no anger, no bitterness. Instead, there came to her a sudden sense of freedom and relief. This woman had escaped from Ralph. Scarred and disfigured, at least she had escaped. He couldn't make her suffer any more. She needn't watch her beauty with sick anxiety, terrified of the marks of weariness, or sickness, or advancing age. This woman had won through to liberty. She felt as if the accident had happened yesterday, and the intervening time were a strange uneasy dream, from which she had just awakened.

Then the door opened, and Ralph entered. She looked at him in silence. Like everything else around her, he seemed to have changed. He had become small, ordinary, rather furtive-looking.

"Had a good time, darling?" he said in that tone of half-mocking affection that she knew so well.

"Yes, thank you," she said. "I'm very tired. I'm going to bed. Good night."

"Good night."

He felt nonplussed and bewildered. She was different somehow, but he couldn't tell how. Then suddenly he knew. That blank, expressionless look had gone from her eyes. . . .

Eleanor Downing opened the door and entered Bella Torrance's room. The girl still sat huddled on the bed, staring in front of her.

"It was your own fault, you little fool," said Eleanor, as she closed the door. "Why did you take her husband?"

The heavy eyes moved contemptuously to Eleanor's face.

"Dozens of women have had him. . . ."

"That makes no difference. . . ."

Suddenly the girl flung herself down on the pillow and burst into a tempest of tears.

"Pull yourself together, you little idiot," said Eleanor sharply. "You aren't hurt. She hardly touched you."

"It's not that," came the voice, strangled by sobs. "I wish she'd killed me. It's—oh, for God's sake, go away."

Eleanor shrugged her shoulders and went away.

The girl still lay there, her thin form shaken by hard, rasping sobs.

She'd let him take her because he reminded her of Simon, and he had left her, not soothed and satisfied, but tortured by desire for Simon, as if her living body were stretched on the rack.

Chapter Twenty

"LADY HETHERSTONE'S coming over this morning," said Judith, looking up from a letter that had been brought to her at the breakfast table. "She's staying at Redmouth, and I suppose I told her we'd be here. What a bore! I'd wanted to start for home this morning. Still—she won't be in Town till just before the pageant, so it's an opportunity to settle things. Get all the papers and sketches ready after breakfast, will you, darling?"

"Yes . . ." said Sidney.

She'd meant to tell Judith about Dickie this morning, but she couldn't now, of course. Judith's mind would be concentrated on the pageant and preparations for Lady Hetherstone's visit. In any case, morning wasn't a good time. Judith was always rather edgy in the morning.

Judith was watching her across the table.

"You're looking pale, Sidney. Do you feel quite well?"

"Yes, quite," said Sidney, blushing guiltily, as if Judith had read her thoughts.

"Well . . . I only hope she won't stay long, and that we can get off early in the afternoon."

"I packed last night, Judith. I can pack for you before she comes, if you like."

"No, my dear, it will take you all your time to get the papers ready. She's coming here at ten. And you know I hate having my room dismantled a minute before it's necessary. I loathe the atmosphere of packing. We can do it together when she's gone. Have you finished?"

"Yes."

"You've eaten nothing at all. I don't think this place has agreed with you. . . . I'm not sorry to be going. I can't think what possessed me to want to come at all. It is, as you said it would be, neither fish, flesh, nor good red herring."

Sidney followed her from the dining-room, across the hall, and up the stairs. Boxes stood piled by the front door. Everyone was going to-day.

Judith opened the door of Sidney's bedroom and looked in. The room was stripped, the box stood packed by the window, on the bed lay her hat and coat ready for the journey, and the dress of powder-blue chiffon that she had worn on Sunday night.

"Oh, you haven't packed 'Sidney,'" smiled Judith.

"No, I didn't want to pack her till the last moment. I should hate her to get crushed. She's so lovely."

"Well . . . let's go and get ready for Lady Hetherstone. Why on *earth* she should want to come this morning!"

They went to Judith's bedroom, and Sidney began to prepare the room for the coming interview under Judith's direction. Judith's irritation increased every moment.

"Take that table from by the bed and put it in the window, and then we can have the sketches on it. My dear girl, it's no use trying to move the table till you've got the chair out of the way. . . . Do use a little common sense. . . . Well, we shall want two chairs at the table, shan't we? Or do you think I'm going to stand? And you'd better move the dressing-table. I'll help you. . . . No, the *other* way. *Really*, Sidney!"

She took her seat at the table and began to sort out the sketches of the pageant dresses.

"Have you got those notes we made the other night?"

"Yes."

"Put them here, will you?"

Sidney put them on the table but not on the exact spot to which the long thin fingers had pointed. Judith's quick frown flashed out.

"I said *here*," she repeated with dangerous distinctness, tapping the spot again impatiently.

Sidney moved the papers in silence, trying to control the sudden trembling that always seized her nowadays at a note of anger in Judith's voice.

Judith glanced up, still frowning, with a half smile that showed more irritation than friendliness but that was obviously intended to compensate for her impatience.

"You're just a little stupid this morning, aren't you, darling?"

"I'm sorry," said Sidney miserably.

She couldn't possibly tell her about Dickie while she was like this. She must wait till she got her in a really good mood. She loved Dickie terribly and, of course, she meant to tell Judith at the first opportunity, but there wasn't any such desperate hurry as he seemed to think.

It would be best to wait till they were at home and had settled down. When one came to think of it, it would be a mistake to try to tell her before the pageant. She'd probably be rather edgy all the time now till after the pageant. It was silly of Dickie to want to precipitate matters. There really wasn't any hurry.

Lady Hetherstone's arrival seemed to restore Judith's good-humour. After greeting her, she turned to Sidney and laid her arm affectionately on her shoulder.

"You've met Miss Lattimer, haven't you? She's my right hand. I don't know what I should do without her."

The smile and pressure of the hand on her shoulder, with their unmistakable message of apology and reconciliation, sent a pang of loving compunction through Sidney's heart. She never really means to be unkind, she thought. She does love me. She'll miss me terribly when I leave her. I must be awfully careful not to hurt her about Dickie. I'll try to explain to him that we mustn't rush things.

. . .

Lady Hetherstone, small and stout and brisk and good-natured, was delighted with the sketches.

"I think you're a genius, Miss Kimball," she said.

"Oh no," replied Judith, with her slow smile, "I'm not. Miss Lattimer's worked awfully hard on these too, haven't you, darling? She's spent hours in the British Museum—a place I loathe more than any other place in the world—and she'll have to spend many more there when we get back. She does all my spade-work for me."

"Well, they're wonderful. . . . I do congratulate you both. It's lucky I was staying near and could pop over. Otherwise I mightn't have seen you till just before the pageant. You're going back to Town to-day, aren't you?"

"Yes. We shall stay a night on the way, of course. . . . Have you told Bennet about the car, Sidney?"

"No. You weren't quite sure what time we'd be starting."

"It will have to be after lunch now. Run and tell him to be ready at two, will you, darling?"

Sidney went downstairs. The Paynters' car stood at the door, and their luggage was just being put onto it by the chauffeur.

The Standfields and a few others of the guests were gathered on the steps as if tentatively prepared to give them a send-off.

"Oh, are you going?" said Sidney to Cicely, who stood in the hall with Mrs. Kellogg. "Good-bye . . . it's been jolly, hasn't it?"

"Yes, hasn't it."

They smiled at each other in shy friendliness.

Cicely was thinking: I wish we'd got to know her. She looks so sweet.

And Sidney: They're darlings. I wish—but, of course, Judith doesn't like young people. . . .

She went outside. Ian and Mr. Paynter were in their places in the car.

Brian Mallard leant against the balustrade at the end of the terrace, where he could watch the Paynters' departure. He was gazing over the garden, however, as if wholly unaware of them.

She sped on to the garage.

Mr. Paynter took out his watch.

"Well, I suppose these women will be ready some time," he said. "It doesn't do to get impatient."

Ian laughed.

"The old car can do it all right, even if they're fairly late," he said. "She goes pretty well still, doesn't she?"

"Still?" echoed his father. "Why the patronising 'still'? She's only two years old."

"Two years is two years nowadays," said Ian.

"Really?" said his father. "Now, that's interesting. I must try to remember that. . . ."

Ian grinned. He and his father were seldom alone together, but, whenever they were, he felt that they would have got on excellently if they had not been father and son. The relationship seemed to stand between them, making them both self-conscious. They couldn't meet simply as two individuals.

"Here's one of them," said his father. "Let's be thankful for small mercies."

Cicely came out, still accompanied by Mrs. Kellogg.

"And I'll always remember you, love," Mrs. Kellogg was saying. "You don't know what you've done for me. I was dreading this first Christmas without Bert, but what with you and I palling up like what we have done I've enjoyed it no end. I took to you the minute I saw you, pet, and you did the same to me, didn't you?"

She's terribly pathetic, thought Cicely for the hundredth time, but she's spoilt everything. I've *hated* it. I *will* be firm the next time I go away. I'll be haughty and standoffish with pathetic people. I'll simply *freeze* them.

Angela came out. She was very pale, and there were violet shadows beneath her blue eyes. She stood for a moment, looking at the youth who was hanging over the terrace balustrade, his eyes fixed ostentatiously in the opposite direction. Mr. Standfield watched her. . . . There was something in her eyes that had been in Alice's when he met her in the street after she had heard of his engagement to Lucy. It was as if Alice had come back to him, giving him a second chance to save her, though it was too late to save himself. He glanced round. His wife was deep in conversation with Miss Nettleton, describing to her the system on which she ran the Band of Hope. . . .

He started forward impulsively to Angela.

"Don't let him go like that," he said. "Speak to him. Tell him . . . tell him . . ."

His voice trailed away. He was appalled by what he had done.

She looked at him steadily, then said, "Thank you," and walked with a firm tread to where the young man stood on the terrace.

He turned to her, and the blood flamed into his face. She fixed her level unsmiling gaze on him and began to speak in a low quick voice.

"You think you're—so right, but you're not. You're wrong. You think that love's ugly and horrible, and it isn't. It's beautiful. I remember in an English lesson at school there was something about someone having 'read God in a prose translation.' That's what you've done. You've read God in a prose translation, and it's left out all the poetry and beauty. You're mean and little, and that's why you think love ugly. I love you, but I'm ashamed of loving you, and I'm going to try hard to stop——"

She swung round on her heel abruptly and returned to the car, without looking back at him. He stood watching her. His face that had flamed crimson while she spoke to him was now colourless.

Mrs. Paynter came out.

"At last!" said her husband.

"Darling, the post has only just come in, and there's the most adorable Christmas card from Jill. Here it is. Nanny says she made the kisses herself. And here's Nanny's letter."

Her husband took the Christmas card, and looked at it, smiling, then read the letter.

Brian Mallard came up to the car with his long loose stride. His mouth was set and tense.

"Will you give me your address?" he said to Angela.

He handed her an envelope and a pencil. She wrote her address on it without speaking.

"Would you—would you let me come and see you?" he said.

"Yes."

"All aboard!" called Mr. Paynter, handing the Christmas card and letter back to his wife.

They packed themselves into the car, and it started off. Brian stood staring after it as it disappeared down the drive. Just at the bend Angela looked out and waved.

Dickie Bennet came out of the garage to meet Sidney.

"Have you told her?" he said.

"No . . . Dickie, I couldn't. She wasn't in a good mood. It would have been stupid to tell her this morning. And now Lady Hetherstone's there. And as soon as she's gone we shall be flying round packing."

"To-day's the last day for me, you know."

"Don't be silly, Dickie. I shall know where you are. We'll meet. Then I'll tell her. . . ."

"When?"

"I think I must wait till after the pageant, Dickie. She'll be—a bit edgy now till after that. And I can't desert her before the pageant. There's such a lot for me to do. She's relying on me. . . ."

"You said you'd tell her this morning. Why didn't you tell her before Lady Hetherstone came?"

"I meant to, but—oh, Dickie, if you knew what she was like. I *couldn't* have told her then. . . . Don't look so serious. . . ."

"I'll go up now and tell her myself."

She laid an urgent hand on his arm. "You *mustn't*," she gasped. "Dickie, I'd never forgive you if you did that. . . . Darling, have patience. It will all come right. . . . Oh, and I forgot. She wants the car at two."

"Damn her!"

He caught her in his arms, and they clung together for a few moments, then she freed herself.

"I must go, Dickie."

"Do you love me?"

"You know I do."

"Not enough to stand up to her. Come away with me now, Sidney. Just as you are. Don't go back to her."

"Darling, be reasonable. Give me time. I must tell her. I *will* tell her."

She kissed him again, then broke from him suddenly and ran back to the house.

In Judith's bedroom Lady Hetherstone had finished looking at the sketches and was discoursing expansively on the economic situation.

"I can't think where the money *is*," she was saying. "I mean, it must be somewhere. Money can't disappear. But no one seems to have any. And there's *nothing* for boys leaving school to do. I dined with the Hatfields at Ottary on Christmas Eve, and they were telling me about a public schoolboy who'd been to tea there that afternoon. He'd actually had to get a job as a chauffeur. To some people staying here, I believe. Bennet, his name was. He took a girl there with him—a friend—and all the young people went out riding. ... Well, my dear, I must go now. It's been so nice to see you, and I'm delighted with your sketches. ... *Good*-bye. ..."

Judith went downstairs with her. When she returned it was obvious that the reference to Bennet had dispersed her precarious good-humour. She was frowning as she closed the door.

"Did you hear what she said about Bennet, Sidney?" she said. "I never liked the man, but this proves that he's a common adventurer." Her lips curled into a sneer. "I wonder which of the housemaids he took with him."

There was a silence, during which the colour drained itself slowly from Sidney's cheeks. Then she said steadily: "It was I who went with him, Judith."

She watched the clear skin turn a dead cold grey, the hazel eyes harden to green, the lips tighten into a thin line.

"*You!*" said Judith between her teeth, in a voice that was little more than a whisper. "How *dared* you!"

Judith's anger, that should have seared and buffeted and blinded. And, strangely, she seemed to stand outside it, as if she watched a storm from some safe place on shore. She realised, to her surprise, that Judith's anger couldn't touch her now. ...

"I'm sorry, Judith. I mean, I'm sorry I deceived you. I ought to have told you as soon as I knew. Dickie and I love each other and are going to be married."

"You and—Bennet?"

"Yes."

Judith was silent for a few moments. The child's eyes still met hers unflinchingly. She wasn't quailing beneath her anger. This monstrous, incredible thing had actually happened. She didn't know how to deal with it. Slowly her anger changed to a panic terror, a feeling of nightmare desolation.

She gave a little cry.

"Sidney," she panted, "you can't leave me. You can't. I can't live without you. If you go I'll kill myself. I swear I will. . . . Sidney"—her voice rose hysterically—"do you hear? I'll *kill* myself if you leave me."

Sidney's clear gaze was still fixed upon her.

"No, Judith, you won't, but—even that wouldn't stop me. Nothing would stop me. You see, Dickie and I love each other. That's all that matters to me now. I was a coward about telling you, but now you know, I'm not frightened of you. . . ."

Judith controlled herself with an effort. Her brain was working quickly, cunningly. This thing had happened. She must face it. She must keep Sidney. Somehow, anyhow, she must keep Sidney. She gave a short breathless laugh.

"Frightened of me? Darling, why should you be frightened of me? I was taken by surprise, that's all. Of course I can't keep you for ever. I never expected to. It's been sweet to have you even for this short time. Of course you must marry your Dickie, if you love him." Time, that was it. Give her time, and she'd manage it. "But not at once, darling."

Already the girl was responding to the note of tender pleading in her voice. The new hard look of detachment had left her eyes, and something of the old devotion was taking its place. Judith followed up her advantage.

"Don't grudge me my last few weeks with you. Listen, darling. Come abroad with me before you get married. Just one last little holiday abroad together. You don't grudge me that, do you?"

"Of course not, Judith. . . . Judith, how sweet you are! I thought——"

There came a knock at the door. Judith frowned.

"See who it is, darling. . . . Send them away. . . ."

Sidney went to the door. Dickie Bennet entered, wearing his chauffeur's uniform, his cap in his hand.

The cold grey tinge crept back again into Judith's face.

"How *dare* you come to my bedroom?" she said.

"I've come to tell you——"

Sidney interrupted him.

"She knows, Dickie."

He put his arm round her, and she stood in the shelter of it, looking at Judith.

There was silence for a few moments, and in that silence Judith knew that she had lost Sidney for ever. The last vestige of her self-control broke down. She turned on her with blazing eyes.

"You brazen little slut!" she spat out venomously. "So you want to go back to the gutter where I found you. I might have known you weren't your mother's daughter for nothing. How long has my chauffeur been your lover? And how many more have you had, you damned little——"

Dickie stepped forward, his face set.

"Stop that!"

For answer she struck him with all her might across the mouth with her open hand. He started back, and Sidney clung to him, trembling.

"Come on out of this, Sidney," he said thickly.

Sidney plunged into her bedroom for her hat and coat, and ran downstairs with him, slipping them on as she ran. He snatched his suitcase from the garage, and they hurried down the drive as if still pursued by Judith's anger. When they had reached the road, Sidney stopped and looked at him. Her face was radiantly transfigured. She held her slight form more upright as if a weight had actually dropped from it. She drew a deep breath.

"Oh, *Dickie!*" she said.

He took her in his arms and kissed her.

"Forget her," he whispered.

"I have already."

"Come along. We can catch the twelve o'clock if we hurry."

"I haven't brought any clothes, Dickie."

"That doesn't matter. My mother will see to that. Come on, beloved. We'll have to run for it."

Miss Wingate leant out of the window of her taxi and smiled her small pursed smile at Celia.

"Good-bye, Mrs. Beaton," she said, "and thank you *so* much for all your kindness."

The taxi started, and she leant back with a faint sigh of relief. It was over. She hadn't enjoyed it. She couldn't even pretend to herself that she'd enjoyed it. It wasn't only the hair-tidy. . . . She'd felt lonely all the time. Lonely and self-conscious and home-sick. She didn't know exactly what she was home-sick for. Somehow she'd seemed here quite a different person from what she really was. Really she was interesting and companionable; here she'd seemed garrulous and boring—so boring that lately people had seemed to avoid her, as if they didn't want to talk to her. Moreover, that something of deference that she was used to—even from her colleagues—was absent, and she had missed it very much. Well, she'd tried getting out of her rut, and she was looking forward to returning to it more than she'd ever looked forward to anything in her life before. She'd never try to go out of it again. She'd learnt her lesson. After all, if you were happy in a rut there really wasn't any sense in trying to get out of it. And it had been very awkward having no hair-tidy. . . .

The Osmonds and Mrs. Lewel and her mother stood at the door, waiting for the taxi they were sharing to the station.

"It's been very nice," Mrs. Osmond was saying, "but so quiet. I mean, nothing's happened. I like a place with more going on."

The taxi drew up, and Celia appeared to say good-bye.

"Good-bye, Patsy darling," replied Mrs. Nightingale. "We have so much enjoyed our stay with you, and I'll be sure to give George all your messages."

Celia waved to them till the taxi had disappeared. Then she turned and went slowly back into the house.

They'd all gone now. Miss Torrance had been the first to go, having an early breakfast in bed, and setting off while the others were still in the dining-room. Then the Downings had gone. There had been some curious difference in Mrs. Downing that Celia couldn't analyse. Just for a second she had had the strange delusion that the disfigurement had vanished; then, of course, she had seen that the features were still scarred and distorted. She had been puzzling about it half unconsciously all morning. Now suddenly she realised where the change lay. Before, Mrs. Downing had been like someone moving in her sleep. Now she looked as if she had awakened. Something in her eyes almost made you forget her disfigured face. Mr. Downing, walking behind his wife and sister to the car, had been unusually quiet, his dapper figure stripped of something of its assurance.

Then the Paynters had gone, then the Standfields and the Fieldens and Miss Kimball. There had been something rather odd about Miss Kimball's departure. Immediately after breakfast she had had a visit from Lady Hetherstone about the pageant that Miss Kimball was dressing for her. And, shortly after that, the chauffeur and Miss Lattimer had left, presumably on some business connected with the pageant, but without taking the car. Then Miss Kimball had come downstairs, dressed for the journey, looking pale and disdainful and aloof, and had ordered a taxi, saying that she would send her chauffeur for the car before the end of the week. She had taken both her box and Miss Lattimer's in the taxi. And the oddest part of it all was that on going into Miss Lattimer's bedroom Celia had found the powder-blue dress that Miss Lattimer had worn on Sunday night lying on the floor torn into tiny shreds. . . .

That dreadful Mrs. Stephenson-Pollitt and her young prig of a nephew had been the last to go, sharing a taxi with Miss Nettleton and Mrs. Kellogg. Miss Nettleton had just discovered that there was a Norman church over at Saltham that she hadn't seen and was in consequence in a state of extreme dejection.

Celia went to the gun-room, where Robert stood by the window.
"They've all gone, darling," she said, closing the door.
He turned to her, but said nothing.
"It's been a great success, hasn't it?" she went on, throwing a dreamy abstracted glance round the room. "You know, Robert, there isn't any reason why we shouldn't have occasional house

parties of paying guests like this. It would pay for the upkeep of the place, anyway. I think it would be quite worth while to have a passenger lift put in and to build an annexe for the servants. . . ."

He knew that she would not be satisfied till she had turned the house into a large residential hotel. The idea would soon so dominate and obsess her that everything that stood in its way would be swept aside.

She looked at him.

"What are you thinking of, Robert?"

Still he made no answer.

She came across the room to him.

"Robert, put your arms round me. I want to feel you near me. I've got such a strange feeling—as if you'd gone right away. . . ."

He put his arms around her, and she clung to him tightly, more tightly.

But still that strange feeling persisted—a feeling that, though he held her in his arms, she had lost him for ever. . . .